KINDRED SPIRIT

S. M. CASHMORE

Kindred Spirit © 2021 S. M. Cashmore

Isbn: 978-1-913746-98-8

Printed by Ingram Spark

Photo © Photo Orlando Florin | Dreamstime.com
Cover Design Mercat Design © 2021
All Rights Reserved

For Zhang Lan

'And the cause?' I said. 'What caused it?'

Carnacki shook his head.

'God knows,' he answered with a peculiar, sincere reverence. 'If that thing was what it seemed to be one might suggest an explanation which would not offend one's reason, but which may be utterly wrong.'

Carnacki the Ghost-finder
William Hope Hodgson

'Finally he began to scratch his head thoughtfully. "Hell, Chris," he said, "this whole thing sounds very familiar," and just sat there scratching his head. All of a sudden he snaps his fingers. "Gone With the Wind," he said. And that was it. This little kid had seen 'Gone With the Wind' eight or ten times until it was part of her unconscious mind.'

The Search for Joseph Tully
William Hallahan

Chapter 1

At twenty to four a slightly overweight curly-haired man came out of Mae's Flower Shop on Bedford Road a few miles north of the centre of Glasgow. The flower shop, sandwiched between a newsagent and a rather shabby Chinese takeaway which didn't open until much later, in the evening, was illuminated by amber autumnal light slanting across the road between two office blocks. The man, whose name was George Viviani, was holding a slim briefcase in his left hand and a bunch of tulips he had bought for his wife pressed between his left elbow and his body. He had raised his right arm to hail a taxi. He was perspiring slightly, not feeling all that great, probably a touch of indigestion caused by the hurried lunch when he'd arrived in Glasgow, but his eyes were shining and he was smiling contagiously. Both the meeting and what had come after had gone really well, better than he had dared to hope; now, he stepped towards the setting sun, smiling.

Two middle-aged women passing by on the pavement saw his expression and could not help smiling back, but he saw neither of them. His eyes were fixed on a distant taxi which seemed to him to slowly emerge from a blur of traffic, like a camel or a safari jeep emerging from rippling heat haze, gradually coming into focus as it turned in his direction. He lowered his arm and ran thick fingers around his shirt collar as if it constrained him, although he was not wearing a tie and his collar was not fastened.

The taxi was cream-coloured and had some sort of advertisement on its side. Still smiling, George Viviani took another step away from Mae's Flower Shop, then another. He thought it was very odd that he couldn't hear his footsteps. He always wore smart black shoes which clacked crisply on wooden floors and pavements and in the echoing stairwells of business offices. He liked to think that the sounds he made as he walked briskly from one place to another announced his presence and the nature of his presence—crisp, clear-cut, no-nonsense. But now, in the red sunlight with the cream taxi swinging closer, almost parallel to the pavement now, he found that he could not hear his footsteps at all. Suddenly alarmed, he looked down to make sure that he was wearing shoes.

Another woman, younger than the two who had returned his smile only seconds earlier, walked behind him, between where he was standing and the tiny shopping arcade. She saw the way he looked down. She saw him stumble slightly and almost lose his balance. Then she saw the taxi pull up in front of him, and she turned away.

George Viviani paused as the taxi came to a stop. He had determined that he was wearing his shoes, but now he realised that not only could he not hear his footsteps, but also he could not hear the sound of the traffic properly, and he could barely hear the rumbling purr of the taxi which, he could see now, was carrying an advertisement for Red Arrow Taxis featuring an orange, yellow and black design and several arrows cleverly painted to look as if they had been shot into the side of the taxi.

And another thing. Where was the fire?

George Viviani looked around, becoming slightly bewildered. He was sure that he could smell smoke, but nothing was visibly burning; nobody came running, screaming, into the street; no crowds were gathering. The sun seemed more intense, hotter. As he looked around something reflected its light at him and his sight dissolved into brightness. He took hold of the cold taxi handle, yanked the door open, put one foot inside and angled himself towards the back seats, and tumbled forwards.

His briefcase fell to the floor.

The tulips were crushed beneath his body and one of the last thoughts that occurred to him was that they smelled so much better than the smoke, wherever it was coming from. His face had jammed into the back of the car seat, down at the base where the back met the seat, where no doubt many coins had slipped from unknowing pockets, slipped into some unseen cavity beneath the seat, perhaps all the way into the boot space. He could see nothing but dark fawn-coloured material, although he could not feel its texture against his cheeks, or forehead, or against his lips. He couldn't feel anything, and it was growing very dark even allowing for the fact that he had just fallen face-down into the back of a taxi.

He knew what was happening, of course, but he didn't want to think about it just now. He knew too that not thinking about it just now meant not thinking about it at all, but that was all right, he had other things to think of. The smell of tulips. The face of his daughter when she was four years old. The first time he saw his wife; she turning around to see who had come into the office, her long ash-blonde hair spilling over her shoulders. A snatched vision of his daughter's tearful face when she didn't know he was looking; her artificial smile when she did. Something about his mother, the top level of a bus, a white handkerchief waving.

He wondered whether Dorothy would ever get the tulips. He worried he had never got to talk to his daughter.

He wished he could have told them both his news.

Next to the silent Chinese takeaway was a convenience store, painted green, which stood on the corner of Bedford Road and Laburnum Crescent. Two men inside the convenience store—one the proprietor and one a casual customer, who had been in the process of buying some cans of beer—watched with interest as George Viviani tottered across the pavement and plunged into the depths of the cream taxi.

The proprietor remarked that it didn't look good, and the customer laughed and joked that the curly-haired man must have been inside the convenience store not so long ago, probably also to buy beer, and what he had bought was now inside himself. Or not, reflected the customer. Perhaps it was now inside the taxi. The proprietor shook his head, denying everything. His gloomy diagnosis was that the whole thing didn't look good, not good at all, and he was glad that he wasn't the taxi driver, a big bald man they could both see in the front of the taxi, who was turning his head and obviously saying something, though of course they could hear nothing from inside the store.

Laburnum Crescent arced round in a long semi-circle and emerged back into Bedford Road half a mile away from Mae's Flower Shop and the green convenience store. At almost half way around the semi-circle, on its outer edge, stood a squalid four-storey block of flats. Graffiti-covered plywood was nailed over two of the three doors which opened onto Laburnum Crescent. Cracked plastic covered the buzzers inset at the side of the doors. Most of the buzzers had nothing written against them, or names or designations written so poorly that they resembled hieroglyphics.

Opposite the block of flats was a row of semi-detached houses, mainly rented out as lower or upper floor conversions, and from one of the upper floors a young man had taken to watching the flats. From time to time he glimpsed a turn of flesh—thigh, or breast, it was hard to tell—and sometimes he saw girls in shiny clothes going in through one or other of the doors, though naturally enough he more often saw men attempting the buzzers or looking warily around the street with a mobile clamped to one ear. Sometimes they approached and then turned away as their nerve broke; sometimes they buzzed or called, stood shifting from one leg to another, and then went away presumably because of a misunderstanding on somebody's part; most often they received word through intercom or mobile, and so pushed up against a door, which would open, and they would slip inside.

When they left a half-hour, or an hour, or two hours later, the young man noted that they were usually smiling, a strange furtive smile which looked as if it had crept unnoticed onto their faces and would be wiped away as soon as its owner noticed it was there. Sometimes their hair was tousled. Sometimes they were no longer wearing a tie that they had been wearing on arrival; once the young man saw a silver-haired man emerge from the block of flats, then immediately ring the buzzer, return back inside, and re-appear moments later with a beige raincoat over his arm that he had evidently left behind.

Infrequently, a girl with red bobbed hair stood in the doorway, on bare tip-toes, for a farewell kiss. She wore a yellow wrap-around, and something glittered on her left wrist. The second, or perhaps the third time this happened, her gaze lifted and she caught sight of the young man watching from across the street. She looked at him for long seconds before stepping back and closing the door, and he reflected afterwards that it was surprising that she had not gasped, and put a hand to her throat, and slammed the door quickly.

It happened again, a few days later. Then, only ten minutes ago, she had stood, both hands grasping the side of the door, her gaze meeting his for the third time across the width of the street. The sun was low; red beams painted pavement and the side of the block of flats, transforming the dirty, grey rectangle into a crimson vision, bright with promise, but he scarcely noticed as they continued to look at each other, and he imagined a glowing representation of their locked gazes stretching across the street, putting into shadow the glowing rays of the setting sun. She smiled slightly before retreating into darkness. By that time he knew that her name was Claire.

The taxi driver's name was Harry McCabe and when he first saw the curly-haired man hailing him from outside the flower shop, he had been in two minds whether to take the fare. On the one hand a fare was a fare, and it looked like this particular fare was probably for Central or Queen Street Station, both of which suited him just fine. On the other hand it was twenty to four already, and he planned to knock off at four. Then he could get home in time to check out his email and online ads before Tommy came home. It wouldn't do to find that the curly-haired man actually wanted to go to Paisley or Clydebank, or somewhere else that was miles away. No, that wouldn't do at all. Still, if that happened he could always say sorry, he wasn't headed that way, sorry sir, bad luck, you'll have to wait for another taxi. True, if that hell-cat Agnes got to hear about it, he'd be in trouble—she didn't like any fare refused—but a man was entitled to some time by himself, wasn't he?

It was possible the man was drunk. He was walking oddly. Harry McCabe watched a young woman with pert legs and a pretty face go past, heard the door open, caught a glimpse in the left hand wing mirror of the curly-haired man falling face forwards into the back, and assumed he had tripped. He waited for the man to recover himself, haul himself upright, close the taxi door and say where he wanted to go. But none of that happened. He turned his head, and was unnerved to see that the man was lying face-down on the back seat, where he had fallen. Harry McCabe jumped out and ran round to the back. The man didn't move. Harry McCabe tugged at his jacket, and shouted, but the man still didn't move. He climbed in, awkwardly straddling the prone figure of the curly-haired man, and fumbled at his wrist, and at the side of his neck, already certain of what he was not going to find.

Harry McCabe had been a taxi driver for nearly six years, and for most of them he had worried about something like this happening. It had happened to other drivers. Johnny Eddolls liked to tell the story of the little old woman who got into his cab outside a church on Winston Street—Johnny Eddolls said he could never remember the name of the church even though everyone always reminded him every time he told the story that it was Theobald's Episcopalian Church—anyway it was just before midnight and the old woman apparently told him to hurry up as it was long past her bedtime.

Johnny said the old woman had sat there, hands clasping a big brown handbag on her lap, and rested her head back and closed her eyes. He said that maybe that was when she died, or maybe it was at some time during the journey, but whenever it was, she was stone cold dead when they drew up outside a tenement in Carstairs Gardens about twenty minutes later, and when the taxi stopped, Johnny Eddolls said, the handbag kept going and landed on the floor with a dull thump, and the little old lady slumped sideways and her head fetched up against the window with another thump, but she never stirred, never moved, and her eyes looked like two pieces of cold glass.

Old Gaw, whose first name might have been Stuart or it might have been Stephen, used to tell the story of a couple of gangsters who flagged him down one evening in Argyle Street. They had seemed on cordial terms, Old Gaw reminisced. That was in the days before taxis had intercom, so with the glass window shut he couldn't hear what they were saying, but he could see them in the mirror, and they were talking and smiling and gesticulating and he could tell they were gangsters, Old Gaw explained, not only because of what happened next, but because they were both wearing ties that were lighter in shade than their shirts.

After a few minutes, Old Gaw noted that the smiles weren't so much in evidence; and after a few more minutes, most of which had been spent idling at red lights at some damned roadworks, Old Gaw noted that the conversation between the gangsters had become considerably more agitated and, glass window or no glass window, he could hear them shouting. Then one of them produced a gun and shot the other one, calm as you like, in the forehead. The shot gangster was flung back, and the window and the back seat were instantly painted in blood and gore. The shot gangster still scrabbled feebly and tried to utter something through the bloody bubbles and foam on his lips, or perhaps he did actually say something, Old Gaw surmised, because the other gangster shot him again, still calm as you like, only this time in the chest.

Old Gaw said that by this time he had stopped the taxi half on and half off the pavement and was blubbering with fear, shock, and a vague sense of outrage that the back of his taxi had been turned into such a disgusting mess. The surviving gangster put away his gun, climbed out of the back of the taxi, then came round to Old Gaw and insisted on paying his fare. Old Gaw liked to say that he had retained enough of his wits to overcharge him, but most of his listeners doubted that was true.

Harry McCabe thought of these stories, and a couple of others besides, while he felt for and failed to find the pulse of the curly-haired man. He had thought that when and if this ever happened to him, he would probably be frightened, nervous, anxious, possibly sickened or dismayed, depending on exactly what had happened. He knew what to do: Red Arrow Taxis was a reputable firm that kept its employees well trained and up to date. Phone the police. Phone for an ambulance. Phone Red Arrow Taxis.

What he had not been prepared for was the irritation swelling almost into anger as he surveyed the cooling body of the curly-haired man, whose name he did not at that moment know, but which he would know before many more minutes passed. He was supposed to be clocking off at four, wasn't he? And what was the chance of that now, with this inconsiderate corpse sprawled across his back seat? He was going to be late; he probably wouldn't get paid overtime; he might miss a response to one of his online invitations. Why the fuck, thought Harry McCabe, did it have to be him?

He returned to the front of the taxi. He radioed Agnes to tell her where he was, told her that he had a body lying across his back seat, asked her to summon the police and an ambulance. Looks like a heart attack, he told her. Then, despite irritation and anger, he panicked that perhaps there had been a faint pulse and he had missed it, so he returned to the back of the taxi and found that no, he had been right the first time, and the body was already growing distinctly cold. He also caught a glimpse of the man's wallet as his jacket twisted open and hung down the front of the seat. He slid it out of the jacket and opened it curiously, feeling an obscure sense of power as he flipped through the personal cards, receipts, tickets of another man, George Viviani to be precise, as he noted on several of the cards. And cash.

Harry McCabe looked around and couldn't see that anyone could possibly see what he was doing, so he removed four of the five twenty-pound notes he found there, and slipped them into his own breast pocket. It wasn't as if George was going to need them, was it? And if there was family, wife, children, whatever, well no doubt he had a life insurance policy which would be worth a damned sight more than eighty pounds. So Harry McCabe thought, as he knelt astride the curly-haired man, thinking that George looked just like the sort of man who would have life insurance.

He put the wallet back. He found himself wondering what George's last thoughts had been, and shivered when it occurred to him that nobody would ever know. He heard a siren approaching, and looked out of the window in time to see a police car run a set of red lights, heading towards him. A little stiffly, he backed out of the taxi for a second time and it was only then that he wondered if the police would fingerprint George Viviani's wallet. He told himself that they wouldn't. Why should they?

While Dorothy Viviani did the ironing and watched her favourite soap, her daughter Melanie was arguing on the doorstep with a boy who wanted to take her out, and forty miles away a doctor and a policeman were having a conversation about the body of her husband. The soap had reached a particularly exciting point, where one of the male lead characters had managed to seduce the daughter of his neighbour, but unknown to the two of them as they lay entwined beneath the covers, the neighbour was on his way home, more than half drunk, having been sacked from his job that morning.

Dorothy's ironing became more and more erratic as successive shots showed the neighbour reeling home, clutching at the garden gate to keep his balance, lurching towards the front door, fumbling in his coat pocket for the key. She didn't know, though she could probably have guessed, that the episode would end just as he threw open the door and discovered a trail of clothing disappearing up the stairs, or possibly even before he actually opened the door. She didn't know, and would have had no way of guessing, that this would be the last time she would ever watch the programme. She would never know or care what happened when the neighbour discovered the errant pair in bed.

At the front door, Melanie Viviani said, 'No, I don't want to. Which word don't you understand?' Melanie had shoulder-length curly hair, a pretty face and eyes which usually sparkled but which at this moment were glinting dangerously, and a figure which in the words of her contemporaries, was to die for.

'No,' said the boy on the doorstep, who combined the superficially unlikely hobbies of playing rugby and writing poetry. He was exactly six feet tall, sturdily built, and tied his blond hair back in a queue.

'And don't,' he added after a moment's reflection. He had fallen in love with Melanie almost a year ago, when he saw her coming down a flight of steps in a local department store. He wrote about it afterwards, trying to infuse his words with the sudden, delicious shock he had experienced when he saw her. Everything, he wrote, focussed on that lone figure; it was as if his eyesight took on telescopic properties as he watched her descend the steps, just behind an old man who, he remembered, was wearing a green beret or hat; the smooth swing of her hips and legs, the way her hair jounced as she descended, the way in which she rested a hand lightly on the stair rail and looked around the interior of the shop with lively interest. She was wearing, he remembered, pale blue jeans and a pale pink jumper, and she was carrying a dark blue handbag over one shoulder. He wrote:

Life is a single drumbeat.
A thousand pities
We do not rebound together

and agonised about how to get these heartfelt words to her, because of course he knew who she was. Ayr was a small enough place that most people knew most people, but he had only just then realised how much she had changed since she had left school. His name was David Wasson.

'Ha ha,' remarked Melanie Viviani. 'Very funny.'

'What, you didn't enjoy yourself last time?'

'One swallow doesn't make a summer,' said Melanie and, as David Wasson's face creased slightly, 'Oh, sorree, I forgot you were a poet,' sketching the last word in quotes, something she felt instantly sorry for as David Wasson's face creased still further, because truth to tell she quite liked his poetry, some of it. She liked 'Drumbeat' and she liked

> *You passed*
> *And the world, as usual*
> *Speeded and swayed alarmingly.*
> *I am only half pleased*
> *I did not fall.*

David Wasson explained on their first date that he had written this after she came down some steps in some shop or other, and he had watched her, rooted to the spot, completely unable to approach her, or try to talk to her, or do anything except stay rooted to the spot and watch her walk past. Now, her face reddened slightly, and so did his for different reasons. They stared at each other in silence. They both heard the phone ring and Dorothy Viviani's voice say, 'What? Oh, well, just a minute, don't go away. Your call is important to me.'

'She does that,' muttered Melanie.

'She does what?'

'When it's advertising. She puts the phone down and carries on with whatever she's doing.'

'Ah. Nice one.' David Wasson nodded approvingly. His pony-tailed hair bobbed in the evening air.

At almost exactly the same time as the telephone rang in the Viviani household, Constable Bob Kirkwood looked at a doctor, who was looking back at him over the top of a pair of very flimsy-looking spectacles, and asked if the taxi driver was right, that George Viviani had died of a heart attack. The doctor, whose name was Muhammad Jamal Rafiq, pursed his lips and said probably, but it was really impossible to tell without a post mortem examination.

Muhammad Jamal Rafiq, who was known as Jammy by other hospital staff, didn't look very tired despite being a junior doctor. This was because he was just back from a week's holiday; he had been working less than ten hours and still felt fresh as a daisy. Constable Kirkwood, on the other hand, looked as though he had slept no more than ten hours in the last week; this was because he had been on duty until late the previous night, and had come across two men fighting outside a pub not far away from Queen Street railway station, and before he could intervene one of the men had pulled a knife and stabbed the other man, high up in his left arm, just below his shoulder, and the stabbed man had squealed like a stuck pig, and carried on squealing as the knifeman twisted his weapon free of constraining flesh and ran away into darkness, leaving the injured man to the ministrations of Constable Kirkwood.

This wasn't much fun for Constable Kirkwood (or for the stabbed man, who was taken to the same hospital where George Viviani was lying, by now as cold as stone, in the mortuary; he was stitched up, given injections and a handful of tablets safeguarding him from tetanus and other diseases, and packed off home, all within a couple of hours), but what was worse was that Constable Kirkwood couldn't get the dreadful squealing noise of the stabbed man out of his head. It played and replayed in his memory, as if it was emanating from an old-fashioned record and the needle had got stuck in a groove.

Was it really a man squealing like a pig? wondered Constable Kirkwood. It seemed odd, on reflection, to liken a human sound to that of an animal. Was it not more likely that the stuck pig made a noise like a stabbed human? And in between the squealing noise in his mind, or perhaps underneath the squealing noise, like some sort of underscore, he heard the sucking, squishing noise that the knife made as it entered the stabbed man's flesh and, scant seconds later, the same sucking noise, only worse, as it came back out.

So Constable Kirkwood lay in his bed replaying the noises in his memory, unable to turn them off. It occurred to him that the knifeman was probably sound asleep by now, untroubled by a guilty conscience, and the stabbed man was probably knocked insensible by a handful of pills, and it was only him, Constable Kirkwood, who had had nothing to do with the fight, who was suffering the consequences. He didn't get to bed until after one o'clock. At five o'clock he gave up the struggle, got up, made himself some coffee, and went back to the station where he was received with unequivocal astonishment by the officers and staff already there.

Doctor Jammy Rafiq reached out, touched his shoulder, and said he looked as though he could do with some sleep. He would fill in the forms, he said. Constable Kirkwood grunted. Doctor Jammy Rafiq asked if there was any problem with identification, adding that he didn't think there was. Constable Kirkwood grunted again, hefted the dead man's wallet in one hand, and said there was only one good thing about the whole damned sorry business, and when the doctor unwisely asked what it was, Constable Kirkwood said that George Viviani had lived in Ayr, so the task of breaking the news of his death to his family, assuming he had one, would fall to some other poor sod of a constable, not him.

At about this point, Melanie Viviani, not knowing that her father's wallet was being carried by the official hand of Constable Kirkwood, rubbed her eyes.

'I'm tired,' she said. 'I've got a part-time job at Bryce and Fenners. The solicitors,' she added when David Wasson looked momentarily puzzled. 'Plus two exams before Christmas. Sorry.'

'Okay,' said David Wasson.

'It's not that I don't want... I'm just too tired,' Melanie said, wondering why she hadn't thought of this before, especially as, now she came to think about it, it was true, even if it wasn't the whole truth.

'Yes, I understand, of course,' said David Wasson, nodding and shaking his head to show understanding and sympathy, trying to keep his face serene despite his heart beating much too fast as he thought he detected a false note in Melanie's voice. 'Another time,' he said.

'Sure. Another time.'

The door closed on Melanie's wan smile, constructed almost as if she was showing him sympathy rather than the other way around.

David Wasson turned and walked away. At the gate which led out onto the pavement, he paused to look back at the house. It was an Edwardian mid-terrace house, a full three storeys, boasting original sash windows set into thick sandstone walls. It was the sort of house which was easy to keep warm in winter, even when a west wind howled in off the sea, but kept cool during summer, not that summers in Ayr were ever unbearably hot.

Jim Eginton, a retired teacher who lived two doors away from the Viviani house, had once tried to obtain lottery funding to enable the entire row of houses to be cleaned, painted and thoroughly restored, so that it could be used for television sets, period drama, and maybe even become a tourist attraction. But the lottery administrators soon discovered that most of the houses were privately owned if not owner-occupied, and regretfully informed Jim Eginton that in those circumstances no funding could be made available because of the vexed question of personal profit.

None of this touched David Wasson's mind as he glanced back at the house. He was, in fact, looking up at what he knew to be the window to Melanie's bedroom. On the one occasion when he had been in the room, when she had invited him up to show him her new computer, he had been astonished at the size of the room, big enough for shadows thrown by the streetlight outside to stretch out on the varnished floor without reaching the opposite wall, and he had been impressed at the marble fire surround, not to mention the fireplace itself, which had not been lit at the time of his summer visit. As if somehow connected to his inner thoughts, the streetlight beside him came on, throwing hazy orange light against the side of the house, turning the dark bedroom window into a glinting mirror. David Wasson closed the gate quietly and moved off through the darkness towards his tiny flat at the other end of the High Street.

Inside the house, Melanie rested her forehead against the door for a moment. Then she went back into the living room.

The half-drunk neighbour in the soap programme had collapsed and all but passed out scant inches before reaching the front door of his house; he had lurched against a porch wall, slid downwards, legs splayed. He was experiencing some kind of flashback, himself being called into an office whose window overlooked corrugated iron roofs stretching away into the distance, sitting down opposite a pudgy man he had known since childhood, who was cleverer than he was, or who had applied himself more conscientiously than he had, or both, because the pudgy man was now the yard manager while he was only one of several charge hands; and the three million or so viewers and Dorothy Viviani all saw expressions pass over both their faces which, although the flashback was shown in utter silence, indicated that it was all his, the drunken neighbour chargehand's fault, whatever it was, and of course three million viewers all nodded and thought yes, that was right, we all saw it coming. Music gradually intruded into the scene, which faded into darkness and then credits.

'I might have known,' said Dorothy Viviani.

Melanie picked up the phone handset, listened to it, shook it, listened to it again, then put it back on its stand. 'Gone. Life insurance?'

'Double glazing. Who was it at the door?'

'David.' Melanie sighed. 'I quite like him but...'

'You still seeing the third year?' Dorothy Viviani's ironing returned to its usual efficient state. She was referring to a boy Melanie had met at university, Graham somebody, and although neither she nor George had met him, they both took an irrational dislike to him, or rather to their daughter's description of him.

'No.'

'Turn that off, will you?'

Melanie picked up a remote control and stopped a shrill game show before it really got going.

'But what?' asked Dorothy Viviani.

'What?' said Melanie. It was hard to keep track of conversations with her mother. She remembered her father once saying that Dorothy had the brain of an Olympic butterfly—she could jump from one topic to another and back again much more often and much more confusingly that anyone else he could think of.

'David. You like him but what?'

Melanie looked at her mother, who didn't look back but folded a shirt in some geometric fashion and ironed a few creases into existence. She wasn't quite sure how to answer. The truth was, she did like David Wasson, probably more than any other boy she'd met, even including Graham— well, especially including Graham now that she knew what a bastard he was. She wondered how long she would be able to conceal her own dark thoughts, whether she would be able to conceal them at all. Surely her mother would sense the black miasma of her mood? Some maternal instinct, an obscure maternal sixth sense represented by a deep unbreakable connection between mother and daughter, would surely reveal how, even as she stood uncertainly in the bright familiar room, her thoughts alternated between the locked compartment of her memory and a dark, beckoning abyss of contrition. But her mother appeared to sense nothing. She folded, ironed, created creases. Melanie felt an unexpected spurt of anger.

'Your father's late,' remarked Dorothy Viviani. 'He must've missed the four o'clock. Late dinner all right, or are you going out?'

Melanie nodded and mumbled. Upstairs, she sat on the edge of her bed, clasped her arms around her chest, and rocked silently in place. She had revision work to do, and she would get to it in a little while. In a little while.

Downstairs, Dorothy Viviani tried to decide whether to turn the television back on to watch the news, as she folded and ironed, folded and ironed, not knowing that most of the clothes travelling the short distance from the emptying basket to the neat piles on the sofa, were those of a dead man.

Chapter 2

The way in which the young man found out that Claire's name was Claire was like this. He bought himself a pair of binoculars and kept them to hand, ready-focussed to bring into instant close-up a view of the panel of buzzers beside the left hand door opening out into Laburnum Crescent, which happened to be one of the doors covered up with plywood. He invested in a note book and pencil and invented a code to keep track of the comings and goings at the block of flats and, more importantly, which buzzers the visitors pressed.

The code worked like this. A/t,b/rc/9.30/12 indicated the arrival at 9.30 of a man who was tall and blond, who wore a raincoat and who, as far as he could tell by squinting through the binoculars, pressed buzzer 1-12. He was only interested in buzzers and arrivals in Block 1, because it was at the door to Block 1 where the red-haired girl sometimes appeared, wrapped in her yellow wrap, to join her gaze with his. A continuation of L/10.17/a indicated that the tall blond man left at 10.17, alone. Sometimes, although he recorded an arrival, he missed the subsequent leaving. Sometimes he saw a man leaving that he hadn't noticed arrive. Sometimes, because of the weather or because the new arrival stood in a concealing position, he was unable to see what buzzer was pressed. But over the course of time he started to build up a picture and on occasion he was able to remove a buzzer number from his calculations.

For example: a man arrived at 10.35, short, wearing a thick overcoat, carrying an old-fashioned briefcase, rang buzzer fifteen away to the right and down near the bottom of the panel, looked furtively around the street before first responding to something from the intercom, and then pushing into the flats as the door released, all recorded in the notebook as A/s,d/oc,bc/10.35/15, but then, scant minutes later, the red-haired girl herself appeared round the arc of Laburnum Crescent and let herself into the flats. This meant it was probably not her that the short man had come to see, and it was certainly not her that had let him through the door, so buzzer 1-15 could be scrubbed from the list.

For example, L/11.05/CD recorded the departure of a young man dressed casually in light trousers and what looked like a thin jacket despite Glasgow's autumnal chill, at just after eleven o'clock one morning, and what was interesting was that he didn't leave alone, but with a tiny, long-haired Chinese girl clinging to his arm, a girl he'd seen before going in and out of the block of flats and who he called China Doll. It seemed reasonable to assume that the young man hadn't come to visit one girl only to leave with another, so it seemed reasonable to cross out the number of the buzzer which he had pressed earlier, which was 12.

While he carried out this detective work, he hardly ever turned the binoculars to any of the windows of the block of flats. This was because almost all of them were permanently covered by curtains or blinds and it was seldom that a stray gust of wind parted them, or somebody inside accidentally brushed up against them, and even when that happened, and even when he was quick enough to whip the binoculars up into place, the chances were that he would see nothing, perhaps just a stray movement which imagination could fashion into the movement of a naked girl but which in reality was nothing of the sort, was probably not even flesh, male or female.

Gradually he narrowed down the possible numbers until there were only three left; five, eleven, and thirteen. On the way back from the shopping arcade where he picked up bread, milk and an assortment of vegetables from the tiny grocers on the opposite end of the arcade from the convenience store, something he did every Monday and Thursday, he stopped off to look at the grimy, cracked plastic covering the Block 1 buzzers, and at the cards beneath.

#5: something old and smudged but might be construed to read *Jimmy Brown*;

#11: *Claire*;

#13: an old but perfectly legible typed legend: *CLAIRVOYANCE MODELLING AND MASSAGE.*

It didn't take much logical deduction to take number five off the list. A few days later, he had a stroke of luck. At three o'clock on an afternoon which was dark and windy, but not cold, the red-haired girl came out of the block of flats, tying the belt of a long jacket which looked as though it might be green although it was hard to tell in the gloom. She was also wearing thigh-length boots and as he watched she finished tying the belt and reached behind to pull a hood over her head. Then she set off towards Bedford Road. She didn't look up.

He sat back and rubbed the heels of his hands over his eyes. When his vision blinked back into existence, the sun had fleetingly appeared between watery clouds, and the red-haired girl was passing a very tall man walking, stiff-legged like a giraffe or a stork, in the opposite direction. As far as he could see, they didn't acknowledge each other's presence; they didn't nod cordially or perhaps abruptly as their eyes accidentally met. When he saw the tall man stalk to Block 1, he picked up the binoculars more out of habit than anything else. He watched as the tall man's thin, slightly bony finger hesitated over the panel of buzzers, and finally settled on number thirteen: *CLAIRVOYANCE MODELLING AND MASSAGE*. The tall man bent down and forward to say something into the intercom system and then without straightening—without even turning—reached out a long arm to push open the plywood door, and seconds later disappeared into concealing darkness.

The young man tried to imagine what was happening inside. Was the tall man climbing the stairs—for surely flat thirteen could not be on the ground floor—taking them two at a time—perhaps pulling himself up even more quickly by means of a banister, perhaps slowing hesitantly, moving through dark corridors towards his destination? Was it dark inside? Was there a lift? Was the tall man genuinely looking for a clairvoyant session, or seeking to employ a model, perhaps for a photographic assignment, or attending an appointment for a massage, not impossible given the man's apparent age and slightly arthritic movements? He crossed number thirteen off the list and circled *Claire* with heavy strokes of his pencil. He glanced up as the sun slid behind the greasy clouds again and darkness swept over the street as if someone, somewhere, had pulled a giant curtain.

As their gaze met through ochre rays a day or so later, his lips murmured *Claire* and even though her own lips formed a slight smile, he did not think it was because she could tell that he had used her name. Nor would she be able to tell that he had put away the binoculars, torn all the used pages out of the notebook and thrown them away, and put the pencil and what was left of the notebook beside the telephone, although he scarcely knew why he bothered, as nobody ever called.

He didn't do anything the next day, because he had lain awake for much of the night, trying to imagine what would happen when he crossed the road and pressed buzzer 1-11. He discovered that not only did he have no idea of what would happen, but also that he had no idea of what he wanted to happen. With his eyes closed, curled up on his left side or his right side beneath the bedcovers (he never slept on his back), he could see himself crossing the street easily enough. Sometimes it was bright; sometimes it was gloomy. Sometimes a car drove past as he reached the distant pavement; sometimes another pedestrian walked past, a middle-aged man bulked out with an anorak, or an older woman walking a small dog which yipped and lunged at his passing heels.

On the opposite pavement, he could see himself pause for a moment and look back at his own window, usually dark and uninformative in a row of other windows (paradoxically also dark during daylight hours, but many leaking cheerful light through curtains or blinds at night). Once he looked back and saw himself staring across the street through a set of binoculars, which he set aside just long enough to make a note, probably, he thought to himself as he drifted between wakefulness and sleep and remembered his own black jacket, something along the lines of A/m,f/bj/10.00/11.

He had no difficulty seeing with his own eyes the panel of buzzers, seeing his own finger pressing 1-11 *Claire*, and seeing the panel swing momentarily closer as he bent forward to hear a voice? a click? a reciprocal buzzing noise? then darkness as the door swallowed him, and nothing until a vertical strip of light showed where another door was open, or was opening.

When he moved, he saw a shadow move on the cold floor, within the rectangular pool of light released by the door. As he moved closer, the shadow bounced and grew bigger, as if it was his shadow representing his own progress through these last few feet of darkness, but he knew that the shadow was cast by whoever was behind the door, coming in the opposite direction, the shadow thrown by light inside the room behind the door, either electric light or sunlight pouring through a window. How did he know the floor was cold? Was he wearing shoes? He was confused, momentarily disoriented: why should he be wondering about shoes, of all things, when the red-haired girl was mere feet, scant inches away?

He turned over in bed and tried to imagine how it would be when she came to the door and saw him, but he found it almost impossible, and when he did make it happen, when he saw her hands and then her face appear around the edge of the door, looking at him as she had looked at him from the street door when they were both awake, he found that he could not understand her expression at all.

The next day he slept late. He had no idea if she was in. He was exhausted and fear tied a knot in his stomach. The day after that it rained hard and he decided not to go out. The next day was a Thursday.

Claire's real name was Samantha Pevey, although most of her friends and all of her family called her Sam. She was twenty-two. Once she saw a psychologist on television say, 'It's a vicious circle. The parents have no structure to their lives, so how can they teach structure to their children? And when the children grow up and have their own family, it is likely that there is no structure to their lives either, so they cannot teach it to their children, and so it goes on.' Claire remembered that the interviewer had looked puzzled. 'So what are you saying?' he had asked. 'Are you saying that these people should not be allowed to have children?' Claire remembered that the psychologist had been an older, smartly dressed woman with a red poppy fixed to her jacket, and the interviewer too was wearing a red poppy, as it was just before Remembrance Sunday.

'No,' the psychologist had laughed. 'Of course not. I'm saying that the government's idea to intervene and support families is a good one, but I would go further and try to impart structure much earlier, in schools.'

Structure.

Claire lost her virginity when she was seventeen. She was working as a shelf stacker in Asda and shared her break with Paul Craig, nineteen, who was actually studying pure mathematics and statistics at university but was trying to earn some extra cash in between semesters. They sipped coffee and swapped sandwiches, and Paul smoked a cigarette which Claire thought looked cool even though she knew that it wasn't very sensible. Her father had told her often enough to 'stay off the fags, they'll do you in', and usually gave a rasping cough to prove his point, though it appeared that he had no similar advice on the dangers of drink, or if he did, he wasn't following it.

At eleven o'clock one night, when their shift finished, Paul approached Claire and asked if she fancied a quick one. Quick one what? she had asked, and by way of explanation he raised his eyebrows, made a circle with his left thumb and forefinger, and pushed his right forefinger through it. Well, said Claire. If somebody had told her that Paul or anyone else would proposition her in this fashion, she would have laughed and said she would just die, she would just curl up with embarrassment, she would cover her face with her hands, or she would run away. In the event she surprised herself by doing none of these things. Where? she said, and licked her lips.

It transpired that Paul had borrowed his father's car, so they drove south, off the main roads, down into some woods and stopped in a gravel parking place underneath some trees which by day saw countless families and dog walkers arrive and depart, but by night was deserted except for the occasional car parked, like them, as far from the road as possible, with its lights killed, sometimes rocking rhythmically or frantically even though there was no immediate sign that anyone was inside. On the way there they said nothing, although the sexual tension in the car rose to such a point that they were both panting slightly when the car finally halted and Paul turned off the engine and the lights. 'You got a condom?' Claire asked. He produced an unopened packet and grinned in the darkness. 'Don't think Mr Asda will miss these, do you?'

Structure.

Men often asked her how she lost her virginity and, when she told them about putting down the back seats and scrambling in, about groping and exploring, without kissing, about the sudden shock of seeing Paul poised above her, ready to push down and in and *take her,* and her feeling of being open to the world when he actually did it, then many men asked whether she had enjoyed it, which she often thought was a singularly stupid question (although she was careful not to say so), because if she had not enjoyed it, why would she be earning money now in Laburnum Crescent the way in which she did?

Some time after Paul had gone back to university, after she had been out with him twice more, and then with a succession of other boys, not all employees of Asda, she had for a prank snatched up the mobile phone of one of her best friends, Caroline Docherty, when it rang. A man's voice said, 'Jade? Jade of GG?' She had disconnected, but when she told Caroline about the wrong number, Caroline turned red partly from anger, partly from shame, grabbed the mobile, and turned her back, pressing buttons to return the call.

Jade? wondered Samantha. When the full story came out, she wasn't upset, or horrified, or disgusted; she was interested and intrigued and soon came to share the flat in Laburnum Crescent, three days one week, two days the next, but always at home at the weekend. That was structure if you like, she often thought, though not one she could share with most of her friends, or her parents, or her sisters, all of whom still knew her as Samantha. So perhaps the psychologist had been right after all.

———●———

The night that the young man dreamed of approaching a door, she also dreamed of a door, though she did not remember it in the morning. She dreamed that a light of some sort was shining outside, on the other side of her bedroom door, so that the small gap between doorframe and door glowed, as if four very thin strips of light had been placed in the shape of a rectangle, and the light, which started off white, slowly turned pink and then red. In the dream, she was curled up in bed, and she ignored the light by turning over, turning her back on it. Either the floor creaked, or the bed did, and she felt very cold.

———●———

When the buzzer rang, she was sitting on a wicker chair, filing her fingernails and watching with half her attention an American chat programme on a tiny television perched on the end of her dressing table. There were only four pieces of furniture in the room: the chair, a double bed, a small bedside table and the dressing table. The programme featured a saturnine presenter arbitrating dissent between on the one hand a young man wearing jeans, T-shirt and a desperate expression, and on the other hand two women who both claimed to have had sex with him and who were both distraught at discovering each other's existence. Neither of them was very attractive. The young man kept licking his lips; his eyes darted this way and that, as if he was searching for an escape route. It looked as if, given the chance, he would leave both women, unlamented, behind.

Claire started. She had no appointment until just after lunch, and she had received no telephone calls. The buzzer sounded again.

'Yes?'

A voice asked if she was Claire.

'Yes.'

The owner of the voice explained, rather nervously, that Claire didn't know who he was, but he lived across the road, in an upstairs apartment.

'Oh, yes? What do you want?'

She did know who it was, of course, and she thought she knew what he was going to say. She found herself wondering how she would react. There was a long pause. She had turned down the sound, but on the television she could see that one of the unattractive women had burst into tears, which had the effect of making her look even more unattractive, and people in the audience were shouting, some of them gesticulating angrily. The boy or young man from across the street said, in a manner which turned the statement into a question, that he wanted to talk to her. Perhaps the intercom wasn't working properly; either that, or his voice was very soft.

'What about?' said Claire.

He didn't know.

'Really?' said Claire. The flat was tidy; the bed was made; she was still dressed in jeans and a sweater but she didn't think that mattered. Who was this boy who watched out for her from across the street? On impulse, she pressed the button which activated the door, and almost immediately regretted it. 'First floor,' she said into the intercom.

She turned off the television, went to the door and looked out, wondering who she could notify. It made sense to tell someone that she was inviting an unknown quantity up to her room. There were six apartments of differing sizes on this floor. The two biggest were numbers seven (an Indian family) and eight (an old lady with lots of cats), both apartments past the stairwell through a glazed fire door. Baz lived in number nine—he often acted as minder in return for the occasional favour, but he would be out at classes. Next door at ten was Lucy, sometimes there, sometimes not, much the same as Claire herself and for the same reason, and on the other side at twelve lived Bailin, a tiny Chinese girl with long black hair who kept herself to herself. Neither Claire nor Lucy knew whether she actually lived there or whether she was in the business.

She got no answer from any of the doors, but when footsteps sounded from the stairwell, Lucy appeared, followed by the young man. Lucy had dressed herself in a shiny red skirt, shiny red boots, and a shiny red plastic raincoat.

'What are you, a fire engine?' said Claire, relieved to see her.

'This one yours?' said Lucy.

'He's just visiting,' said Claire, employing their code. A visitor, by definition, was nothing to do with the business.

'Just as well, eh?' said Lucy, putting the key to her own door. 'After last night?'

'What?'

'Don't be trying it on,' said Lucy.

Claire looked at her, puzzled. Lucy must have sensed that it was genuine, because she said, 'Ok, right, never mind, talk to you later, all right?' and waggled her eyebrows towards the young man, who was standing patiently in the hallway. She closed her door and Claire turned around.

She saw that the young man had a slim build and was an inch or so taller than she was. He had fair hair, neatly cut. His eyes were grey and curiously fixed, as if he never blinked. Although she wouldn't call him handsome, neither would she call him unattractive. He was wearing blue jeans and a black leather jacket, and was carrying a plastic bag featuring the logo of the tiny grocers up on Bedford Road.

While she looked at him, he looked at her. He saw a girl of about his own age, hair dyed red and cut in an old-fashioned straight bob. Her features were regular and attractive, but her eyes looked tired, as if either she had not had enough sleep, or she had seen too much of life, or both. Her light blue sweater was an inch or so too short, revealing the pale flesh of a thin body.

'Well? Like what you see?'

He tried to smile.

'You better come in.'

———————●———————

Afterwards, she sat with Lucy in the ground floor kitchen, both of them clasping hot mugs of coffee in their hands.

When Lucy asked what had happened, she described how the young man had followed her into her room, and she had sat, legs curled, in her wicker chair, and he had looked around helplessly until she had indicated the bed, and he had sat perched right on the edge in such a stiff-backed precarious position that she felt she only had to purse her lips and blow at him and he would slip right off onto the hard uncarpeted floor.

'Did you tell him you were used to having men on your bed?' asked Lucy, straight-faced.

'That reminds me,' said Claire, 'what did you mean, after last night?'

Lucy blew steam away from the top of her mug and took a sip of coffee before replying. 'Well, I heard him. The man. I heard his footsteps across the hall last night, I can always tell a man's footsteps from a woman's footsteps, well you know that as well as I do. I heard him at your door—did I hear him at your door? I'm not sure if I did, now I come to think of it, but I did hear him walking across your room, I always hear them walking across your room, no carpet, you said it yourself, no carpet. Didn't hear him leave, mind you I went to sleep so I might've missed it I suppose, but anyway I thought you must've had an overnight.'

'But,' said Claire, 'I wasn't here last night. I was at home.'

The two girls stared at each other across the kitchen table, over the tops of their mugs.

'Oh,' said Lucy, mystified. 'Well. It must've been Jade, then.' But Claire shook her head uncertainly, and said she thought Jade was away for a week. 'Oh,' said Lucy again.

'You sure you heard footsteps?'

'Yeah.'

'In my room?'

'Yeah.'

'P'raps it was Jade,' said Claire rather helplessly, although even as she said it, she remembered how neat and tidy the room, the bed and the tiny bathroom had been when she arrived that morning, not that Jade made an undue amount of mess, but the flat had looked exactly as she, Claire, had left it two days ago.

After a few moments when neither of them said anything and the mystery was no closer to being solved, Lucy asked again about the boy. Claire explained that he had launched into a long story about how he had identified her, even from across the street, something about binoculars, code, deductive reasoning and luck but, admitted Claire, she lost track of his explanation almost immediately. 'I kind of stopped listening,' she said. 'I watched his fingers, and his legs, he was all kind of tense. He kept licking his lips,' she added. 'You know what they're like,' she said. Lucy nodded. 'But his eyes were very calm,' said Claire. Her own eyes unfocussed slightly as she remembered how he had looked at her in a composed fashion, even though the rest of his body language shouted that he was uncomfortable and out of his depth.

'Did you like him?'

'Hmm-mm,' answered Claire as if she was thinking, but the truth was that she felt deeply uncertain about the young man with the black jacket, blue jeans and serene gaze. She didn't know whether she liked him or not, and she wasn't sure she could explain to Lucy why he made her as uncomfortable as she obviously made him. She wasn't completely sure she could explain it to herself. She had structured her life, as the psychologist would say, into two halves; business at Laburnum Crescent; everything else at home. Friends knew her as Samantha. Clients knew her as Claire. And here was

41

this boy who was not a client, or at least she supposed he wasn't a client, she supposed he had just caught sight of her and wanted to make friends, but he knew her as Claire, who didn't have friends, only clients. His presence made her uncomfortable, as if he was challenging the order she had imposed on her own life, as if he was pushing at barriers merely by being there. But was that his fault, or hers?

'Well, did you?' insisted Lucy.

'Not sure,' Claire answered. 'Don't know. It was kind of hard to get anything out of him. I kept asking, what do you want? And he kept saying he didn't know. I asked if he knew what I did and he said he had guessed, so I asked did he want me then, was that it? and he said he didn't know and eventually after going round in circles I pulled up my jumper and showed him my tits and shouted, is this what you want, then, is it?'

'You what?' laughed Lucy.

'But even though he looked at them, he looked right back at my face, Lucy, I swear to you I was sitting there with my boobs out and he just looked at my face and said he didn't know, and this wasn't quite what he expected, and when I asked what he expected, he said he didn't know, so I lost my temper and told him to get out.'

'And he went?'

'He went,' confirmed Claire. But what she didn't say was that he glanced back at her just before he went out of the door. She didn't say that their eyes met for just a second, or maybe two seconds, but that was all the time it took for her to understand that he would come back. She didn't say that the glance was wrapped in layers of meaning, something she found both wonderful and disturbing; she knew he would return, and he knew that she knew, and when she said nothing but let him go out of the room in silence, that

42

represented an understanding, that she knew he would come back and had not rejected the idea out of hand. How could all that meaning have passed between them, in a glance lasting no more than two seconds, without a single word being spoken? She didn't know, and she didn't say anything about it to Lucy.

'Weird,' said Lucy, shaking her head. 'Weird.'

Claire nodded and said, 'It certainly was.'

It certainly was.

———◆———

By the time he got back to his own rooms, he was trembling violently and felt nauseous. He had screwed up the courage to press buzzer 1-11, and look at what had happened. She had invited him in, shouted at him, showed him her breasts and nipples. Voice trembling, she had ordered him out, but he had seen that her nipples were engorged, and her eyes had lost their tiredness and were shining and, when he had looked back at her before leaving, as she smoothed her sweater into place, her eyes had been complicit. She was at once more and less than he had imagined; less perfect, more alive. She wasn't at all what he had expected. He found it impossible to decide whether this was a good thing or a bad thing.

Still shaky, he put away his bread, milk and vegetables.

Chapter 3

Harry McCabe sat in the dining room of his tiny house and stared at the business card he had thrown carelessly onto the mantelpiece some days before. He wondered why he hadn't thrown it away immediately—it wasn't the sort of thing he usually kept. Maybe, he thought, he had known even then that he might need it. He wondered how it was that Stevie had a spare card to give him, then remembered that Stevie had said that Cheyne had given him a handful of cards, a whole lot of cards, he said, to spread around so that he could be famous even if he couldn't be rich.

Cheyne was Cheyne Tully, the name on the card, a made up name if Harry had ever heard one. The card was black, with just the name: Cheyne Tully, in white block letters, and just underneath it, also in white but not in capitals: Ghosthunter. And then, in much smaller letters, also white, down in the bottom right-hand corner of the card, an email address: <u>ctully@gdomain.com</u>. It was an elegant card, Harry had to admit. He had stared at it for some time before realising that the white text on the black background was supposed to reinforce the ghosthunter message, and perhaps it did; perhaps that was why he hadn't thrown it away. The back of the card was just unrelieved black, but he turned it over and looked anyway, in case more white words had materialised in some ghostly fashion while he had been staring at the front of the card. None had.

He didn't know what to do.

On the evening when Stevie had given him the black business card, he had been nursing a lager in the Lag's Hand—only a lager because he would be driving the next day and Red Arrow Taxis were as conscientious about warning him of the staying power of alcohol in his system, which could affect his driving even on the day after he had been drinking, as they were about making sure he knew what to do if a fare took ill, or worse, while in his cab. Not that he had followed any of the advice after George Viviani had plunged onto his back seat, inconsiderately dead. *That* evening he had felt the need of something considerably stronger than a lager and on the following day he had rung in to say he wasn't well enough to drive, and Agnes for once didn't say anything catty but just hoped he would feel better soon.

On the next day, or maybe the day after, he picked up a woman near Kelvingrove Park, who wanted to be taken to the Buchanan Galleries shopping centre. She was about thirty, not unattractive but not his type, and anyway he spotted straight away that she wore a wedding ring. About halfway there, she asked him to turn up the heater, which he did.

Later on he picked up two businessmen going to some sort of seminar at the Adam Smith building. The pair of them argued all the way there, and he heard them using words like stimulus, fiscal and quantitative easing, together with words like unemployment, benefits policy, and student grants, from which he gained the impression that they were economists of some sort, although whether they were on their way to give lectures to students at the university, or whether they were going to some sort of meeting of other economists like them which just happened to be hosted by the university, he was unable to tell. They tipped well and he wondered whether the level at which economists tipped taxi drivers was itself some sort of economic indicator. He remembered thinking he was pleased he had taken the trouble to clean the back of the cab after George Viviani's untimely demise, even though George had left no visible mess, no indication that he had ever been there, alive or dead.

That evening he picked up two half-drunk women who wanted to go to some obscure address in Dalmarnock, and on the way there they interrupted their giggling to ask him to turn the heater on. Three more customers asked him the same thing on the next day, which was a Thursday. One was a middle-aged man who wanted to be picked up at the City Chambers and taken to a restaurant in Berkeley Street. He spent most of the trip reading a magazine, apart from a few minutes calling someone on his mobile to let whoever it was know that he was on his way. Another was a woman wearing an old-fashioned coat with a fur collar and leather gloves, who wanted to be taken out to the airport. She was accompanied by an enormous suitcase which sported handles and wheels, and Harry McCabe surmised that she was going on holiday somewhere.

And later that evening he picked up a girl, not much more than seventeen or eighteen, who had studs set into her lips and at the corner of her eyes, a style which Harry McCabe always thought looked ludicrous and sometimes downright unpleasant, although he also had an accompanying and worrying thought that perhaps this was because he was no longer seventeen or eighteen. The girl was wearing jeans and a thin jacket and as soon as she jumped in, wanting to be taken to a club in Charing Cross, she said, 'Jesus it's frigging cold in here, can't you turn the frigging heating on?'

Harry McCabe might normally have responded with a tart comment of his own, but truth to tell, he had noticed a draught of cold air on the occasions when he had gone to the back to open the door of the taxi, almost as if he had opened the door to a fridge or a freezer. As far as he could tell the heater was working. It was certainly blasting out heat into the front of the cab; he had turned it up to maximum and drove the taxi wearing a short-sleeved shirt even though the Glasgow weather was dark and chilly, and even though he could see passengers in the back shrugging shoulders deeper into coats, or blowing into their cupped hands.

On Friday he told Agnes he was popping into the garage to get the heater fixed, but when he got there, and after he had waited for a bit in the designated waiting area drinking coffee out of a plastic cup and reading all sorts of certificates of attainment which appeared to prove that the garage was the best in Glasgow, if not in Scotland, the mechanic emerged from the depths of the garage wiping his hands on an oily rag to tell him there was nothing wrong with the heater. Harry McCabe informed him that the back was cold, that one of his customers had even referred to it as 'frigging cold', and the mechanic shrugged and said aye, he noticed it was a bit chilly too but it was nothing to do with the heater. Then what? Harry had asked, and the mechanic had just shrugged again.

'Yo, big man.'

He had been jolted back to the gloomy interior of the Lag's Hand and the lager he'd been nursing. Stevie joined him, together with two other drivers, one of who was Paul somebody, but the other was a stranger. On hearing the story, Stevie had produced the black business card.

'What's this?' Harry had asked.

'It's this guy,' said Stevie, 'who knows about ghosts and suchlike.'

Harry snorted, and the stranger guffawed.

'You got a guy snuffed it on the back seat, and then you get all this cold?' asked Stevie. The stranger stopped laughing and said, 'You had a guy snuffed it?' and when Harry McCabe nodded and said, 'Heart attack,' the stranger rearranged his features into a more sombre expression and muttered something about being sorry to hear it.

'See, I had this friend,' said Stevie, 'his original name was Michael but he got fed up with that and started calling himself Richard. He got married to a nice Welsh girl called Rhona and they lived in a cottage down near the A55 somewhere—you know where I mean?—on the north coast, along near Conwy. Anyway, they was happy as Larry until Rhona took their dog out for a walk one evening, I remember it was a crazy dog, some sort of hound about nine feet tall but daft as a brush, anyway some kid in a souped-up mini lost control round a corner and killed it instantly, and Rhona too.

'I went to the funeral,' said Stevie in a quiet voice, 'seeing as how I had known Richard ever since he was Michael, and afterwards we went back to the cottage, and that was when he told me about the music. See, Rhona had loved a particular piece of piano music—he told me what it was but I could never remember, a bit like Eddolls and Theobald's Church, remember that?—anyway it was an old record that her father had given her, and it was scratched in one particular place. Course they don't play records much now, in fact they didn't play them much then either, so the church got hold of a cd recording from somewhere for the funeral and, so Richard told me but I confess I didn't notice at the time, when they played it as the coffin was being carried up the aisle out of the church, it clicked and clicked in exactly the same place, as if there was a scratch on the cd in exactly the same place as on the record.'

'Yeah?' said the stranger. 'Nah, you're full of bull.' Harry McCabe picked up the black business card, turned it over to discover that nothing was written on the back, and put it down again.

Stevie shrugged his shoulders.

'You want another one of those?' asked the man Harry didn't know, a small neat man who looked as if he would be more at home sitting behind a desk in a bank rather than driving a taxi. Harry McCabe made a gesture which said thank you, no, and put a hand across the top of his glass. Light glinted on his bald head. The stranger made the same enquiry of Stevie and Paul whatever his name was, and having ascertained that only Stevie wanted a refill, pushed back his chair and made his way to the bar.

'About a week later,' said Stevie without waiting for him to come back, 'I got a call from Richard, he sounded strange on the phone, though I couldn't put my finger on why. He said he had something to show me, and when I went to see him—this was in the days before I lived in Glasgow, I lived just over the border in Chester—he showed me that whenever he put a record on, it always made a noise like it was scratched even when it wasn't. He said he'd tried everything. He'd taken the records round to a friend's place, and they all played fine except for the original piano thing. So he borrowed the friend's record player and took it back to the cottage, and played the records again. Scratch. He borrowed some records from his friend. No scratch. He played records that he had listened to with Rhona. Scratch.

'I stayed there that night,' said Stevie. 'I noticed that Richard didn't sleep in his bedroom but on the couch downstairs, and I assumed that he just hadn't got over everything and couldn't bear to sleep in his own bed that he had shared with Rhona, but he gave me a funny look, almost a desperate look and said, I know what you're thinking, but the reason I'm not sleeping in our bedroom is because it's so cold.

'When he said this, I suddenly realised that this desperation was why his voice had sounded funny on the phone. It was a quiet, concealed desperation; he concealed it because he didn't believe anybody would believe the story about the records, and the cd in the church, and the cold bedroom. It was obvious what he was thinking.

'In the night, he came in and shook me awake, and said, listen. In the next room, in the room that had used to be Richard and Rhona's, we could hear what sounded like a faint sobbing. I've heard it before, Richard whispered, but I didn't want to say earlier. I pulled on trousers and a jumper and we went out, and opened the door to the next room. It was like a fridge in there. I swear there was ice on the windows, and the white light of the moon was broken into slivers so that parts of the room were bright white and others were black.

'There was no sound,' said Stevie. 'No sound, and nothing to see, just cold air where we was breathing and bright moonlight, but neither of us believed nobody was there.'

The man Harry didn't know returned. 'What?'

'The guy's place was haunted,' summarised Paul.

'Thanks,' said Stevie. 'Cheers.'

'I stayed in a place where it sounded like a kid was crying, a baby, something like that. Cheers.' The man Harry McCabe didn't know waved his beer vaguely and took a swallow. 'Turned out to be the pipes, water blockage, something like that.'

'Yeah?' said Paul, not sounding very interested.

Harry McCabe picked up the black business card again and waved it in a questioning fashion. Stevie nodded.

'Yeah. Well, it turned out that Richard's friend, the one with the record player, knew this other guy Cheyne Tully. I'm not sure why, I think it was something to do with his mother, who had some sort of problem when her husband, the friend's father, died. Anyway Richard was desperate enough to get in touch with Tully, who came round—I heard all this afterwards, I wasn't there, you understand?—I only met the guy once, in a pub when it was all over. He seemed normal enough, tall, thin, black hair, black clothes, he gave me a bunch of business cards and told me he had fame but no fortune, I think he was a bit drunk as Richard had been buying rounds for some time before I arrived.' Stevie took a breath, then swallowed some of his own drink.

'He came round?' prompted the stranger.

'Yeah. He came round, got the full story, like I did. And then, according to Richard, he just hung around. He told Richard to go to bed as he always did, and then went into the cold bedroom. Stayed there all night, Richard told me. He listened to the music. He listened to Richard.' Stevie nodded to himself. 'I wonder now if that wasn't the most important thing. He listened to *Richard*, who told him all about Rhona, how they met at some karaoke club, how they got married, how they bought the daft dog, what their plans were. Had been.

'Richard said he told Cheyne Tully everything, more than he had told anyone before. And after he had heard everything that Richard had to say, Tully told him that he had to let go. Richard said he had laughed hysterically when he heard that. *Me?* he shouted at Tully. *Me?* And Tully nodded and said, a little sadly, that they both had to let go. He gave Richard a microphone, although it wasn't plugged in or anything, and said he should speak to Rhona that very night, and that he wouldn't stay.

'Richard said it was the sadness that got through to him in the end. It was like Tully knew exactly what he was talking about, and knew exactly what to do and what would happen. And because he knew what was going to happen, he was sad about it.'

Stevie fell silent.

'What?' said Paul.

'I just remembered I'm not supposed to tell you what happened next.'

'What!' said Paul, and Harry McCabe looked up.

'I promised Richard,' said Stevie obstinately.

'You can't do this,' said Paul. 'You can't tell us a whole fucking story and then not tell us how it finished.'

Stevie swallowed more of his drink and remained silent. Paul turned up his palms in a beseeching gesture, and looked at Harry McCabe. Harry turned the business card over and over with the fingers of one hand. He said, 'But it worked?'

'Yeah,' said Stevie. 'It worked. He talked a lot. He got mighty sad, then he got mighty angry, which was not what he expected, and then he got mighty sad again. I won't tell you all the things he said, 'cos I promised not to, but at the end he said something like, Rhona, I know you can't leave me alone, and I can't leave you alone either, but we have to be apart, don't you see? We have to be apart, for a little while. And when he woke up much later—not that he ever remembered going to sleep, so he told me—she was gone. No funny clicks. No cold room. No sobbing. Nothing, except the perfect imprint of a set of lips on the microphone.'

Stevie drained his glass and set it down gently.

'Aw, you're full of bull,' said the stranger after a few moments.

Stevie shrugged again. Although he didn't remember doing it, Harry McCabe must have slipped the business card into his breast pocket about then, because he found it there later. Paul had been staring at Stevie intently.

'Why did you move from Chester to Glasgow?' he asked.

'Personal reasons,' said Stevie.

He got up, grabbed a coat because it was raining, and went outside. The cab was parked on the other side of the road, about two doors down. He skipped across the street, holding the raincoat up over his head, unlocked the cab using the automated key fob while he was still ten yards away. The cab's indicator lights flashed orange, reflecting on wet tarmac and in shallow puddles nearby. He could hear the rain bouncing off car metalwork, could see it slanting down through the illumination of a streetlight. He reached the cab, yanked open the back door, and recoiled at a blast of cold air. 'Fuck you, George,' he muttered, and slammed the door shut.

Back inside, he logged on to the internet and wrote an email to Cheyne Tully, explaining that he had got a copy of his business card through a mutual acquaintance, that he (Harry) had a problem with his car and he would be grateful if he (Cheyne) could call or visit as soon as possible. He added his address and telephone number and then sat in front of the computer screen for quite a while trying to make up his mind whether to send the message.

He finally decided that before very much longer he was going to find it impossible to induce customers into his fridge-like cab, if indeed he had not reached that point already, and when that point was finally reached, be it tomorrow or the next day or the day after, he would suddenly find himself without means of support. So the sooner he started trying to solve the problem, the better, especially as he had already mentioned what was happening to the company, Red Arrow Taxis, and catty Agnes, after consulting with unnamed superiors, merely reminded him that the upkeep of the vehicle was his responsibility. When he pointed out it wasn't really upkeep, or the lack of it, which was causing the problem, she didn't bother to reply.

Having reached a decision, he clicked on the send button and momentarily imagined the email message zapping its way through wires to emerge almost instantaneously on Cheyne Tully's computer screen somewhere else, maybe in Glasgow, maybe not; it was impossible to tell from the bland email address and there had been no other means of contact displayed on the business card. Then he yawned and stretched, and with Tommy away for the weekend and tiredness creeping over him like rising floodwater induced by the rain outside, he decided to turn off the computer without even checking his personal ads, and go to bed.

———●———

Not very far away, Constable Bob Kirkwood was curled up alone in his own bed (Constable Kirkwood had never married, although once he had proposed to and been turned down by a girl called Jennifer Cowell, who he had met at a party and then went out with on a number of occasions, but it seemed she had bigger fish to fry because, he discovered afterwards, she had also been going out with a banker and an estate agent, and had finally married the banker and moved away to California, and he had never heard of her again).

The Constable's eyes were tightly shut and he was beginning to twitch and quiver as he started to dream his recurring dream. He wasn't quite sure when he had first dreamed the dream. It must have been two or three days after the incident of the knife fight when the assailant had run away and left his bloody victim behind; three or four days after attending the death of George Viviani and the subsequent discussion with doctor Muhammad Jamal Rafiq; four or five days after his phone call to Constable Gillian Sargent in Ayr. (Not surprisingly, Constable Gillian Sargent was universally known as Constable Sargent, and was widely tipped for promotion.) The trouble was that it wasn't until six or seven days had passed that Constable Kirkwood realised that his dream was recurring, by which time he had forgotten exactly when he had first dreamed it.

In the dream he was standing in a queue of people, outside, on roadway somewhere. There were houses on both sides, very tall houses, so tall that they started to lean over at the top in such a way that houses from the left hand side of the roadway met houses from the right hand side and they propped each other up, almost horizontal above the roadway like some sort of roof. Constable Kirkwood stared up at these crazy houses. He could see people in windows far above his head, sitting in defiance of gravity as if chairs had been affixed to walls and they could saunter up and sit on them without any danger whatsoever of falling through the window to land on Constable Kirkwood or some other member of the slowly moving queue. In the dream there was always one man at one window drinking tea or coffee from a cup, without spilling a single drop.

The queue meandered slowly through a number of turnings, and Constable Kirkwood shuffled after the person in front of him, a small woman wearing an all-in-one jumpsuit, while wondering who was shuffling along behind him, but he never turned around to see who it was. Sometimes he thought about turning around to see who it was. But dream logic or dream knowledge told him that if he tried, his neck would seize up with agonising cramps and pain would shoot down the nerve endings of his spine, although he wouldn't stumble in shock and fall out of the meandering line, but rather would freeze in place for long seconds while, or so it seemed, red hot needles danced up and down his body, before disappearing as quickly as they came, allowing him to shuffle after the jump-suited woman, who had gained several feet on him while he stood stationary in excruciating pain.

Constable Kirkwood didn't know whether this had actually happened in an early enactment of his dream, planting a memory for later dreams, or whether the dream knowledge had always been there, welling up in some arcane fashion from his subconscious.

After a while, he became aware that the head of the queue was in sight. It ended in the middle of a space outside a pub and he could just make out another queue, facing in the opposite direction to his queue, which ended in the same space, rather like two tug of war teams except that neither team had a rope, but merely shuffled towards each other. It was at about this time that Constable Kirkwood noticed a red liquid running down either side of the roadway, in the gutters. He wondered if it might be blood. Dream knowledge suggested that it was, in fact, blood, but he rather wished that it would be something else. In the darkness of his bedroom, he shifted and quivered and moaned gently, trying to deny the existence of the blood even though he could see it, plain as day. In fact he could see more and more of it because as he shuffled forwards the amount of visible liquid seemed to grow.

The young blond man in front of the jump-suited woman reached the head of the queue and was given a knife by another man who stood to one side, with a flat box hanging in front of him, suspended by two straps fastened up behind his head. Constable Kirkwood didn't recognise him, although he thought he recognised his hairstyle. The young blond man stepped forward, and a man at the head of the other queue stepped forward to meet him. This man wasn't carrying a knife and Constable Kirkwood was surprised to notice that he didn't appear to have a face, either. The peculiar thought struck him that perhaps the young blond man was sharing the same dream, was perhaps curled up somewhere dreaming that, armed with a knife, he was advancing towards another man, but that in his version of the dream, the other man had a face, was recognisably someone which gave added meaning to his dream, but which would mean nothing to Constable Kirkwood.

And then, as Constable Kirkwood had subconsciously expected, the young blond man stabbed the faceless man high up in his left arm. The knife made a wet gristly sound as it went in and the victim threw his faceless head back and Constable Kirkwood imagined that surely he would be screaming in agony if only he had a mouth to scream with. Perhaps, he thought, he was screaming in the young blond man's dream. And then the knife made another wet gristly sound as the young blond man yanked it back out, and Constable Kirkwood saw that his hand had become covered with blood.

While all this was going on, the man with the vaguely familiar hairstyle had passed a knife to the jump-suited woman. She stepped forward to meet a girl coming in the opposite direction, a thin girl with long black hair but no face and no knife. Constable Kirkwood noticed that the young blond man and the faceless man he had stabbed had both vanished, in the manner of dreams, but that the level of blood in the gutter had risen slightly. He saw the blood swirl and run through both shadows and light. He looked up to see what was causing the shadows, and saw that the pub was reaching high into the sky and was bending over at the top just like the houses further down the street, except that it just hung there without leaning on anything. Spectators were clustered at the windows, peering down at the bloody action on the bloodstained ground directly beneath. As Constable Kirkwood watched, a man quaffed from a mug of beer and he was convinced that it was the same man he had seen earlier drinking tea or coffee.

Because he was looking up at the pub building stretched against the sky, he didn't see the jump-suited woman stab the faceless girl, but he heard the familiar wet gristly sound; and then he heard it again at the same time as the man with the box proffered a knife and he took it with what he felt to be cold, listless fingers.

He stepped forward.

Ahead of him, just three paces away, then two paces away, then only one pace away, was George Viviani. He appeared to be alive, although his features were slack and unmoving, as if the myriad tiny muscles which should direct the movements of his face had all been numbed and all the corresponding nerve connections severed. Constable Kirkwood didn't like it. In the back of his mind he knew that George Viviani was dead, and yet here he was just one pace away, a zombie intent on getting its own back on the living world, which at that precise moment equated to Constable Kirkwood.

With a terrific, terrified effort, Constable Kirkwood hefted the knife and stabbed George Viviani high up in the left shoulder. The wet gristly sound repeated itself. He rather expected that George Viviani would then start squealing like a stuck pig, but in actual fact he merely clutched at his chest, rather than at his stabbed arm, and his expression moved for the first time. He looked surprised. His eyebrows rose in surprise, his dead eyes widened in surprise, and his bloodless lips formed a round O of surprise. Constable Kirkwood pulled the knife back out again, feeling rather sorry that he had ever stuck it in now that it was obvious that George was a human being and not a zombie, even if he was dead. The thought struck him that, according to the rules of his dream, he ought now to vanish, he and George Viviani both.

He woke up.

In the darkness of his bedroom, he decided that the most important thing about his dream, which he recalled with perfect clarity, was that it recurred. He also decided that he probably ought to talk to someone about it, and in fact when he got to the station the next day he applied for some counselling.

A week or so later he was summoned to a small building not far from Pitt Street, which was where the police headquarters used to be. After filling in the inevitable forms and questionnaires, he was ushered into the presence of the counsellor, a woman of about his own age who introduced herself as Sarah McPherson, who had thick red hair and an infectious smile, and who Constable Kirkwood instantly took a fancy to. By this time his recurring dream was recurring less frequently, as he dutifully told Sarah McPherson, but she insisted that he come to talk to her a number of times over the next few weeks, which he did, and by then not only had the recurring dreams stopped completely, but they had been replaced by dreams of a different nature altogether.

When the last counselling session came to an end he, greatly daring, asked Sarah McPherson if she would perhaps like to see him in the outside world, outside the tiny building where she worked, somewhere in the greater part of Glasgow such as, he suggested, a bar or a restaurant. He was both relieved and surprised when she accepted, and they started going out on a regular basis, as regular as his police work allowed, and after another six or seven months had gone by, by which time they had slept together and he was more often in her flat than in his own, he proposed to her, and she accepted again, and they married without further ado.

It was sobering to think, Constable Kirkwood often said in future years, even as he rose through the ranks to become first a Sergeant and eventually a Chief Inspector, that the brutal misery caused by a knifeman outside a pub, and the untimely death of George Viviani in the back of a taxi cab, should ultimately lead to the happiness of two other human beings.

Meanwhile, long before any of this happened, Harry McCabe also dreamed. He dreamed that he jumped out of bed, flung on his raincoat, and went outside into the cold, dark street where it was still raining. He could still hear raindrops landing on the parked cars, although now they were pattering out the beat of some tune that he recognised but could not quite put a name to.

The windows of the taxi were covered with frost on the inside, while rain ran down them in rivulets on the outside. He yanked open the door and saw that the whole of the inside of the taxi was coated with ice and frost, and on the back seat sat his wife who had died at the time Tommy was born. She was wearing nothing but a thin hospital gown. She looked at him, her face suddenly frightened, and opened her mouth to scream. He watched the thin muscles of her arms bunch as she clenched her fists, and she took a shuddering breath, and screamed. Again. And again.

He opened his eyes and discovered that she was still screaming in the darkness of his bedroom. No, it was the phone. Tommy? He eyes sought the red numbers of his digital clock: 23.45. Had something happened to Tommy? He fumbled the receiver to his ear. Croaked out a query. Licked his lips.

'My name is Tully,' said a voice. 'You asked me to call?'

Chapter 4

Dorothy Viviani never remembered much about what happened in the few weeks immediately after being visited by Constable Gillian Sargent. There were great gaps of time when she remembered nothing at all, and then her memory would furnish a few pictures, a few events, before lapsing into darkness again, rather like a film reel where three-quarters of the images had been erased, leaving only grey flickering static, but every now and again scenes would flash into brilliant life.

She remembered opening the door to find Constable Gillian Sargent standing on the other side. She remembered that the Constable opened her mouth and said something like, 'It's about your husband. Can I come in for a minute?' and that her heart had instantly started to pound, and her vision had momentarily blurred. She wasn't to know that Constable Gillian Sargent was intensely worried about what effect her words were going to have on Dorothy; twice before she had been the bearer of bad news.

On the first occasion the woman who had opened the door—a woman, now that Constable Gillian Sargent thought about it, not unlike Dorothy Viviani—had said, 'No, you must have come to the wrong house,' and promptly shut the door again, when of course she hadn't gone to the wrong house at all, and it had taken repeated knocking and eventually prolonged telephone calls before the woman, whose name Constable Gillian Sargent had forgotten, finally accepted that her husband was dead.

The second time was even worse, when an older couple learned what had happened to their son on the main road just coming home from work, because she had managed to get inside the house without giving away anything too traumatic, and even got the couple to sit down with cups of tea. But as soon as she told them what had happened, the woman still toppled out of her chair and struck her head against a wooden surround, and had to be taken to hospital, while the man didn't try to help or react in any way, but sat motionless in his chair, except that every ten seconds or so he would violently shake his head, as if in disagreement with something which kept occurring to him.

So Constable Gillian Sargent watched Dorothy Viviani anxiously while they went inside, and a young girl came down the stairs, who Dorothy Viviani introduced as her daughter.

'Could you go and make us all a cup of tea?' Constable Gillian Sargent asked Melanie and, when Melanie had disappeared out of the room, not without a curious backward glance, she said, 'I'm afraid I've got some rather bad news.'

It was at this point that Dorothy's memory started to play tricks. Something would happen; she would do something, or somebody else would, or she would say something or somebody else would; whatever happened, it was recorded on her memory and should have been available for future retrieval, but in the instants after the event happened her memory would default to another, much earlier memory which would overwrite or wipe current events.

So, in the future, instead of seeing Constable Gillian Sargent perched on the edge of a chair, looking at her anxiously, she saw herself sitting in an office, turning to the door as it opened, and seeing George for the first time. And although Constable Gillian Sargent actually said, 'I'm sorry to tell you that your husband had a heart attack and died, Mrs Viviani, while he was getting into a taxi in Glasgow this afternoon,' and although Dorothy understood every one of these words as they were being uttered, in the future she had no recollection at all of Constable Gillian Sargent saying them. Instead there was a complete blank, and the next thing she remembered was opening the front door again to find, not Constable Gillian Sargent, but her brother-in-law James who came in to embrace her and that was the first moment, or so she thought but of course she could not quite remember, that she cried.

The next thing she remembered was standing in a tastefully furnished but very small room, with an open coffin, resting her hand on George's face one last time. She said afterwards that he had felt hard, like marble, and very cold. She knew, without knowing quite how she knew, that Melanie was sitting in the corridor outside, because she was frightened of seeing a body but really, Dorothy said afterwards, it wasn't frightening at all. George looked peaceful, as if he was just asleep. There was no sense of fear in her as she rested her palm against his cold cheek. She said afterwards there was only infinite sadness and, although she never told anybody this, a vague sense of boredom, the urge to get out of the tiny room into the sunlight, to go about the business of living.

She slipped a small teddy bear into the coffin, a parting gift from Melanie, the first teddy bear George and Dorothy had bought her when she had been born, which she called Roger although neither Melanie nor anybody else could remember why. Dorothy pushed Roger down at George's side where perhaps his arm would eventually fall... and her memory failed after that moment, apart from thinking that she smelled a faint fragrance of flowers. Perhaps it was just the roses placed strategically around the viewing room, although it did cross her mind that the fragrance smelled different from that produced by roses.

Flickering images of a hospital room. She didn't know where they came from. Sometimes she wondered if they were her memories at all, or whether they belonged to somebody else but her faulty memory had somehow picked them up and recorded them, albeit faintly, rather like being able to use somebody else's access to the internet.

At the funeral service she glimpsed James' two sons, Petey (twelve) and John (nine) standing wide-eyed and only semi-comprehending, and felt her face stretch in what was supposed to be a reassuring smile, while in the background, as if it was part of another event altogether, she heard the minister say '... worked for the local Council, a valued member, though what he really wanted..', before more darkness.

Then the hearse in front moving at first sedately through the streets. A tall man on a corner doffed his hat; that was one thing she always remembered, always wishing there was some way to track down the man to thank him for his courtesy. Then the hearse surreptitiously speeding up, until it was bellowing through urban roads and some in the convoy behind struggling to keep up, all because the minister had long overrun the time allotted for the service, and they were going to have to go quickly to get to the burial on time. Dorothy thought George would have appreciated that. He would have put a hand across his stomach, creased up his eyes, and laughed and laughed. She didn't remember anything about arriving at the churchyard, or the burial itself, not even tossing a tulip down into the grave, a final farewell, even though everyone told her afterwards that she did so. She didn't even remember where the tulip came from.

James was very efficient, and dealt with all the paperwork. A woman from somewhere came to counsel her, but everything she said was lost. Somebody else came with George's briefcase and the other things he had with him on his last day, and she remembered asking whoever it was to take the things through to George's office because she felt she could not bear to touch them herself, but she couldn't remember anything about the person who brought them, not even whether it was a man or a woman.

Upstairs she slept curled up on her own side of the bed, not wanting to venture onto George's side, though she did not quite know why. Every time she woke up, she was surprised that she had been able to go to sleep. She had no dreams, or if she did her faulty memory failed to record them. Once she thought she heard Melanie sobbing in her own room, but when she held her breath to listen more intently, the sound had stopped. It occurred to her that she ought to talk more to Melanie.

James called in almost every evening, sometimes only briefly. One of her next door neighbours, Trudy, a Canadian woman who ran a small bed and breakfast concern, called in most mornings for a cup of coffee and a chat, and part of Dorothy was grateful, and another part wished she could be left alone. Most of what Trudy said was lost in the darkness between memories, but at one point Dorothy could replay her pouring out tea, not coffee, very carefully, and saying equally carefully that 'George would have wanted you to cry, of course he would; but he would also have wanted you to dry your eyes, and carry on.' And she said, at the same time or possibly at a different time, 'George wouldn't have wanted you to stay alone, now would he?' and part of Dorothy would be dully resentful that this woman, who had barely known George, could presume to know what he would have wanted, while another part of her acknowledged that she was probably right.

Actually, for most of the time Trudy had no idea what to say to Dorothy. She just felt it was only right to pop over and try to take her mind off things, to find out whether there was anything she could do to help. Mostly she talked about her own life, about how she originally moved from Canada to England after meeting a young man while on holiday in Toronto; but the young man tired of her soon after, and she moved to Scotland after chatting to another man on the internet.

Trudy passed over what happened next, about getting married to this second man, whose name was Gordon McInnes, about how they set up the bed and breakfast business together, and then found that Gordon had an inoperable tumour in his stomach which killed him six months after their marriage, none of which information, she thought, was likely to improve the mood of Mrs Viviani as she sat there gazing vaguely about her, sometimes nodding, sometimes letting her eyes drift shut, not, thought Trudy, because she was going to sleep, but because she was replaying some image, some memory, in her own mind.

One day Dorothy remembered to set out a plate of biscuits before Trudy rang the doorbell, and after that Trudy came less and less often. Dorothy never really thanked her next door neighbour for taking the time and trouble to come and visit her. This was partly because she could not remember very much about the meetings; she couldn't remember very much about their conversations, and nor could she remember just how often Trudy came round to talk to her, to try to cheer her up, to gently chivvy her into picking up the fragments of her life. It was also because she didn't quite know how to thank Trudy; she really didn't know how to go about thanking someone for helping her to cross an apparently endless sea of despair.

In the end she resolved to recommend Trudy's bed and breakfast establishment as often as she could, to friends and relatives who wanted to visit the west coast of Scotland, or who wanted a staging post on their way up to the Highlands and who, for one reason or another, could not or would not use Dorothy's single guest room, perhaps because the travelling party was too large, or because their travelling times were too awkward.

Trudy's bed and breakfast establishment was called the Seashore Guest House despite being two or three hundred yards from the sea front, and benefited from having a large dormer extension built on its third floor, something which George Viviani had wanted to install onto their house, but had been prevented from doing by current building control regulations. Dorothy remembered that he had complained bitterly about how it had been acceptable to build a dormer in the days when Trudy and Gordon had wanted to build one, but by the time he came round to wanting one too, the goalposts had been moved.

When Melanie found out what had happened to her father, she rushed upstairs and flung herself on her bed, and wept bitterly. At first she wept because she could not bear the thought that her father was dead. Then she wept because she had never talked to him about the darkness inside her, about what had happened to her to cause the darkness, although truth to tell she had never really decided to tell her father, because it would have been a very difficult conversation. After more than an hour, when her head started to ache abominably and her tears had almost run dry, she wept because nobody had come to find her, to find her weeping. And at last she wept herself asleep, thinking that nobody had come, and her father would never come, never again knock gently on the door to come in and put an arm around her and ask what the matter was with his favourite daughter, never again, never again, never again.

One afternoon, not long after lunch, Dorothy Viviani told her daughter that she was sorry, that she should have paid her more attention, but that she had felt so empty and drained of energy that she had been unable to give anything her attention, unable to focus on anything but the emptiness itself.

'It's okay, Mum,' said Melanie, thinking that she didn't feel empty at all. She felt taut and full, her skin stretched tight. It didn't matter how often she tried to relieve the pressure, still she felt that one more trauma would increase it to such a point that she would be unable to contain it any longer. What would she do then? Scream? Cry? Confess? What would happen to the outpouring of her emotions? Would it coat the walls and ceilings, as if a paint bomb had exploded in the exact centre of the room, smearing red and black paint into every crevice where it would drip slowly, slowly and then more slowly, as it congealed?

'No, I'm sorry,' said Dorothy.

Mother and daughter were embracing in the middle of the bay-windowed front living room. Dorothy could see out of the window, at rain slanting down from a slate sky. She wondered when she had last embraced Melanie. Had they embraced during the last few weeks, before the funeral, at the funeral, after the funeral? She couldn't remember, but she didn't think so. What about when that policewoman came to tell her about what had happened? No. She had been in shock, she remembered that much. She remembered the policewoman heaping sugar into her cup of tea, and she thought she remembered the policewoman putting an arm round her shoulders, so that was an embrace of sorts, but it wasn't an embrace with Melanie who, Dorothy now remembered, had run upstairs on hearing what had happened to her father.

She couldn't remember what happened after that. Had she embraced Melanie when they had left her at the university at the start of the term? She didn't think so. Melanie's room had been so small that there was barely room for the three of them; she, Dorothy, had been standing by the door when the time came to leave, so Melanie had embraced her father, who had been standing just inside the tiny room, and had not embraced Dorothy herself. Perhaps, mused Dorothy, watching the rain change direction slightly and beat against the window, she and Melanie hadn't embraced since Melanie was very little. Now, her chin rested against her daughter's shoulder.

'How did you get so tall?'

'What?' Melanie had been imagining the inside of the room coated with an invisible, obscene patina that would leave the room forever dank and dismal, like some of the caverns beneath the streets of Edinburgh.

Dorothy straightened and pushed Melanie away.

'Why are you here?' she asked. 'Why aren't you at university?'

'It's okay, Uncle James sorted it.'

'Haven't you got exams or something?'

'He rang them up. I couldn't ring them up. I couldn't possibly do exams.'

'Them?'

'The university people, my tutor, Professor Lamberton, the loans board.'

Melanie reflected that when the loans board had in fact refused to talk to Uncle James, and had insisted on speaking to her personally, she had spoken rationally for two or three minutes until sorrow and hysteria had overtaken her in equal measures, and she had shouted and cried down the telephone until it finally dawned on the woman on the other end that she wasn't going to get any sense out of Melanie, and had decided to talk to Uncle James after all. But none of that, thought Melanie, was likely to be of much interest to her mother.

'Ah,' said Dorothy vaguely.

'I've got some special leave, like a gap year,' explained Melanie. 'I'll do the last few weeks and then the exams next year.'

'Oh good,' said Dorothy. She turned away from her daughter, putting a hand to her forehead as if she knew there was something she was going to do, or say, but for the moment whatever it was escaped her. Melanie watched her. She had watched her do the same thing time after time over the last few weeks, watched her turn off from reality and revisit her own empty space. She wished she could put her arms around her and say, Mum, don't worry, it'll be all right, everything will be all right, but she couldn't, because she wasn't sure that everything was going to be all right. She felt helpless compassion, as if their roles had been momentarily switched, and she was the mother watching her child deal with the anguish of grief, but she suppressed it. She felt too taut, too tight. She felt that one more surge of emotion could blow her apart.

The telephone rang.

Melanie wrapped her arms around herself, instead of her mother, and walked to the window where she stood staring out at the dreary weather.

'Yes?' said Dorothy. The voice on the other end of the telephone, which Melanie couldn't hear, asked whether it was talking to Mrs Dorothy Viviani.

'Yes,' said Dorothy. 'Who is this?'

The voice explained that it was Robert Barker, of Barker Associates, based in Glasgow.

'Oh?' said Dorothy. She was about to say that she would be back in a minute, that this call was important to her, before putting down the receiver and leaving the caller to his own devices for ten minutes or half an hour, when the voice said that he, Robert Barker, may have been one of the last people to see George Viviani alive. 'Oh?' said Dorothy again.

Melanie had no idea of what was being said, but she detected the change in her mother's voice and looked up sharply to see Dorothy, receiver clamped to her ear, slowly sitting on the sofa, her face white.

Yes, said the voice, and went on to explain that Barker Associates worked in the field of proofing and editing, and also acted as agents for various types of manuscripts, usually non-fiction, said the voice pedantically, but on occasion it had been known to take on works of literary fiction, particularly by local authors. Such as, said the voice diffidently, the book of short stories written by Dorothy's late husband.

'I see,' said Dorothy. The colour returned to her face, and Melanie turned back to the window, which was shuddering slightly in a strong westerly wind. Judging by the thick, dark clouds looming beyond the tops of houses opposite, the worst of the storm was yet to come. On the telephone, Robert Barker commiserated with Dorothy for her recent loss, and Dorothy murmured her thanks. Mr Viviani had been a fine man, a fine man, reminisced the voice, and she, Dorothy, could only imagine the surprise and shock he had received when he had rung, oh, just over a week ago, and a Mr James Viviani had answered the phone, and had explained what had happened, and had suggested leaving it a week or so before calling again. Which is what he was currently doing, explained the voice.

'I see,' said Dorothy. She glanced across at Melanie and saw that she was looking out of the window but because it was getting so dark outside, the window acted as a mirror and she could see Melanie's face looking sad—no, not just sad, but utterly bleak. Her heart jumped into her throat. What was the matter with her daughter?

The point was, explained Robert Barker, that George had sent them his collection of stories, and at their meeting (at this point Robert Barker hesitated for a fraction of a second and Dorothy instantly divined that he had been going to say that the meeting had taken place on the very day that George had died, but at the last moment had realised that this would not be very tactful) a few weeks ago, they had reached an agreement to the effect that Barker Associates would represent the collection of stories to publishing houses in an effort to get the book commercially published.

'I see, I see,' said Dorothy. 'I didn't know that.'

No, said the voice, and the conversation descended into a natural silence as both Robert Barker and Dorothy brooded on just why it was that Dorothy had never known about her husband's arrangement with Barker Associates.

'You all right, Mum?'

'What? Oh, yes. I'm fine. I'll tell you about it later.'

What? inquired the voice of Robert Barker.

'My daughter,' explained Dorothy.

Outside, the black clouds stretched out on either side and started to pile up directly overhead. Melanie gave a slight start as all the streetlights on one side of the road suddenly came on. Paradoxically, the rain seemed to ease, but she could tell by the way in which the trees bent and swayed, and the way in which the old sash window continued to shudder, that the wind was growing stronger. Lights were coming on in various rooms of houses across the street.

Robert Barker informed Dorothy that a certain publishing company had in fact expressed an interest in acquiring the rights to her husband's collection of short stories and in a small way he hoped that this piece of good news would um. The voice paused. Clearly Robert Barker was not quite sure how to express his notion that his news about the short stories might help to cheer Dorothy, but Dorothy understood readily enough and rescued him by saying, 'Yes, yes, thank you. That is a good piece of news for a change.' Melanie glanced across at her, surprised, and she smiled. She really did feel a slight lifting of the darkness around her, a slight filling of the emptiness.

Rain abruptly clattered against the window, a heavy persistent pounding. Melanie turned back and saw that all the streetlights were now shining. It was two o'clock in the afternoon but outside was as black as midnight. As she watched, car headlights turned into their road, which was a cul-de-sac, and started to move forward cautiously through the storm.

'What?' asked Dorothy. 'I'm sorry, I didn't catch that.'

Robert Barker said that the publishing firm and Barker Associates would need Dorothy's permission to go ahead with publication, assuming that she was happy for the stories to be published. Robert Barker's voice added a question mark to this sentence, and Dorothy found herself nodding.

'Yes, of course,' she said. Out of the corner of her eye she saw Melanie lean forward and rub at the window, trying to make it easier to see outside. Robert Barker wondered if it would be in order for Dorothy to come to see him in his office in Glasgow. 'Yes, I expect so,' said Dorothy, getting up off the sofa and moving over to stand by Melanie. 'Where are you?'

'It's a taxi,' whispered Melanie, pointing outside.

'What was that?' asked Dorothy. 'Stable Side Street... Stableside all one word, right. Eight Stableside Street. I'm sorry, someone's coming to the door, I—what?'

She and Melanie watched as the taxi doused its lights. A big bald man jumped out, hunched against the rain, and at the same time the rear door opened. A tall man wearing a long dark coat of some sort climbed out and stood looking at the house—looking, Melanie suddenly realised, directly at them. The taxi driver opened their garden gate and bustled up the path, but the tall man made no immediate move to follow. He stood directly beneath a streetlight. The beating rain appeared to have no effect on him. Despite the darkness and sheets of water, Melanie and Dorothy had no trouble seeing how his gaze shifted from them to the upstairs windows, to the front door which the taxi driver had almost reached, fleetingly to the guest house sign next door, which Melanie knew would be gyrating wildly in the wind, and the overgrown front yard of the house on the other side. Then he nodded once, as if satisfied of something, and started after the taxi driver.

'Yes, that would be best,' said Dorothy.

The front doorbell pealed. Melanie went quickly into the hall. Dorothy noticed something strange. The tall man had not bothered to close the taxi door, but even as she noticed this curious fact, the door moved back and forth in the gusting wind, and then slammed itself shut. Melanie must have opened the front door, because as she hung up on Robert Barker, who had promised to send an email giving the full details of his address and a handful of possible meeting dates, she heard the wind howling outside in the hall, and the living room door slammed shut too, though not before she felt a blast of colder air and not before she thought she smelled the fresh smell of flowers. Footsteps on the stairs. Had Melanie run upstairs for some reason? The feeling of unreality which had been creeping over her ever since the sky turned black and Robert Barker made his phone call deepened into unease.

She opened the living room door again to see that Melanie had not gone upstairs but was confronting the two men, the taxi driver and the tall man, who both stood in the covered porch. Who had gone upstairs? Dorothy unconsciously shook her head, thinking that the sound she had heard could not have been footsteps. It must have been something rattling in the wind when Melanie opened the front door. It struck her as very odd that the taxi driver had come to the house. Why had the taxi driver come to the house, and not just his passenger, whoever he was? Was the passenger somebody that Melanie knew from Glasgow? As she moved closer, the tall man lifted his eyes from Melanie, and Dorothy saw that he was quite young, perhaps in his early twenties.

'Mrs Viviani?'

'Yes,' she said. She was confused, and still uneasy. First Robert Barker, and now this. She noticed that the taxi driver, a big, bulky man with sad eyes, was staring at her intently.

'My name is Tully,' said the tall man. He held out a card. She reached out automatically but as she took hold of the card, he covered it with his other hand. Melanie shifted sideways, awkwardly, as his arm brushed against her. 'Look at it in a minute, when we've gone,' he said. His voice was soft and difficult to hear over the storm. 'Now that we have been here, you may need this. You may need to contact me.'

'Now that you have been here?' said Dorothy wonderingly. The taxi driver suddenly reached inside his coat and produced another card, which he handed to Melanie. She looked down at it. *Red Arrow Taxis* and a Glasgow telephone number.

'I'm Harry,' said the taxi driver. 'You can always ask for me.' He had handed the card to Melanie, but his eyes were still fixed on Dorothy, who was becoming more and more confused. Why on earth had two men turned up in the middle of a storm, apparently just to give her their business cards? The tall man—what was his name? Tully?—released her hand and backed away, into the rain. Both of the men turned and went quickly back to the taxi. The driver hoisted his coat over his head in an attempt to keep dry but, as before, Tully ignored the weather. They both got into the taxi. Two doors slammed. Melanie and Dorothy watched as the big bald man, Harry, started the engine of the taxi and turned on its headlights. They watched as the taxi made a neat three point turn, and nosed back out of the cul-de-sac.

As Melanie realised that she was holding the door open, and closed it, Dorothy looked curiously at the tall man's business card, which was entirely black apart from some elegant white lettering. An expression of distaste crossed her face.

'Was that weird or what?' said Melanie. 'What does yours say?'

Dorothy showed her daughter the black business card and, after Melanie had also made an expression, not exactly of distaste but more to show baffled wonderment that anybody could be so crass as to deliver such a card at such a time, she dropped it into a bin. Melanie also wondered how the tall man in the long black coat who, now she came to think of it, was not unattractive and certainly had more charisma in his little finger than the bastard Graham had in his entire body—how the tall man had known that her father had died recently. This question did not occur to Dorothy, but she continued to wonder why the taxi driver had bothered to get out of his cab into the pouring rain, and make his way up the path through the storm, all the way to the front door, and all for no apparent reason except to stare intently at her.

'What was the phone call about, Mum?'

Dorothy's thoughts were jerked away from Harry the taxi driver and Cheyne Tully, and focussed again on the thin, dry voice of Robert Barker of Barker Associates, and on his piece of good news. As she relayed the story to Melanie, she felt a faint stirring of excitement. What better way to remember George than by publishing his beloved collection of stories?

At that time, neither Dorothy nor her daughter made any association between the Glasgow taxi and the exact location, which they both knew but had perhaps blocked from their conscious thoughts, of George Viviani's death.

Chapter 5

Neither of them spoke as Harry carefully negotiated narrow streets. Rain swept across the windscreen in torrents which the wipers were hard put to sweep away; orange streetlight illuminated sheets of water blown almost horizontally by wind bludgeoning in from the west, off the sea. In his rear-view mirror Harry could see cracks of light far behind, but approaching, as the huge mass of clouds was forced further inland and daylight followed.

The narrow streets ended in a roundabout next to a police station, whose blue light shone out with surprising brightness in the unnatural dark. After that a wider road took them past a racecourse and a Tesco where signs, also shining with unnerving brightness, announced that the store was open twenty-four hours, and finally the wider road disgorged them on to a large roundabout which accessed first a dual carriageway and then a motorway leading to Glasgow.

As the taxi swung on to the dual carriageway, the rain lessened, and the thin cracks in the sky widened as they rushed in from the west. Harry McCabe relaxed slightly, and glanced in the mirror at his passenger in the back seat. He flipped on the intercom.

'So what's it like?'

He watched as the dark figure of Cheyne Tully glanced up, then looked around the interior of the cab carefully, and finally nodded to itself.

'Getting warmer,' said Tully.

Harry also nodded, more to himself than to his passenger. A plume of bright sky had appeared not far ahead. Already he could scale down the activity of his wipers to intermittent.

'Didn't you feel it?' asked Tully, his voice tinny.

'Feel what?'

'When the girl opened the door, he went in.'

'Yeah?' said Harry McCabe. Briefly, he met Tully's gaze in the rear-view mirror, before returning his attention to the road ahead. By now the darkness of the storm had almost vanished, but spray from other traffic created its own problems.

Harry McCabe pursed his lips. He hadn't felt anything strange at the old house in Ayr, only rain battering on his unprotected head and a cold wind blustering at his back as he hurried up the path and rang the front doorbell. Had he felt anything brush past him, hastening invisibly into the house? No. Only the wind, rushing into the space created by the opening door, feeling almost as if it was tugging him forward as well as pushing him from behind. Still, if Cheyne Tully said that something had happened, and if the back of his cab was really warming up after the visit to the Viviani household, then he was prepared to believe that something really had happened.

What he had noticed, taking him completely by surprise, was the appearance of the woman in the hallway. Mrs Viviani. If somebody had asked him what Annette would have looked like, if she had survived and stayed with him for the last eighteen years, then he would have said that she would have looked exactly like Mrs Viviani. Ash-blonde hair. Wide eyes. Thin arms, slender body. Too thin, perhaps, Harry McCabe thought to himself. Perhaps Mrs Viviani hadn't been eating properly since her husband's death. He remembered losing almost two stone after Annette died.

A lorry splashed past, its lunatic driver hurtling along at almost seventy miles an hour despite the quantities of surface water. Spray engulfed the taxi for long anxious seconds.

'Bastard,' muttered Harry McCabe and heard a chuckle from Cheyne Tully. He thought about telling Tully how much the recently bereaved Mrs Viviani stirred up memories which, truth to tell, were never very far from the surface, but thought better of it. There were pictures of Annette in the house, and he did not think very much escaped Tully's sardonic gaze.

'She'll be in touch,' said Cheyne Tully for his own reasons, but to Harry McCabe it felt as though Tully had read his mind.

Some thirty miles ahead of the Red Arrow Taxicab, in the drab block of flats by the side of Laburnum Crescent, the buzzer to apartment eleven rang, as Claire had known it would. When she answered, the voice belonging to the young man from across the street announced itself, and Claire immediately hit the button which opened the downstairs door. This time she allowed the young man entry without trying to work out whether or not it was a good idea. She knew, or at least she thought she knew, that the young man posed no threat, so she didn't bother trying to find someone to let them know that he was coming to visit her. She remembered the last seconds of their previous meeting, when their eyes had met, when they had somehow come to an agreement that he would come again. Now he had come again, expecting her to hit the button to give him access to the building; she knew he expected it, and felt somehow obliged to adhere to their unwritten, non-verbal agreement.

She couldn't tell whether the door had opened, but he hadn't buzzed again, so that must mean he was inside the building, climbing the stairs. In any case, she had already finished with one client, and nobody else was due until the evening. She had been sitting in her wicker chair, trying to decide whether to go out, where she would go if she did go out, whether Lucy was around and if she was whether she'd like to go out too; and she was mentally calculating how much money she could put into her second bank account, the one that she had set up for her own purposes, after she had put aside the money she needed to keep the family going, an amount based on the salary she was supposed to be getting as Samantha, a part-time clerical assistant in an unspecified building firm on the south side of Glasgow.

She was also thinking about the last visit from Social Services, which focused first on her father and then on her youngest sister Paula, just fifteen, though she could have told Social Services that Paula was probably the most sensible member of the Pevey family, and the social workers would probably do better to focus on the middle sister Jenny who was eighteen and spent most of her time sharing a bedsit with an older man called Raymond O'Donnell, who had no visible means of support, but lived in the bedsit with another man that Claire had never met and didn't know the name of, and for that matter Social Services would probably do better to focus on her, Claire, because of the way in which she had structured her life, as the television psychologist would put it.

She was shivering. She was looking around the flat nervously. She was filling her mind with these thoughts because she didn't want to think about what had happened on the two previous nights, Tuesday and Wednesday. It was good that the young man was coming to visit her, because he could occupy her thoughts for a while. In theory she could stay in the flat on Thursday night too, and hand over the key to Caroline in the morning—that was their usual arrangement—but tonight she had decided to go back home after her second and last appointment of the day, unless someone rang up with an offer to the contrary. Her father would never notice that she was back on a day when she was supposed to be staying over at her friend's flat; Paula would readily accept that she had just managed to get off her shift earlier than usual; Jennifer probably wouldn't be there and in any case she had no idea of Samantha's shift patterns.

A knock at the door made her jump. She realised that she had been sitting hunched in the wicker chair for long minutes, her thoughts going around in circles. She got up, went to the door and opened it, and found the young man almost completely obscured by a huge cardboard box which he had somehow managed to carry up the stairwell, and which he immediately started to manoeuvre through the doorway.

'What the fuck?' she said, stepping back.

He succeeded in getting the box through the doorway, and struggled across the room towards her bed. He was wearing trainers, she noticed, rather than shoes, so he made an irregular squeaking noise as he lurched across the uncarpeted floor rather than crisp, clicking footsteps, but nevertheless the sound triggered her memory again. She covered her face with her hands and started to tremble, but the young man didn't notice as he had his back to her, and all of his concentration was directed towards getting the huge box safely onto her bed.

On Tuesday she had gone to bed early, at half past eight, tired and a little depressed after seeing three clients during the day. The first was an older businessman who was perfectly straightforward and liked to chat, so that by the time he left, she knew all about his family life and his wife who was actually five years older than he was, and she had heard all about his two grown-up children, one of whom had a lucrative job in Japan while the other worked as a teacher just outside Edinburgh, and she had heard all about his plans for early retirement after which, he told her, he intended to travel widely, but especially to New Zealand because he had always been a fan of the *Lord of the Rings*. Claire had responded monosyllabically, not disliking the man exactly, but wondering whether he realised that the children he was so proud of were both older than she was.

After the businessman she saw a middle-aged man who arrived wearing jeans and a denim jacket, and who spoke hardly a word but just handed her an envelope and got right on with what he wanted, with minimalistic grunts and movements of his hands and knees to guide her, almost as if he was riding a horse, and she allowed her mind to wander during this meeting, so that while her body was kneeling on all fours on her rumpled bed, her thoughts took her to an imagined countryside scene with huge pines shadowing a ground covered in needles, a scene so vivid that she wondered whether she had actually been to such a place when she was much younger, when she had been so young that only her unconscious mind had retained any memories of that time.

The third client of the day had been about her own age, or perhaps even younger. It could have been so much better than it was between the two of them, but he was so nervous that he had been almost unable to do what he had come there to do, and he was constantly asking whether it was all right if he did this, or touched her there, or if he did that; and he asked her so many times whether she was enjoying herself or whether it was just a job for her, that she almost snapped at him with irritation, and it was this wound-up irritation which left her feeling tired after the door closed for the third time, and left her feeling down and generally miserable.

Afterwards she was not quite sure if what happened that night had been a dream. She had been lying curled up in bed, mind drifting, perhaps trying to dredge up more memories from a time when she had not consciously remembered them, or perhaps trying to predict the course of her life, to extrapolate some sort of lifeline into the future, bisecting other places and other lifelines. Drifting, or dreaming, she noticed that a light must have come on outside in the hall, because the shape of the door was suddenly marked in the darkness by four thin illuminated slices, two vertical and two horizontal. She vaguely remembered seeing this before, possibly in another dream, and she vaguely remembered that she had turned away by rolling over on to her other side, but this time she didn't move.

The light brightened and dimmed, as if someone was moving on the other side of the door, and then it turned pink, and then red, and at the same time she heard footsteps, or something like footsteps. At this point she sat up, shivering.

There was no light at the door. Disoriented, she looked at the red digital numbers of her clock. It was only eleven o'clock, much earlier than she thought, until she remembered that she had gone to bed early.

She was about to lie back down again when she thought she heard a footstep, two footsteps, on her uncarpeted floor. Her heart pounded and she fumbled desperately for the bedside light switch, and while she did so she thought she heard a third footstep, but that might have been the crisp click of the switch on the light, which flooded the room with impersonal radiance, and showed nothing at all out of the ordinary. Still, she sat for long minutes, tugging the bedclothes up around her shoulders as her breath misted in cold air, and waited and watched, only reluctantly lying back down again and still more reluctantly turning off the light. She lay unmoving, eyes wide open, trying to see through the darkness and listening fearfully for more sounds, but nothing further happened. Eventually she came to the conclusion that she must, after all, have been dreaming.

On Wednesday she had lunch with an unattractive but charming man of about thirty, who was not English but she couldn't immediately place where he came from, not that it mattered especially as she had no difficulty about working with men of any race and he spoke perfectly good English. Over lunch he explained that he came from Malta and lived six months in the UK to work with clients and promote his computer business, which meant that for six months every year he was away from his wife and children, who couldn't come with him because of financial considerations and school commitments.

They went back to his hotel room after lunch, and Claire was pleased to discover that it was not one of the string of what she thought of as cardboard hotels, but was one of the more luxurious hotels in the centre of the city. She delighted in taking a long, hot shower with the man from Malta, and afterwards almost fell asleep in the huge double bed during their three-hour appointment.

That night there was no question of whether she was dreaming. She had exchanged some text messages with Caroline, come out of the tiny shower with a towel wrapped round her body, dried her hair, and climbed into bed at about eleven o'clock. She had not been thinking about lights at the door, or footsteps; she had been thinking about Caroline's invitation to join her with a single client on Wednesday the following week, something which Caroline, as Jade, had done before with different girls but which she, Claire, never had.

As she turned off the bedside light she was trying to imagine how it would all work out, whether she would be embarrassed with an audience, even if it was only Caroline; what sort of man it would be, and how it would benefit her financially. She was still thinking about these things when she realised that the four strips of light were there again, though she wasn't sure whether they had always been there and it had taken a while for her eyes to accustom themselves to the darkness, or whether the strips of light had come on at some point after she had settled down.

The light shadowed and shifted. Gradually it changed colour to an angry red, and the temperature inside the flat unmistakably dropped. Claire shivered with more than cold and reached out again for her bedside light, but before she switched it on she heard again what sounded like a footstep not far from her bed, and as the light came on she was almost sure she saw the panel of the door shiver as if from a heavy but soundless blow.

But there was nothing and nobody in the flat, and there were no further sounds, except that as the strangeness slid away and the room, and the furniture, and the doors all regained their normal identities, she heard a rhythmic noise from Lucy's flat next door. She decided then that Lucy and her client must be the explanation for everything. They must have turned on the light in the hall outside, and turned it off again, and been responsible for the sounds she thought she had heard; and as for the light apparently turning red, that must have been the result of looking through her own tired eyes, and the panel on the door hadn't moved at all but when she turned on her bedside light the momentarily dancing shadows must have made it appear to flex and shudder.

So she told herself, though she didn't turn off the light again that night, because as well as telling herself that Lucy and her client were responsible for it all, she was fairly certain that they weren't.

Enough time had passed that the young man had put the cardboard box on the bed and started to unwrap it, before he realised that she had not come back into the room. He turned to see her standing by the open door, hands over her face. At first he thought she was crying, but when he moved closer he discovered that she seemed to be frozen in place, unmoving, as if she had been captured and immobilised by her own thoughts. She was so rigid that when he took hold of her forearms and tugged them gently, she resisted and he had to pull more strongly, and then yet more strongly. When his tugging finally overcame her resistance, her arms suddenly came free and shifted down and out to the side, and she stumbled forward so that their faces, almost on a level, were inches away from each other. He saw her glazed eyes return to the present; saw how she took in his own placid gaze so close to her own; saw her expression harden. In a soft voice, he asked if she was all right.

She pulled pack, breaking his hold on her forearms.

'What's it to you?'

He had been right. She was at once more and less than he had thought. She was hard to reach and harder to understand, but at the same time she was more vibrant, more alive than he had imagined. He could see now that he had only imagined her as a pretty girl with red hair who he had seen across the road, who he would be able to meet, and talk to, and bring calmly into the circle of his existence, but now he understood that the reality was much more complicated, that she would react in ways he had not imagined, that she would speak or move in ways that he had not considered, that her character would be different and that her outlook on life was totally different from his own.

He told her then, that when he was three, his mother had killed his father.

The expression in her eyes changed to one of uncertainty. He made a small gesture which indicated that he would tell her this story, a verbal equivalent of laying his throat bare. The gesture indicated that he knew she too had a story of some kind; her glazed eyes and rigid body told him clearly that something was wrong.

He went on to say that, apparently, he saw it happen, the thing that had happened between his mother and his father, but he didn't remember it. Claire raised trembling hands to her lips. Her gaze was locked with his and she was unable to look away. His mother, he explained, hit his father with an iron. Grotesquely, he pressed one ear close against the side of his head, laid the other side of his head against his shoulder, and surveyed her from this awkward position. He said that the police said it had been just one blow. He straightened and added that it was hard to see how it could have been an accident. His brow furrowed and for the first time she saw expressions in his placid eyes, puzzlement, dismay, and a sense of loss.

'What—what happened to her?'

He didn't answer directly, but told her that he had been discovered sitting by his father's body, and he knew that must be true because he had old newspaper clippings with pictures of himself, aged three, looking puzzled and lost, and sensationalist stories of how he had been found. His eyes regained their usual placidity. His mother had been located upstairs, sitting on her bed. She never spoke again; she was catatonic. He inquired whether Claire knew what that meant, adding that he hadn't known, but he had looked it up.

'Yes,' said Claire.

The young man stared at her for a few moments, as if trying to decide whether this was true, as if perhaps she had just said yes so that he would get on to the end of his story and be done with it. Then he looked away. He told Claire that his mother died two weeks later, in hospital, but nobody knew exactly why. There was no trace of sadness in his voice, Claire thought; it was merely a recital of facts which, now she came to think of it, he must have been reciting in his own mind since he was three, or at least since he was old enough to understand what had happened, so perhaps it was not surprising that his tone was dull, matter-of-fact, after all those years. She asked his age, and he told her he was twenty-four. She nodded slowly, thoughtfully, as if his answer had provided some interesting information for her to consider.

For the first time, the young man hesitated, and then he disclosed that he thought he knew why his mother had died; she had died because of what had happened, he told Claire, and then made another small gesture to indicate that these words didn't quite convey the message he intended. He said that he thought the whole thing was an accident, or perhaps it wasn't an accident, but after it had happened, then that was when she died. He was struggling. He paused to think. Claire looked at him curiously as he fought to find the right words; it was almost as if he wasn't used to talking. Finally he said that he didn't believe his mother died because of guilt, but because she was so sad at what had happened; he was sure it hadn't been guilt, he was sure that she had been overwhelmed by sadness and remorse.

Claire moistened her lips and said, 'She died of a broken heart.'

He looked away again. Claire heard a door bang in the next room—not Lucy's room, but on the other side, where the tiny Chinese girl lived. Footsteps clicked across the hall and faded in the direction of the stairwell. The young man said that he had been brought up by his aunt in Luton. His hesitancy was gone. These were well-rehearsed facts. He told Claire that when he was eighteen, he came into quite a lot of money, as neither his father nor his mother had been poor, and he went on to explain (in case the point had been lost on Claire, which it hadn't) that he didn't have to work. He glanced at Claire, then looked away again.

'Why live here?' asked Claire. She meant, if he had money, why would he choose to live on Laburnum Crescent in Glasgow, of all places, rather than in a nice cottage out in the country, or a flat in a city centre, or even in a white-walled house in a warm, far-off climate? When he said that he was doing a course at the art college, she understood immediately. The college was only half a mile away, on Bedford Road.

'You're an artist?'

For the first time she saw him smile, shyly. He shook his head and said that he wished he was. If he was a real artist, he said, then he wouldn't have to go to college.

Claire thought back over what he had said, about his parents, about not needing to work. Her eyes drifted to the package on the bed.

'What is it?'

They both moved over to the bed and she saw for the first time what was written on the side of the box. Side by side, they wrestled it open excitedly, she anticipating what she thought was going to be inside, he anticipating her reaction to what he knew was inside. Finally the new acquisition was exposed as a brand new thirty-inch flat-screen television. She covered her mouth with her hands again, and stared at him. He shrugged and tilted his head at the tiny portable television sitting on the end of her dressing table, and she understood that he meant that he had noticed it the last time he had been in the flat, and thought she might fancy something bigger.

He liked it when she didn't jump up and down with excitement, squealing *for me? is it for me?* and she didn't whisper in solemn disbelieving tones that really, he shouldn't and she couldn't, and her eyes didn't suddenly flood with tears at the thought that someone was unexpectedly being kind to her, a reaction which he would have interpreted as a form of self-pity. Instead, she walked over, kissed his cheek and said, 'Thank you,' and then unplugged the old television and started to clear a space for the new one. He helped her to carry it over; they plugged it in; discovered that the aerial wire was a fraction too short and so shifted the entire dressing table about a foot closer to the window. They sat together on the end of the bed to press buttons on the channel changer and follow arcane instructions in the user manual.

When the television was finally working properly, they watched five minutes of the news, which was reporting terrible floods in India and revelations about the sex life of an MP from a north-west constituency, and was about to reveal the weather forecast when Claire pressed more buttons on the channel changer so that they saw in quick succession a children's cartoon, two documentaries about something to do with archaeology, a brooding moment from a drama during which they saw nothing but an attractive middle-aged woman staring out of a window at the moon and silhouetted trees, and finally a whole raft of sports channels showing mostly football, but one was covering a snooker tournament in Beijing and another was broadcasting clips of skiers coming to grief in various ways as they hurtled down snow-covered hills.

They watched in silence. He sometimes looked as her fingers pressed buttons on the tv remote, and sometimes he snatched a glimpse of her face. She was entranced at the way in which the big television transformed the interior of the flat; she reflected that it was even bigger than the television they had at home, and she also wondered if any of her clients were politicians, and, if any of them were, whether she could make any money by selling the story of their visits to the media.

Clients.

She suddenly realised that it was already half past four and a man she knew only as Brian was due to arrive at five o'clock. She turned off the television halfway through a commercial for a brand of running shoes and jumped to her feet.

'I've got an appointment,' she said.

He liked the fact that she was not apologetic; she was merely stating a fact. He nodded. He got to his feet, squeaked back to the door to the flat, opened it and then paused to look back at her. Without inflection, he told her the number of his apartment, but didn't add that he was telling her in case she needed him, or go on to explain that it was no good her protesting that she wouldn't ever need him, because he knew, having seen the glazed look of panic in her eyes and felt the rigidity of her limbs, that something had happened to her. Then what happened when he left her at the abrupt end to his previous visit happened again. He saw that she understood him and, exactly as it happened on that previous occasion, she said nothing, made no effort to deny his unspoken implications, so that when he turned to leave without a further word being passed between them, another agreement had been made.

As he left, a message arrived on Claire's mobile phone which read *r u up 4 it?* She banged on Lucy's door, but there was no reply. She knew the Chinese girl was out, and Baz, it seemed, had gone away for a few weeks. She wasn't too concerned as she had met Brian before, although she was pretty sure his name wasn't Brian as he was a coloured man from India or perhaps Pakistan, and he enjoyed not only being massaged but also giving her a massage, and he was quite good at it. Somehow the thought of a coloured man good at massage being called Brian was so ridiculous that she frequently started giggling during his visits. She showered, and towelled her hair. Before she had time to change her mind she messaged Caroline: *All right what time? Brian here 5pm.*

Two things occurred to her soon after. As she sat in front of the new television screen, watching a comedy programme which appeared to be based in a suburb of London where the sun was always shining, she realised that she had not told the young man why she had been seized with a panic attack. She thought about what had happened to his parents and what had happened to him. She supposed it was not too surprising that he had grown up to become—what? Not shy exactly. Not nervous exactly. Awkward. He was awkward with her and she suspected he would be awkward with other people as well. It wasn't just a case of being shy with girls, it was more a case of stepping back from social interaction altogether; not too surprising, Claire thought to herself again, given what the two people closest to him had done to each other and to him.

Anyway it appeared that they had exchanged another non-verbal message just as he was leaving. She still didn't see how that happened in the space of a glance lasting no more than two seconds, but regardless of how it happened she knew that he expected her to tell him why she had been so frightened. She smiled to herself at the antics of the family on television, thinking that she was not so frightened now.

The second thing that occurred to her, popping into her mind for no apparent reason as she was kneeling astride Brian, kneading his hirsute shoulders and spine, was that Lucy had said she had heard footsteps in her flat, Claire's flat, but that she hadn't heard Claire go to the door. She shivered, her thighs rubbing against Brian's hips. For a moment she considered offering him an overnight at a reduced rate, but then remembered that she had decided to go home after the appointment.

When Brian had gone, she took another shower and sat back in front of the television to watch a film about an ex-marine who came out of retirement to sort out trouble in his neighbourhood, and Caroline messaged her with *3 2 4 c u tom*. So by the time the film had finished she changed her mind about going home, partly because the tough, brutal nature of the film had filled her with vicarious resolve, partly because Caroline was expecting to see her in the morning to swap news, check dates, and go through the ritual of turning over the card by the buzzer by the front door, and partly because it was getting to be too late to go home anyway.

She had some supper while watching the news, then turned off the television and didn't like the way silence invaded the flat. She went to knock on Lucy's door again, but still there was no answer. When she climbed into bed a little earlier than usual, the evening film was no more than a memory, and the resolve it generated was no more than the memory of a dream. Reality was darkness, silence, the fervent wish that she was in her small bed at home with her sisters nearby and the sudden blooming, as she turned off the bedside light, of fear.

Chapter 6

When Colin Taylor was six he woke up in the middle of the night a few days before Christmas to see a hamster on his window sill. This was surprising, since neither Colin nor anyone else in the family owned a hamster, but what was even more surprising was that the hamster, after sitting for a while washing its face with its tiny paws, turned round and scampered through the window, even though it was securely shut. At the time Colin Taylor blinked sleepily and decided that either he must still be asleep, or that he had only just woken up and had dreamed the hamster.

Some years later he discovered that the twin sisters Pamela and Pauline living not next door but two doors away owned a hamster, in fact they owned several hamsters over several years and, not realising that they hibernated, had religiously buried them in their garden at the onset of each winter.

Many years later, at about the time Colin Taylor changed his name to Cheyne Tully, he bumped into Pamela on Princes Street in Edinburgh. Over a cup of coffee they caught up on what had happened to each other, and Tully told Pamela about the incident of the ghostly hamster. He remembered that it had happened when he was six, so Pamela dug into her own memory and worked out that it must have been the ghost of Marmite, their third hamster, the previous two having been called Sugar and Spice. Pamela said the shock of discovering that they had been burying their hamsters alive had made her decide to take up a career as a veterinarian, a sort of penance, she said, which involved dedicating her working life to those poor lost tiny souls.

Tully asked what had happened to Pauline. Pamela shook her head and said she had suffered no such pangs of conscience, but had studied to become a lawyer, and was now working in a junior position in an office near Aberdeen.

As Colin Taylor grew up, he came to realise that occasionally he saw things that other people didn't. Once he was sitting in the back of his father's car, with his mother and father in the front seats and his older brother sitting beside him and the car itself sitting at the head of a queue waiting at a level crossing, when he saw a man wearing old-fashioned clothes walk through the crossing gates as if they weren't there, straight into the path of the oncoming train. Nobody said anything. He didn't say anything. At about the time when he changed his name to Cheyne Tully, he could no longer recall if he didn't say anything because he hadn't seen anything strange in what the man in old-fashioned clothes had done, or whether he had thought it strange but kept quiet because everybody else did.

Another time he saw an old woman standing at a bus stop, the only person waiting, and he noticed her because her clothes were dark grey, her skin a pasty white, her hair was completely white, her handbag was completely black, as were the gloves she was wearing. It was as if somebody had cut a life-sized black-and-white photograph out of something and propped it up by the side of the road, although Colin Taylor also noticed that nobody else paid any attention to the old woman and by then he knew enough to know that she probably wasn't there.

Part of the library where his mother took him at least once a week always seemed bitterly cold to him, and the fluorescent lighting overhead appeared to flicker with streaks of blue. His mother noticed neither of these things. When he was twelve, a boy who he didn't know very well because he went to a different school but whose name was also Colin, and who lived almost opposite, on the other side of the road, was knocked over and killed by a lorry. Naturally the police were involved in trying to sort out the consequences of the accident, as were the local roads authority, several lawyers, the parents of the dead boy, the company which owned the lorry, and the lorry driver himself, who had to be counselled for months afterwards because of recurring nightmares resulting from the accident, and who eventually gave up his job and retrained as a call centre operative for a manufacturing firm.

Colin Taylor knew none of this, but he did see the dead boy on several occasions immediately after the accident, when it was not too dark. The boy stood on the pavement just outside Colin Taylor's house, gazing across at his own home, but was obviously unable to cross the road, either because that was where his life had ended, or for some other reason that Colin Taylor was unable to fathom. One evening he slipped out of the house and went to stand by the phantom where he said in a quiet voice, 'Let's cross the road now.'

Although the other Colin did not turn, or nod, or in any way acknowledge that he had heard these words, as soon as Colin Taylor stepped out into the road, he followed, moving smoothly, and once they had both reached the opposite pavement, Colin Taylor was able to watch as the silent boy continued to move right on up the garden path of the house where he used to live, and through its closed front door. He never saw the dead boy again, and as far as he knew, the fact that the other Colin had returned home went completely unnoticed by his family.

About five years afterwards, the family decided to move away, and it was only after they had gone that the new owners of the house opposite started to complain about the sound of footsteps, and muffled sobbing, and of one room which seemed to be permanently cold no matter how much they turned up the heating. They had no idea of what to do, but one day Colin Taylor visited them from across the road and suggested that they pinned up the forwarding address of the dead Colin's family on the front door, and possibly on the door of the cold room as well. They scoffed at first, but eventually tried it. As if by magic the footsteps and muffled sobbing disappeared. The cold room was cold no longer. Colin Taylor often wondered if the dead Colin ever found his way back to his family at the new address and, if he did, whether anybody noticed.

When he was just fourteen, his grandmother died. He was upset, but truth to tell not desperately so, because his grandparents lived over a hundred miles away and tended to keep themselves to themselves. Some time after the event he overheard his grandfather telling his father that he was frightened to go to bed at night, because almost invariably his wife of more than fifty years joined him and the bed grew cold and uncomfortable, and he was terrified that he would roll over in his sleep onto her side of the bed, and even more terrified that she might move over towards him in her everlasting sleep. But I don't want to turn her away, Colin Taylor overheard his grandfather say. I don't want to move.

Some days later Colin Taylor remarked to his father that he had overheard this conversation, and wondered why grandfather didn't consider getting rid of the double bed and replacing it with two single beds. His father had looked at him strangely. Why two single beds, he had asked. Why not just one? Colin Taylor hadn't replied, sensing that his father already knew the answer to his own question, and some months later his father told him that it had been a good idea to switch the beds, and that his grandfather was now sleeping well.

Over a period of ten years Colin Taylor made a number of suggestions. To one family he suggested that they set an extra place at the dinner table on a particular anniversary each year; to an old woman who was at her wit's end because the front door banged and crashed every evening at the time her recently deceased husband used to take the dog out he was able to suggest that she simply left it open for a few minutes, which solved not only the problem of the noises, but also the problem of walking the dog, a task which she had become too frail to undertake.

He solved a problem on a local bus service by suggesting that the driver left a ticket on one particular seat where a spectre was regularly reported to appear—visible, it seemed, on certain occasions at the top of the bus late at night, but only visible from outside the bus, never from the inside. He had worked out that the reason the figure kept appearing was that it felt guilty it had not bought a ticket for a ride taken more than twenty years before.

Once he suggested that a woman changed the curtains in her room; to another woman he suggested leaving for work ten minutes later every morning. Sometimes he charged for giving advice. Sometimes he didn't. He also worked as a freelance reporter and reviewer and on occasions it was hard to know where one job finished and the other one began. When Harry McCabe mentioned the case of the newlyweds in Conwy he remembered it well, although that was by no means the only time he had worked in Wales.

His first conversation with Harry McCabe, it has to be said, did not go well. Harry McCabe had irritably asked whether he knew what time it was. Tully had replied that it was almost midnight, whereupon Harry McCabe had made an indeterminate noise which expressed weariness, disgust, amazement and a sprinkling of doubt as to whether he had done the right thing to contact anyone who was so bereft of social skill that he could make a phone call at such a late hour. Tully mentioned that Harry McCabe had asked him to make contact as soon as possible, but didn't add that therefore he was simply doing what Harry had asked, although that was the clear implication. There was a long pause, and then Tully heard Harry McCabe say, 'Yeah, yeah, whatever,' and understood that this was the verbal equivalent of erasing the last few minutes and starting again.

'Where are you?' Harry McCabe asked.

'Edinburgh,' Tully replied. 'I'm tied up for a bit, and then I was going to go back to London. But...'

'I'm in Glasgow,' said Harry McCabe.

'Shall I come over?' asked Tully.

Harry McCabe gave him his address.

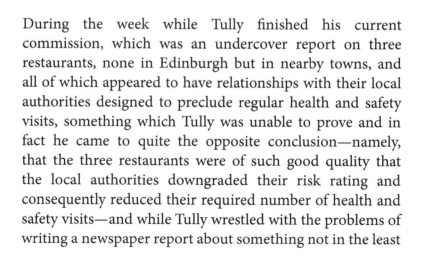

During the week while Tully finished his current commission, which was an undercover report on three restaurants, none in Edinburgh but in nearby towns, and all of which appeared to have relationships with their local authorities designed to preclude regular health and safety visits, something which Tully was unable to prove and in fact he came to quite the opposite conclusion—namely, that the three restaurants were of such good quality that the local authorities downgraded their risk rating and consequently reduced their required number of health and safety visits—and while Tully wrestled with the problems of writing a newspaper report about something not in the least sensationalist and of no public concern whatsoever, Melanie Viviani took to her room with the notion of keeping on top of her university work. She had textbooks; she had notes; she had material on the internet, both random and specifically placed there by her course tutors. But more often than not she found herself crossing her arms and pulling off both her jumper and blouse in one practiced motion.

She would sit in front of her dressing table mirror and run her hands over her scars, seven on her left arm and only three on her right as she was right handed, plus the puncture mark close to her shoulder created when she had attempted to relieve the pressure in a different way. The earliest scars were fading. Once she took off her bra as well, and allowed her hands to run over the scars and then down to the soft skin of her breasts, which she kneaded thoughtfully, and stroked her thumbs over her nipples, wondering whether scars on her breasts would heal as easily as those on her arms.

On two occasions she took out a small box decorated brightly in yellow and red, originally used for curved triangular shortbread biscuits packed in tightly according to some abstruse mathematical principle, but now used to store razor blades, iodine and plasters of various shapes and colours. Twice she put the box on the dressing table and looked into her own eyes, asking herself questions, but on both occasions she picked it up again, unopened, and replaced it in the dressing table drawer, pushing it to the back, out of casual sight.

On impulse she logged onto the internet and looked up Dr Graham Rowbotham, who of course she had blocked from her email and all her social networking sites, and found out a few things which she hadn't known. He was twelve years older than she was. He had been born in Camberley, Surrey and had gone to a boy's school which called itself a grammar school, though Melanie had thought that grammar schools even then were a thing of the past. A boy's school, thought Melanie as she looked at the neat paragraph onscreen, now that might explain a thing or two, and she could not help glancing at her wrists, though any scars there had long since faded.

On reflection she decided she didn't want to know any more about Graham Rowbotham and certainly didn't want to look up the two pamphlets he had written, called *The future of Cartesian Theory* and *Topological Spaces: A view from the Boundary*, the existence of which was the sole reason why any entry for Graham Rowbotham appeared on the internet in the first place.

Trying not to think about the pressure bloating her body, she put the laptop to one side, wrapped her arms around herself, and rocked backwards and forwards with her eyes closed, something which she tried to avoid doing because whenever it happened she could not help thinking of an animal in the zoo, caged, pacing backwards and forwards, backwards and forwards, perhaps a tiger, or a leopard; or she could not help thinking of a bear chained to a wall, rocking backwards and forwards with a mad, puzzled look in its eyes; or worse still she could not help thinking about some traumatised children she once saw on television, the survivors of a massacre, who wrapped their arms around themselves just as she was doing, and rocked backwards and forwards, just as she was doing, though they had their eyes wide open to reveal blank inhuman incomprehension whereas she squeezed hers tightly shut; and the common link between the tiger or leopard, bear, traumatised children and herself, apart from the obvious similarity of physical movement, was a feeling of being trapped and, for all she knew, was also a feeling of pressure building inside with no immediate prospect of it being released.

She opened her eyes. She could no longer talk to her father, and she didn't feel this was something she could share with Uncle James, and the thought of telling her mother was just something she couldn't even contemplate. But she needed to talk to somebody. She picked up her mobile phone and searched for David Wasson's number. She hesitated, then put down the phone again. She did this several times during the week while Tully struggled to meet the deadline for his article. By the time she finally plucked up courage— or perhaps felt desperate enough—to press the call button, Tully had made arrangements to meet Harry McCabe and had boarded the train which would take him from Waverley Station to Glasgow Queen Street.

Harry McCabe wasn't sure whether to be surprised that he and Cheyne Tully got on well, almost from the moment that they met. Over a cup of coffee he picked up the black business card and said, 'Cheyne Tully?' He was a professional taxicab driver so it was in his own best interests to develop a knack for getting on with all kinds of people. It increased the size and number of tips if nothing else.

Tully struck a pose and said in a dramatic voice, 'Colin Taylor, ghost hunter!' and quirked his eyebrows at Harry McCabe, who conceded the point.

'Naff,' he said.

Tully was a professional ghost hunter and, as Harry McCabe learned later, a newspaper and magazine reporter, so he assumed it was also professionally expedient for Tully to develop the same kind of knack, to get on well with clients or interviewees, depending on what occupational hat he was wearing at the time. But still. It might be predictable that they would get on at a superficial, professional level, but Harry had a feeling that it was more than that. He found that he liked Tully, despite having serious reservations about the services he professed to offer.

'I read somewhere, people choose another name, they nearly always pick something with the same initials. You know, subconsciously.'

'You read that?' asked Tully, meaning: 'You read?'

Harry McCabe grinned. 'Sometimes I pinch one of Tommy's books and hide it in *The Sun*.'

'Tommy?'

'My son.' Harry McCabe made a curious, defensive gesture which Tully filed away in his memory. 'He's away on a trip just now.'

'I chose Cheyne Tully deliberately,' said Tully. 'I've got CT sewed onto my underpants and I didn't want to have to buy a new set.'

'That'll be right,' grunted Harry. 'But, Tully?'

'Read a book a few years back,' said Tully. 'Sort of a ghost book, sort of a horror story. The reviews said it was a great example of Grand Guignol writing. I'd never heard of that so I looked it up.'

'Yeah?'

'Meaning, drama or dramatic prose which emphasises the horrific or macabre.' Tully sketched quote marks in the air.

'And the hero was...'

'... Tully,' confirmed Tully. 'It made quite an impression on me.'

'But, Cheyne?' said Harry McCabe.

'Read some short stories a few years back,' said Tully succinctly. 'About a man who solved supernatural mysteries, and he lived in...'

'... Cheyne Walk?' guessed Harry McCabe.

Tully nodded.

'Where've I heard Cheyne Walk before?' wondered Harry McCabe.

'Maybe in *The Sun*.'

'And these stories, they made an impact on you too?'

Tully nodded again.

'Cheyne Tully,' said Harry McCabe. 'Jesus.'

'No, I didn't consider Christ Tully,' said Tully, deadpan. He put down his cup. 'You said something about a problem with your car?'

'Yes,' said Harry McCabe. 'It's a taxi. You want to see it?'

'You want to tell me what the problem is?'

'No,' said Harry McCabe. He had thought about this, the inevitable question and how he was going to answer it, and now he looked levelly at Tully, who looked back and nodded.

'Sure, I understand,' said Tully. 'Let's go take a look.'

It was late afternoon. Not very far away the Maltese client escorted Claire down three flights of wide, carpeted stairs; past the reception desk where he was entirely unaware that two of the three receptionists looked at Claire as she clicked across the polished floor, looked her up and down before exchanging a significant glance; at the entrance to the hotel a taxi appeared as if by magic, and the Maltese client pressed some notes into Claire's hand for her fare, pressed his lips to hers, and whispered his thanks and fervent promises that he would call on her again during his next six-month stay in the United Kingdom, promises which Claire did not believe for one moment, although it warmed her to hear them. The notes in her hand warmed her still further.

In Ayr, David Wasson noticed he had missed a call from Melanie but when he called back her mobile was switched off and a recorded voice suggested that he leave a message after the tone, which he didn't.

Harry McCabe's taxi was parked in its usual spot across the road. Harry pointed his key and unlocked it as they approached, then stood with his arms folded to watch Tully. It wasn't raining. A bus growled past, jouncing over a traffic-calming bump in the road. Harry watched it thread between cars parked on both sides of the road and tried to remember if he had ever seen a bus pass in front of his house before. He was fairly sure he hadn't. When he looked back at the taxi, Tully had opened the front door and was sitting in the driver's seat. He had his hands on the steering wheel and he was smiling at Harry McCabe. He wound down the window and called out that he had always wanted to sit in the driving seat of a taxi, and Harry retorted that he was glad he had been able to assist Tully achieve his life's ambition, but then went on to enquire whether Tully felt anything odd about the taxi.

'No, not at the moment,' said Tully.

Harry McCabe had told himself that he would not give anything away, but he could not resist asking Tully if he could see anything unusual.

'No,' said Tully. He got out of the taxi and walked around the front to the pavement, where Harry McCabe was standing. He put his hand to the handle of the back door, and jerked, as if he had received an electric shock.

'What?'

Tully didn't answer. He pulled open the door and leaned inside. As he did so, Harry McCabe had a momentary vision of George Viviani as he toppled into the back of the taxi, which he originally saw happening in his wing mirror, but in the vision George Viviani froze just as he was half way through the door, suspended several inches above the back seat in midair, and while he was fixed in place Harry's point of view swung across the front of the taxi rather like computer graphic turning an image this way and that until it had swivelled around to give a view from the position where he was standing while Tully leaned forward. For an instant the two figures of George Viviani and Tully were superimposed one on top of the other. Harry McCabe blinked. Tully had crawled right inside the taxi and the door had swung almost closed behind him, so that all Harry could see was a blurred outline of hunched shoulders and unruly hair.

'Anything?'

'It's cold.'

'Yeah.'

'Someone died in here, didn't they? Recently.'

'Yeah.'

Tully backed out of the taxi, straightened.

'You see anything?' asked Harry McCabe again.

'No.'

'I thought you saw—you know...'

'No. Well, hardly ever. Just as well,' said Tully absently, with the air of having said the same thing many times before, 'or I wouldn't be able to see anything else, eh?'

Harry McCabe thought about it. Pursed his lips grudgingly. 'Yeah. I suppose.'

'It was a man, wasn't it?' said Tully.

'Maybe.'

Tully put a hand to his forehead. 'I think... I think his name began with G. Yes, it's coming to me. G E... O... George!' Harry McCabe stared at him, dumbfounded. Tully's eyes took on a distant look, and his voice seemed to change. 'An unusual second name. V... V something. V I V I. Vivienne? Vivian? Viviani! George Viviani!' He shook his head, as if shaking himself back to the here and now of the ordinary world. Harry McCabe wondered if there had been a report of George Viviani's death on the internet, or in a local paper. It seemed unlikely, and even if there was, it was even more unlikely to mention Red Arrow Taxis or identify the particular taxi driver unfortunate enough to be driving past the wrong place at the wrong time. Tully was looking at him, the distant look in his eyes replaced by one of amusement.

'How—?'

Tully reached out to show a rectangular piece of card held in his long fingers. Harry McCabe took it cautiously. It was a business card with the name George Viviani printed in capitals neatly in its centre and a telephone number and address in smaller letters underneath. Harry McCabe raised his eyes. Tully shrugged. 'It had slipped in between—you know, in the middle part of the seat, but I reckoned you'd have cleaned the taxi pretty thoroughly after—well, I took a chance and when I saw your reaction to the letter G I knew I was on to a sure thing.'

He grinned. Harry McCabe turned the business card over to see if there was any writing on the back, remembering as he did so that he had done the same thing with Tully's card. The result was the same. Nothing. The card must have fallen out of George Viviani's wallet when he had looked through it. 'Very clever,' he muttered.

Back in the house over another warming cup of coffee Tully asked for the full story and Harry McCabe told him all about picking up the curly-haired man, who turned out to be George Viviani, and the way in which he died, and the way in which, two or three weeks later, the back of the taxi had started to feel cold. He mentioned several of his passengers who had complained about the cold, not forgetting the girl with studs set into her lips who had complained more forcibly than any of the other passengers, not without some justification, Harry McCabe had to admit, and he went on to describe how he had taken the car to an unsuccessful garage appointment and soon after had been presented with Tully's business card by another taxi driver in a local pub.

Tully said nothing for a while, but sat staring into space as he considered Harry McCabe's story. Harry McCabe sipped his coffee, slightly surprised that he felt no concern, no awkwardness, over the silence that had descended on their conversation. He glanced at his watch.

'You want to stay over?'

'Ah-huh. That okay?'

'Yeah, sure.'

More silence. Tully was thinking about the sensation he had experienced when he had grasped the handle on the back door of the taxi when, despite the fact that it was a grey and chilly afternoon, his vision had momentarily disappeared in a bright flash of sunlight. When he pulled open the door and the inner light of the taxi came on, he was almost sure it had glowed bright blue, just for an instant, but he wasn't completely sure because he was still recovering from that unexpected burst of brightness.

He was, however, quite certain that the back of the taxi was cold with a chill that reminded him of the library where his mother used to take him, many years ago, where he and another man seemed to be the only people who noticed the cold. The man wore a suit and his hair was white and surprisingly long, and he was often in the library at the same time as the young Colin Taylor, often in the very same aisle where the cold seeped between the rows of books, and he often glanced curiously at Colin Taylor as if he was something strange to be remarked at and not, as Tully had come to realise in later years, the other way about. But he had seen nothing in the taxi, only his questing fingers had been lucky enough to find the business card.

'He said nothing?'

'No.'

'Never gave you an address?'

Harry McCabe shook his head.

'What was he carrying?'

'Briefcase, some flowers.'

Tully's eyes narrowed. 'Flowers? What, roses? A bouquet?'

'Uh.' Harry McCabe struggled to remember. 'Not roses. I think it was tulips.'

'Tulips?'

'Tulips.'

'Okay,' said Tully. 'And the taxi didn't start getting cold right away?'

'No,' said Harry McCabe. 'Can't remember exactly when, probably didn't notice when it started. Couple of weeks.'

'About a week ago?'

'Maybe a little more.'

'When did your son go off on his holiday?'

Harry McCabe stared. 'What?'

'You'd be surprised,' said Tully, 'at how often something happens or seems to happen, when there's a young person involved. Especially if they're aged between, oh, about fourteen and twenty. You know, I once suggested that a young boy went away on holiday, not quite what the family expected when they asked me in to check out noises from their attic, especially as the boy, Peter I think his name was, had his bedroom on the ground floor nowhere near the attic. But he was unhappy, rebellious, angry; somehow he awoke something which would otherwise have been dormant. He went away on holiday, with his grandparents or his parents, I can't remember now, somewhere abroad anyway, and the noises, whatever they were—not footsteps but some other rattling sound—just stopped.'

Harry McCabe stared at Tully. Tully shrugged.

'But—a taxi?' said Harry McCabe, meaning that the location shifted about and was not connected to the house.

Tully shrugged again. 'I read about a case in France, in the north somewhere. The windows in a trailer caravan thing kept cracking with cold and apparently the door handle got so brittle it kept just snapping off, and it turned out to be connected to a girl living in the village a couple of miles away who had been abused by the owner of the trailer thing, probably inside it. You sometimes give Tommy a lift in the taxi?'

Harry McCabe nodded.

'See, it's not as if it's a place where he's never been. Was he here when the cold started?'

'No. Though from what you're saying, does that matter?'

'Oh, it matters,' said Tully. 'It would be very unusual for something like this to be caused by someone who's—well, where is he? On holiday somewhere?'

Harry McCabe sighed, pinched the bridge of his nose and ducked his bald head momentarily. 'Sort of. Tommy's mildly autistic—a form of Asperger's—he's away for a month with a group, France as it happens. Organised by a local autism support group.'

'Ah, I see,' said Tully.

'He'll actually be helping out some of the others.'

'Sounds good,' said Tully, sounding not in the least interested.

'Anyway I took him to the airport a couple of days after Viviani died. He's back Thursday after next.'

'Oh, good,' said Tully. 'We should have this little problem sorted out by then. Let's go get something to eat.'

As he climbed to his feet, a few miles away Claire jumped off the bus in Bedford Road and popped into the grocer's to buy herself some milk; she would walk up Laburnum Crescent soon after but she would not be observed by the young man living opposite the block of flats, as he was hard at work in his back room, painting a portrait of Claire from memory, replacing the door and impenetrable background of the block of flats with a clean, straight bole of a tree, possibly a conifer or pine though he did not pretend to know anything about trees and it was just something out of his imagination, as was the way Claire peeped from behind the tree, her hands and her face on one side, one leg thrust out for balance stretched out on the other. He painted a vague green-brown background with the suggestion of other trees, and smeared a blue sky with the merest hint of clouds at the top of the canvas.

As Tully and Harry McCabe went back to the taxi, this time to make use of it to get to a restaurant in the city centre, Melanie Viviani took a long hot bath, not knowing that David Wasson had made another attempt to reach her. While she was lying there she heard her mother come in and the sound of her footsteps fade in the direction of the kitchen. Later, she would watch a movie on television, taking in none of it but glad to stop thinking.

In Glasgow, Claire first took her shower, then came out to exchange texts with Caroline before going to bed.

Tully and Harry McCabe enjoyed their meal. Afterwards they sat up and talked of nothing in particular, except that Harry was unable to resist asking for ghost hunter stories, and Tully obliged. At about half past eleven Harry McCabe showed Tully to the tiny guest room and went to bed himself, later than Claire but before Melanie Viviani, who decided to watch a second movie about three women, all recently divorced, who met up regularly to tell each other about their latest conquests and affairs, and who ended up, entirely predictably, marrying each other's ex-spouses.

Harry McCabe went to sleep almost immediately and as far as he could tell, he didn't dream except that for a few moments he thought he was standing on a wide plain under heavy black clouds waiting for thunder, and when the thunder came he opened his eyes to discover that someone was banging on his door.

'What the fuck?' he mumbled. The door opened and Tully came in. Harry McCabe knuckled at his eyes and discovered that it was past one o'clock and had time to hope that Tully wasn't going to make a habit of waking him up at unearthly hours, before Tully said, 'How well do you know Ayr?'

Chapter 7

It struck Dorothy Viviani that for the first time she could remember, she wasn't thinking about George. Usually, as she went into her suddenly lonely bedroom to get ready for bed, she couldn't help thinking about all the years when he had been getting ready at the same time, showering while she got rid of makeup, cleaning teeth and fixing the lights while she showered, a nightly routine they danced without thinking, arriving in bed at the same time to read, or make love, or talk, or settle straight down after a long, tiring day.

She wasn't thinking about George because she was thinking about the two men who had turned up in the middle of a storm to give her business cards, and she was thinking about the phone call from Barker Associates, so in a way she supposed she was thinking about George because it was his stories they wanted to publish, although she was thinking more about the trip to Glasgow than she was about the stories. Why on earth would somebody hire a taxi to come all the way from Glasgow to Ayr, apparently with the sole aim of presenting her with a business card? And why did the taxi driver come up the path to ring the doorbell? That was odd and it kept nagging at her. It made no sense.

She climbed into bed and turned off the bedside light. Now it was impossible not to think about George, because it was impossible to ignore the empty half of the bed, and she rubbed at tears in the darkness.

Steve Eginton's wife, from two doors away on the other side of Trudy, whose name was either Carol or Carole, had bumped into her on the High Street and insisted on buying her a cup of tea and a cream cake. Every Christmas, Dorothy remembered, she would ask George whether it was Carol or Carole Eginton, and every Christmas he would say he couldn't remember, and she would address the Christmas card to *you both*.

She smiled and sniffed at the memory, the darkness of the room pressing against her eyes. Why was she thinking about Carol(e) Eginton? Oh yes. Over the tea and cake they had talked desultorily, Carol(e) saying that she, Dorothy, only had to ask if she ever needed help, and they both said all the usual things, except that towards the end of their conversation, Carol(e) said she hoped Dorothy didn't mind her asking, but was she ever frightened in the house on her own, particularly at night? The answer to that was no, although there had been one occasion, not very long after George had died, when she had been getting ready for bed as usual and she thought she saw him in the bathroom, but when she turned to look properly, heart pounding, she found that she had glimpsed the reflection of her own bathrobe in a full-length mirror.

No, she wasn't frightened. Why should she be?

She remembered the first time she had met George, when he had walked into her office by mistake. She had been working as a benefits assistant in those days, taking calls, filing claims, conducting interviews, she and Helen what was her name? Gainsborough, that was it, and the young boy they'd taken on as a trainee, Bob somebody, who had a ridiculous goatee beard. One day the door had opened and George had come in, although she hadn't known his name was George then, of course; he was looking for the benefits manager and had come in to the wrong room, except that when she turned and met his gaze, both of them instantly knew that it was not the wrong room at all. They went to lunch. He bought her flowers, he always bought her flowers, all through their long and happy marriage he bought her flowers, always tulips and not roses as he was allergic to their scent.

The last time she had seen him, he had kissed her and waved, and was gone. If only she had known that was going to be the last time. No, it wasn't. She had seen him once more, in that small sterile room, and she remembered that there had been the smell of flowers but she couldn't remember now whether it had been the smell of roses because if it had been, well, that would have amused George, to be laid out in a room suffused with the scent of roses.

George. She saw him sitting in front of the fire while she sat with Melanie, aged about five or six, on her lap; curiously, she saw herself and Melanie as if she had been a fourth person in the room, although nobody else had been there. George was reading out one of his stories, a child's ghost story or a story about a monster, and Melanie's eyes were as big as dinner plates and she was furiously sucking her thumb. She saw Melanie aged about eight or nine, curled up in front of the same fire, listening to the latest story, her serious face turned up towards George, firelight gleaming in her eyes.

Melanie.

With a jolt that almost woke her, Dorothy Viviani remembered seeing the bleak expression on her daughter's face reflected in the window, with the black storm coiling behind. The big taxi driver was running up the path towards the front door, but she wasn't sure whether he was running to help Melanie, because he had seen her desperate face from outside, or whether Melanie's expression was caused by the sight of the taxi driver running up the path, or whether the two events were entirely unconnected.

A little unexpectedly, she heard Trudy reminding her that George wouldn't want her to stay unhappy, that he would expect her to laugh again. But what was there to laugh at, she wondered. Rain was slanting down from heavy skies, a taxi driver was running towards the house, his passenger, the tall younger man dressed in black, was standing on the pavement with the open door of the taxi quivering behind. Now the tall young man jerked into motion, but Melanie remained unmoving, a dark silhouette against the window. The door. The wind. Footsteps on the stairs? No, it wasn't Melanie; it was a silent figure standing in the corner of her bedroom, watching her from its furthest corner as she slept.

Confused, she sat up and stared at the figure, her breath misting in cold air. Then sleep left her, and she reached frantically for the light, almost knocking it over in her anxiety. When she turned quickly to look at the far corner of the room, where the built-in wardrobes met the curtained windows, there was nothing there, not even a chair or pile of clothes or anything that could have been mistaken for a watchful figure.

Dorothy Viviani leaned back against the headboard, her right hand clutching at the duvet which she had dragged up to cover her chest. She thought now that she could smell tulips, but when she took a deep, shuddering breath, the scent was gone. She must have imagined it. She must have imagined the figure, or dreamed it; after all she hadn't been able to see the corner of the room until she turned on the light, so how could she possibly have seen a figure standing in the darkness? George had once screamed himself awake, and clawed on the light, shouting about spiders on the ceiling. Then he had woken up and scratched at his head in embarrassment, muttering that he couldn't possibly have seen spiders in the darkness and he must have dreamed them. So now Dorothy must have dreamed the figure because she couldn't possibly have seen one in the darkness; but nonetheless she decided not to turn off the light immediately.

She woke in the morning neither sitting nor lying, but in an awkward posture somewhere in between, with morning sunlight spearing through gaps where the curtains didn't quite obscure the outside world, and with the bedside light still shining, although it seemed but a pale imitation of itself in the morning light. The confused memory of her dream about a figure in the room was already fading, and the memory or illusion of briefly smelling the scent of tulips had already gone.

———◆———

Claire went to bed nervously, blinking her eyes in the direction of the door until they became accustomed to the darkness, straining her ears for any unusual sounds. But nothing happened that night, or if it did she went to sleep and completely missed it happening, and she woke up the next morning with no added memories of any strange events. It wasn't until later that morning, after Caroline had arrived, that anything strange happened.

She had breakfast, watching the news on her giant new television where she learned that a bomb had gone off in a city she had never heard of and the news presenter had trouble pronouncing, and that between thirty and forty people were feared dead, none of them British, but another soldier had been killed in Afghanistan, or in some other country that Claire thought of vaguely and generically as *out there*, bringing the total killed to a number Claire didn't catch as she was fetching her toast at the time. She thought, as she always thought, that it was awfully sad for a soldier to be killed, but after all they were in the army and armies fought battles and soldiers sometimes died in battles.

She listened to a labour politician spouting figures about unemployment and then a conservative politician spouting different figures, both of them claiming that the other party had turned their back on the unemployed and she thought, as she always thought when she heard politicians, that if one of them said one thing and the other one said something else, then surely one of them was just plain lying, or being economical with the truth as the politicians themselves would probably put it, and wouldn't governing the country be a whole lot simpler if politicians learned to tell the truth?

The weather, it seemed, was going to be cold, drizzly and grey, so there were no surprises there.

At a little before nine she turned off the television and tidied up the flat. At just after nine, the buzzer gave three short and two long buzzes, the code which told Claire that Caroline was on her way up, and she went to the door to wait there, the arrangement being that if one of them had a client when the other arrived, then the incumbent wouldn't go to the door and whoever it was that was arriving would get the message and wait in the kitchen, or pop in to see Lucy if she was around, or go back out to the shops for a little while.

'Wow,' said Caroline when she came in and saw the new television. Caroline was slightly taller than Claire, with a fuller figure. Her hair was dyed blonde and she liked wearing thigh-length boots and short skirts.

'A guy gave it to me.'

'You must be good.'

Claire giggled and explained it was a present from a friend. She didn't say which friend. She found herself

121

curiously reluctant to tell Caroline about the young man from across the street. 'Not a client,' she insisted.

'Uh-huh,' said Caroline, clearly not believing a word of it. She was clearly thinking, with friends like that, why would you be working? but instead of saying it she started to rummage in her handbag.

'You turned it?' asked Claire, meaning, had Caroline turned over the card by the buzzer, so that it now read Jade instead of Claire.

'Uh-huh,' said Caroline again. She found what she was looking for, retrieving a crumpled newspaper cutting which she passed to Claire. 'Here. Wasn't he one of yours?'

As she reached for the cutting, Claire shivered. Some sixth sense told her she wasn't going to like this. What she saw was a photograph of a curly-haired man smiling at the camera, a man she recognised instantly as one of her favourite clients. He was always on time, always clean, always had a friendly smile and never bored her with long drawn-out excuses as to why he was visiting her in the first place. He was one of the few clients she liked to see off at the door to the block of flats, something she did because, for some reason she hadn't thought through properly, she thought it more likely that they would come back again if she accompanied them down the steps to the plywood street door. He called himself George.

She remembered that the last time she had seen him was about three weeks ago, and now that she was thinking about it, she remembered watching him walk away, and then meeting the gaze of the young man across the street, who at that time had been a stranger to her.

Underneath the photograph were a couple of paragraphs which described how George Viviani, who apparently lived in Ayr and worked in a senior accountancy post, had died of a heart attack as he got into the back of a taxi on Bedford Road. The article gave the date and time of this tragic event and noted that Mr Viviani left a wife and a daughter. Without saying anything Claire got out her appointments diary and was unsurprised but unnerved to discover that George had died a scant half hour after he had left her.

'Was he?' asked Caroline.

Claire nodded dully.

George had a set routine. Used to have. He liked her to leave her door open and then wait for him, lying in her bed as if asleep. He told her it was nice to come in—like coming home, he said—making his own way in to find her waiting for him, perhaps asleep, he told her winningly, but not for long, not for long. So she would press the button to open the street door, open her own door, and slide, naked, into bed.

Lucy's voice: Just as well, eh? After last night? I can always tell a man's footsteps from a woman's footsteps, well you know that as well as I do.

Yes, she knew that. George walked with firm footsteps, she could always hear him approaching the door; she always lay curled with her back to the door, pulling the sheet to her shoulders, smiling into the pillow. She recognised his footsteps, in the same way that she recognised those of Adrian, another of her favourites, who walked so quickly across the hallway that he almost ran, so eager was he to see her; the same way, she suddenly realised, that she recognised the squeaking footfalls of the young man from the other side of the street. But Adrian and the young man would have to knock at the door. George didn't, because she would already have opened it. She wouldn't hear George at the door, or even hear him easing through it, although sometimes she would hear a faint snick as he closed it behind him.

Lucy's voice: Did I hear him at your door? I'm not sure whether I did, now that I come to think of it.

'You're okay for Wednesday, then?' said Caroline.

'What? What?'

Claire was staring at the newspaper cutting, but her gaze was unfocussed. After the door closed, she would hear George walk across her uncarpeted floor, pause, make a muffled sound of annoyance at the way his shoes clicked briskly on the floor; then there would be a longer pause while he carefully removed his socks and shoes. Claire could hear the rustle of clothes and balancing noises against the wall; she would smile at his total failure to hide his approach.

Lucy: I always hear them walking across your room, no carpet, you said it yourself, no carpet.

She sat on the bed, hands trembling.

'Here, are you all right?' asked Caroline.

She wasn't all right. She remembered the crisp, firm footsteps that she thought she had heard, or that she had dreamed. She remembered how George would stand by the side of the bed, usually in the afternoon, sometimes it was almost dark, sometimes light was still streaming into the flat around the edges of the drawn curtains. She could hear him breathing, then feel him gently drawing away the sheet. Not waking her, he said, if she was truly asleep, so she would pretend to sigh sleepily, and stretch, rolling onto her back, and quite often he would chuckle softly.

'I'm sorry, I'm sorry,' Caroline said in a slightly bewildered voice. 'He was just a client, wasn't he?'

'What have we here?' George would ask throatily.

On one occasion, instead of staying at the flat, he took her out for a meal. He came in through the door and instead of striding across the floor to the bed he stopped just inside the room and said, 'Never mind all that, Miss Claire. I'm hungry.' He always called her Miss Claire. They went to an Italian restaurant further up Bedford Road, where Claire had once been taken by another client, a big, beefy man who called himself Seamus O'Malley although he had not the slightest trace of an Irish accent, and who turned up twenty minutes late because, he said, his damned meeting had overrun and he hadn't had any dinner and he wasn't in the mood now and forty minutes was scarcely enough time anyway, so how about going out for a meal instead?

When she went to the restaurant with George, he had ordered a lasagne, and she had chosen pizza, and they both drank cokes. George didn't say much, although he mentioned that he had written some stories and was trying to get them published, but he asked her lots of questions and she found herself telling him more about her life, and her family, and why she was doing what she was doing, than she had ever told anybody else, including any social worker.

George asked her about her mother, and she told him that she had run away when she, Claire, had been only eight, and when George asked why she had run away, Claire nodded and said yes, that was the question, did her mother *run away from* or *run away to*?

George didn't say anything at this point, but just took a forkful of lasagne as Claire told him that her father had started drinking, but she couldn't remember whether he was already drinking when she was eight, or whether he started after her mother had left. She hastened to add that her father wasn't in any way abusive or violent or even unkind, it was just that he drank too much and that left him... She fumbled for the right word. Ineffective, she said eventually. Ineffective.

Harry McCabe went out before breakfast to open the back door of his taxi and was delighted to find that it was no colder inside than it was in the front of the taxi. He sat there for some time, thinking not so much about George Viviani and the way in which he plunged into the taxi, but more about the dream he had of his wife sitting there in her thin nightdress while the windows, seats, floors and even the ceiling were rimed with ice.

Over breakfast he told Tully the good news, but Tully seemed distracted. The previous evening they had reached an agreement, which was that Tully wouldn't charge Harry McCabe provided that he could stay on for a couple of days, and that Harry would provide a lift down to Ayr should Dorothy Viviani call.

'You think she'll call?' Harry had asked, more than a little hopefully.

'There's something not right,' Tully had said.

Harry McCabe remarked that, on the contrary, everything seemed to be getting back to normal. 'I mean, you said we should drive down to Ayr, and when we did, the cold went, didn't it?'

'Yes. The cold got left behind,' said Tully significantly.

Harry McCabe blinked, then ducked his head slightly and ran the palm of his hand over his bald skull. 'Whatever. The thing is, well, I didn't exactly laugh at Stevie when he gave me your card, but I didn't really, well...' He trailed off.

'And now you're a believer, eh?'

Harry McCabe nodded cautiously. If there was one thing he had learned over the past two days, it was that conversations with Cheyne Tully seldom went the way he expected. Tully looked at him thoughtfully for a moment, then gave a description of the case of the old woman's husband who, or so it seemed, wanted to keep taking the couple's dog out for a walk. It was one of Tully's favourite cases, although he often wondered what happened when the dog itself died, as it surely must have done by now.

'The dog went out by itself and came back by itself?' said Harry McCabe.

'Yes.'

'And the banging noise stopped?'

'Yes.'

Harry McCabe's face creased in an expression of mild disbelief. 'That'll be right,' he muttered.

'The thing is this,' Tully told him. 'What if I told that old woman about a man dying in the back of a taxi, and how the taxi was cold afterwards, until it had been driven on the journey that the man wanted to take...'

'Yeah, yeah,' said Harry McCabe.

'There was something wrong with the taxi,' Tully said.

'What?'

'That's what the old lady would say. There was something blocked, something not working quite right, and the long drive down to Ayr unblocked it, fixed it somehow. Sure, you took it in to the garage, but they didn't spot the problem.'

Harry McCabe looked at him.

'There's always an explanation,' said Tully.

'What about...?' Harry McCabe thought back to their conversation on the previous day. 'What about John whatsisname, you helped over the road?'

'Colin, not John,' said Tully. 'I dreamed it.' He shrugged. 'Or even, after all these years, my memory thinks something happened but I only imagined it.'

'You could say that about anything.'

'Exactly.'

'The hamster?'

'I dreamed it.'

'The ghost on the bus,' said Harry McCabe triumphantly.

'I never saw it,' said Tully. 'I never spoke to anyone who did. Could've been made up. A prank.'

'Yeah?'

'No,' said Tully. 'But that's what people will say.'

There was a pause while Harry McCabe digested this information.

'So you think Mrs Viviani will call?' he asked finally.

Cheyne Tully nodded thoughtfully and said he was almost sure of it because, he said, there was something not quite right about the Viviani household, even allowing for the fact that the head of it had just died; or maybe there was something wrong about the way in which the wind blustered furiously when the young woman, presumably George Viviani's daughter, opened the door. He was beginning to wonder, although he made no mention of it to Harry McCabe, whether his sense that something was wrong emanated from the young woman. He wished now that he had paid more attention to her, but he retained no more than the impression of a nice figure and a pretty face.

'Between fourteen and twenty, you said,' said Harry McCabe.

Tully looked up sharply and thought, not for the first time, that Harry McCabe was far from stupid. He nodded. They stared at each other.

'The dog?' said Harry.

Tully shrugged. 'Dogs are creatures of habit. No reason one couldn't take itself out.'

'But the door? The banging?'

'Bad weather.'

'Jesus,' said Harry McCabe. 'Whose side are you on anyway?'

Tully grinned. 'Nobody between fourteen and twenty in that house, anyway.'

'Yeah?' grunted Harry McCabe. 'What about the dog?'

'You must've imagined it. You must've been dreaming,' said Caroline.

'But, Lucy,' said Claire. 'She heard footsteps.'

'Oh, Lucy,' said Caroline, making a gesture that indicated Lucy's contribution was not reliable, that anything Lucy said was to be taken with a pinch of salt, and all of her opinions were debatable if not ridiculous. 'Footsteps,' added Caroline disparagingly, and made another gesture which reminded Claire that there were always footsteps to be heard in the block of flats; footsteps could be heard in the hallway, in adjoining rooms, in the room above and usually in the room below, not to mention in the stairwells. 'Lucy heard footsteps, okay, so what? And you had some bad dreams, so what? What did you have to eat, anyway?'

Claire remembered going out to lunch with the man from Malta, when she had chosen some sort of chicken stuffed with cheese and it was true, she also remembered reading somewhere that cheese could cause nightmares, but she shook her head mutely and looked down at curly-haired George smiling for the camera.

'Anyway,' Caroline said, 'you won't be here tonight, will you?' Claire looked up. 'Or tomorrow night, eh?' Claire nodded slowly. 'I'll text you if I hear fucking footsteps, okay?'

Claire nodded again. Perhaps Caroline was right. Perhaps it had all been in her imagination. At the time she thought she had been awake, but perhaps she really had been asleep, and only dreamed everything.

She had done it before, now that she thought about it. A long time ago she had dreamed that she had got up, dressed, had breakfast and caught the school bus as she did every weekday, only this time the bus started to speed up until it was zooming along towards a busy junction at a terrific speed. Everybody else on the bus behaved perfectly normally, reading, or staring out of the window or chatting to friends or fighting with somebody on the seat behind, and only she saw how the bus was shuddering and shaking as it went faster and faster towards cars queued not far ahead, and it seemed only she saw pedestrians crossing the road in front of the cars. Her stomach had churned with terror and she had opened her mouth to scream, in fact perhaps she did scream because as she woke up in the darkness of her bedroom, she fancied that the air trembled as if in the aftermath of some shock, some sound, such as it might have done if she had screamed in her sleep.

'Okay?' asked Caroline.

At the time Claire nodded, more than half convinced by Caroline's cheerful practicality and her own memory of dreaming that she was awake. It was only when she was on the bus back home that it suddenly occurred to her that Lucy had heard footsteps (but had not heard the door) before she, Claire, had dreamed her strange dreams, if they were dreams, and more importantly before Caroline had produced the newspaper clipping. On the bus, doubt assailed her again, but she was able to watch the housing estates and shopping arcades pass by outside, reflecting that she was travelling away from and not towards any strange lights or footsteps. Funny she had remembered her dream about being on a bus, and here she was on a bus again.

She wondered whether anything would happen to Caroline as she became Jade and slept at the flat for two nights. On the one hand she hoped that nothing would happen, because she didn't really want Caroline to be frightened in the same way that she had been frightened, and also because she didn't want to go back to the flat knowing that something strange really was happening. On the other hand, she half hoped that something would happen, to vindicate her own memories and prove to Caroline that she wasn't quite as stupidly imaginative as Caroline seemed to think.

When she got back to the flat two days later, on Wednesday morning, it was to discover that nothing at all had happened, although Caroline admitted she had found it harder to get to sleep than usual. You and your stories, she told Claire. But in Ayr that same morning, Dorothy Viviani woke up disoriented, thinking that it was summer because the window was open and a wind blew into the room, carrying the scent of tulips. In the moment of awakening, while she saw the summer sun paint shadows on the wall, she knew that George had only just left; he was on his way downstairs to fetch her a cold drink, or perhaps he was already on his way back up. In the next moment the bright sunlight was gone and a watery replacement showed her the curtains not drawn and one window standing open, but still she smelled tulips and the terrible sense that George was on his way down or up the stairs remained.

At the corners of her vision, one of the shadows—black now rather than grey—moved. Or she thought it moved. It grew as it moved, silently and swiftly, as if it planned to engulf her.

She screamed.

In the next room Melanie lay awake, wondering what she was going to say to David Wasson later, wondering whether it was a good idea to talk to him at all. When she rushed through to her mother's room it was to find Dorothy cowering on the bed and a chill wind blowing in through an open window. Dorothy shrieked something about the scent of tulips but Melanie could detect nothing, especially as opening the door set up a draught which sucked the air directly from the window out of the bedroom, out into the hall where it was strong enough to disturb something, because Melanie heard a series of small bangs rather like the noise a book or ball might make as it bounced down the stairs, though afterwards when she checked, she found nothing.

'It's all right,' she told Dorothy. 'There's no one here. There's nothing.'

'The window,' whispered Dorothy.

Melanie went over and looked outside, down into the small enclosed garden at the back of the house, before latching the window shut. She could see the top of the shed. She could see that the back gate was closed. There was nobody in sight. 'It blew open,' she said. 'Or you opened it in your sleep.'

'He was here,' whispered Dorothy.

Melanie felt fear tighten her stomach. She sat down on the bed and took her mother's hand in hers. 'Don't be silly,' she said as brightly as she could. She had a flash of inspiration. 'Anyway, even if he was, you don't think he would ever hurt you, do you?' As she spoke she could not help thinking of her father; tears came to her eyes and her voice faltered as she tried to hold back an unwanted flood of emotion. Dorothy didn't seem to notice, but shook her head, although it was not clear whether she was agreeing or disagreeing with the notion that George would never hurt her.

'I'll get you breakfast,' said Melanie, but Dorothy shook her head again. They put on dressing gowns and went downstairs together, Melanie expecting to find something fallen to the foot of the stairs, but there was nothing.

Chapter 8

'I wasn't very good at statistics,' explained Melanie. 'Oh, I could do the theoretical stuff about probability and combinations and frequency distributions and like that. But I wasn't very good at the number crunching side—you know, one-sided tests, t tests, confidence levels and like that. You know.'

David Wasson reflected that if somebody had asked him to calculate the likelihood that he would invite Melanie Viviani around to his flat where they would end up talking about statistics, of all things, then he would no doubt have calculated a very low probability, not that he knew anything about statistics.

'The point is,' said Melanie, 'that Professor Lamberton recommended that I should get some individual tuition on practical statistics. Which is how I came to meet Graham Rowbotham. Doctor Graham Rowbotham.' Melanie paused and chewed at her lip, avoiding the gaze of David Wasson. She was wearing a thin pink jumper, blue jeans, and ankle length boots. Back home, Dorothy Viviani was standing in the kitchen looking with surprise, bewilderment and a little sadness at the two mugs she had just taken out of a cupboard. She always used to take out two mugs; she took tea without sugar, George with one spoon of sugar but very little milk; she might have expected, in the days after he died, that she might have automatically taken two mugs out of the cupboard, but she hadn't, not once in the previous three weeks or so, not until now, presumably because she was still upset and confused by the events of earlier that morning.

David Wasson's flat was a tiny affair above what used to be a video rental shop but had been transformed into a vaping retailer, not far from the railway station. The flat consisted of a small bedroom, just big enough for a single bed, a wardrobe and a desk, and an even smaller kitchen which contained a fridge and a hob but no oven and a sink which doubled up as a washbasin. It had frequently occurred to David Wasson that Melanie's room in the Edwardian terraced townhouse at the other end of the High Street was probably bigger than his entire flat.

'The first couple of times were okay.'

'What's he look like, this bloke?'

'Tall. Slim. Very pale. Very black hair. He likes to wear bow ties.'

'Bow ties,' repeated David Wasson, with no particular emphasis, as if he was taking a mental note.

'Then he suggested having the tutorials at his place,' said Melanie, also without emphasis, although the reason she was speaking in a flat, colourless voice was that she wanted to keep emotion at bay. She met David Wasson's gaze for a moment, and instantly understood that he had already anticipated some of what she was going to say. She looked away, out of the window. A row of taxis, some of them black and some white, lined up outside the railway station, looking like a slice cut out of a chess board. She could see one of the taxi drivers reading a newspaper in the front of his vehicle, and remembered the big, bald taxi driver—Harry, that was his name—running up the path towards the house while the storm crashed and rolled overhead.

In the house, Dorothy finally plucked up courage to return to her bedroom and adjoining bathroom, where she found a towel left in a dry heap in between the shower and the sink, which was just where George always used to leave his towel after showering. She stood and looked down at the towel, her thoughts a confused jumble; she wondered whether it had been there earlier; she remembered continually nagging George about leaving his towels there; she tried to remember if she could have knocked it down from the towel rail, although if she did, she must also have slid it several feet across the tiled floor to its present position. George always mumbled something about remembering next time, but he never did, and she knew that he wouldn't remember, and he knew that she knew, but she nagged him anyway.

A noise came from just behind her and she jumped and whirled, finding that the bathroom door had swung to, and she breathed rapidly and shallowly, not liking the sudden enclosed space. She pushed it open and barged out into the wider space of the bedroom, and to her muddled whirling frightened thoughts she added the question of whether, in all the years she had lived in the old house, that particular door had ever swung closed before.

Melanie shrugged. 'I wasn't quite sure about whether it was right, but I mean, he's a university lecturer for God's sake.'

'So you went.'

'I went.' She shrugged again. 'We did some stats, but it was kind of obvious, I mean at one point he drew a bell curve and then I saw him looking at me. It was pretty pathetic I suppose, but after a while he offered a drink and he showed me some of the stuff round the flat. Some of it,' she added defensively, 'was really interesting...'

'He seduced you,' said David Wasson. When she nodded, his mind conjured up an image of a pale, thin naked man lying between Melanie Viviani's parted legs and he felt such a surge of jealousy and rage that he was hard pressed not to stand up and smash his fist through the window, or against the wall, and he hurriedly brushed away tears that unexpectedly ran from his eyes, before Melanie Viviani could turn and see them.

'We did it in his bed,' whispered Melanie, still staring out of the window, where a red taxi had joined the end of the chessboard line, spoiling its pattern. 'The next time, we did it on the sofa.'

David Wasson gripped the arms of his chair, not sure that he had heard correctly. Wood creaked. He didn't know whether or not to ask the obvious question, so he stared at Melanie's face in profile as she gazed, apparently calmly, out of the window. He saw her swallow; the silence stretched until it was broken by the raucous shriek of a seagull outside. Melanie turned and met his gaze.

'He told me he would be marking my paper,' she said.

She searched David Wasson's eyes, not sure what she was looking for; understanding, disgust, sympathy, shock, revulsion, anger, support. Did David Wasson even want her in his flat after this disclosure which, though he did not know it, was itself only the first page of a longer, more sordid tale? Absently she heard the seagull squawking again, two seagulls, probably they were arguing over a scrap of food. Something rumbled past, between the flat and the railway station, a lorry or a bus. She didn't turn to see what it was. David Wasson smiled very slightly and reached out to squeeze her shoulder. He stood up and said, 'I'll make another cup of tea.'

As he did so, Dorothy Viviani ran to answer the doorbell, to discover a ginger-haired, freckle-faced teenager almost obscured by the bouquet of flowers he was delivering. She reached inside transparent plastic to extract a card from where it had been wedged between two stems. It read: *No special reason. James.*

'How long did this go on for?' asked David Wasson as he manoeuvred about the tiny kitchen with the ease of long practice.

'Nearly five months.'

David Wasson considered asking whether she could have told somebody, but he could anticipate the answer easily enough. Who could she tell? Who would believe her? What would happen to her exam? For that matter, if she tried to complain and the whole thing blew up into some sort of investigation which would probably hit the newspapers if not the local television news, how could she possibly have concentrated on any of her subjects and passed any of her exams, never mind statistics? He made the tea, remembering that she took no sugar, and went back to the window where she was sitting perched on the edge of his bed.

'Here.'

'Thanks.'

They sipped. Movement caught Melanie's eye. Arrivals were coming out of the station, first a handful of people walking quickly, then a group all carrying or wheeling suitcases, then a pause before a couple came through pushing a buggy, and a whole stream of people behind. The taxi driver who had been reading a newspaper folded it up and shifted in his seat in anticipatory fashion.

'I guess,' said David Wasson, 'there wasn't much you could do.' The simple act of getting up to make the tea had calmed him down, but he could not get the image of Melanie Viviani having sex with a pale-skinned man out of his mind.

'It got worse,' whispered Melanie.

'What?'

'He didn't just like, you know, I mean after a few times of doing it... two or three weeks, I don't know, he, I went round mostly on a Tuesday in the afternoon, or Thursday in the evenings, I suppose that fitted in with his timetable, anyway, he wanted to do more even though I said no, he made me... he made me...'

Melanie was trembling violently and as David Wasson suddenly reached over to pull her close, she saw her tea fall in slow motion, cartwheeling away from her and then downwards, the liquid at first staying inside the mug but eventually spraying free in a clearly defined arc, and even as she started to cry, so that the window and the outlines of the flat blurred and merged behind a curtain of tears, she found time to notice how strong David Wasson seemed, and even found time to think that David Wasson pulling her close in no way resembled the way in which Graham Rowbotham pulled her close, or pushed himself up against her.

David Wasson stroked her back and made some small noises of comfort while her mouth was close to his ear; she choked, spoke some words, cried achingly, whispered some more, her breath caught and she coughed as she tried to speak, and repeated her words before dissolving into tears again.

In this fashion, gradually, piece by piece, David Wasson learned that Dr Graham Rowbotham liked to tie Melanie up, usually naked, sometimes wearing just underwear which he would painstakingly remove or cut away while her wrists and ankles were fastened, and sometimes she was even blindfolded; and he learned that Dr Graham Rowbotham not only became extremely excited on the Tuesday afternoons or Thursday evenings when he had Melanie fastened to his bed, but that he liked to do just exactly what he wanted under these circumstances—although, Melanie said at one lucid point, he never hurt her, he just did whatever he liked with her. If he had hurt her, Melanie said, or if she had been frightened of being hurt, then she would have gone to someone, the Professor, or the police, or someone, and to hell with the examinations which, she added with a hysterical laugh, she never got to take anyway.

It took half an hour or more for her to choke out the story. All the time David Wasson held her in his arms and stroked her back, and didn't interrupt or ask questions. He stared past her ash-blonde hair towards the window, but he was sitting too far back to see anything except some kind of aerial device affixed to the top of a hotel next to the railway station. Instead he saw into the future.

This event, this outpouring of emotion by Melanie as she sat cradled in his arms, was not destined to transmute their relationship into something closer and more permanent. They would go different ways, and perhaps even eventually lose contact altogether, but he would never forget these moments which were both dreadful and wonderful at the same time. He never forgot the way in which she clutched at him, and how her lips were so close that they sometimes brushed his cheek, or moved against his ear. He never forgot the way in which her body trembled and how it felt to hold her in his arms. He never forgot the story she told him, although he never knew that she didn't tell him everything.

In particular, he never forgot the name Dr Graham Rowbotham.

About six months later a local Glasgow newspaper carried a story about how a university lecturer, a mathematics lecturer by the name of Doctor Rowbotham, had been caught up in a pub brawl after a rugby match, although he hadn't been to the match and, the newspaper reporter had somehow discovered, had no interest in rugby. The brawl apparently surged around Dr Rowbotham. Bottles were thrown, chairs were broken, lights were smashed. After the brawlers had spilled out into the street and dispersed at the sound of approaching sirens, the unfortunate mathematics lecturer was discovered huddled at the foot of a nearby wall, in an alleyway, with a disfiguring cut on his face, a broken arm and several broken fingers, together with several bruises about his lower body, the cause of which was never properly ascertained but which, the police suspected, were probably the result of somebody repeatedly kicking the unconscious lecturer in the groin.

The person who found the damaged Dr Rowbotham was Constable Jerry Harkness, who happened to be a good friend of Constable Kirkwood. The article in the newspaper concluded with the disheartening news that the police had no leads, and noted that Dr Graham Rowbotham was likely to make a full recovery, although the lightning-shaped cut across his face would probably leave a permanent scar.

Melanie Viviani pushed herself away from David Wasson. He fumbled in his pocket and produced a handkerchief which she used to wipe her eyes and nose. She was still sitting in his lap and they both felt suddenly embarrassed at each other's close proximity, especially given what Melanie had just been describing. They avoided each other's gaze as Melanie pushed herself further away, stumbling back to the edge of the bed. She made an apologetic gesture at the spilt tea, and David Wasson muttered that she should forget it, and they almost collided as both bent to pick up the mug.

'Leave it,' said David Wasson. Melanie clasped her hands on her knees and looked at him, and he looked back. It would be unreasonable to suggest that nothing had happened between them, or that their relationship had not changed, although exactly how it had changed was hard to define. They did not feel closer despite the intimate nature of Melanie Viviani's confession, rather they felt complicit in that they both knew something that the world in general did not, and both felt the same constraints that the nature of that knowledge imposed on them. In those few moments Melanie Viviani decided not to tell David Wasson the last distasteful twist in her story, and he did not detect any evasion in her gaze.

'Sod it,' he said. 'Let's go out, have lunch, talk about something else.'

They went out in search of a cafe.

At the other end of the town Dorothy Viviani was too tired to do anything more than make a sandwich for lunch, and a cup of tea. She sat down and flipped through tv channels, settling first on the news and then, when that proved too depressing, switching to a documentary about a group of explorers boating up some broad, slow-moving river in Africa or New Guinea—somewhere where thick, impenetrable jungle still existed and there was still a chance of meeting a last outpost of humanity that had never seen a white man and had no idea that the world had moved on from poisoned arrows, mud huts, and the complete absence of any clothing.

Sometimes the intrepid explorers could be seen taking a detour round some shallow rapids, or disembarking beneath the shade of a gigantic tree with the intention of lighting a fire, hunting for food, and eating al fresco, and Dorothy thought, as she often thought when she saw this type of documentary—which she enjoyed, she wasn't really criticising in any way—but she did wonder how they managed to get camera shots such as these unless the intrepid explorers were actually accompanied by another boat stuffed with cameramen, equipment and (or so her cynical mind insisted on thinking) a secret store of Western food.

On being reminded of food, she took a bite of her sandwich, and looked down at it with surprise. It had pickle in it. She didn't like pickle. Of course George had always liked pickle in his sandwiches, but she never put it in her own, and she didn't know why she had done so on this occasion, unless it was another symptom akin to taking two mugs out of the cupboard. She took a sip of her tea and was relieved to find that it had one sugar in it, and plenty of milk, just the way she liked her tea.

She went out to the kitchen to check whether she had absentmindedly made two sets of sandwiches, but she hadn't. When she went back into the sitting room, it was to discover that the television was no longer showing images of exotic flora and rare animals, but was instead tuned to a football match. Dorothy Viviani stopped just inside the door and stared. She saw that the channel changer was on the floor, and although she didn't remember it dropping off her lap when she got up to go to the kitchen, that was what must have happened. It must have fallen onto the carpet and bounced on buttons which changed the channel and it was just coincidence that the new channel was football, an unhappy coincidence because George had always enjoyed watching football on television.

She decided to eat the sandwich anyway. A bit of pickle never hurt anybody.

Irritatingly, she heard Carol or Carole asking her, in a decidedly smug voice, whether she was afraid of being alone in her own house. Two days ago she would have thought that a silly thing to ask, but now she didn't like to think about the question; she avoided thinking about it, as she avoided thinking about any alternative explanations for finding a towel on the floor, for the way in which the bathroom door gently swung closed, for finding pickle in her sandwich, and for the way in which the channel changer apparently bounced in just such a way that football bloomed on the television screen.

She slept. She imagined that she was going upstairs, or possibly she was going downstairs, it was hard to tell, but what she could tell was that for some strange reason her shoes were clicking loudly, firmly, crisply on each carpeted tread.

She imagined that she pulled the curtains to her bedroom and unaccountably found herself looking into the room, instead of out over the back yard. She could see the bed and vaguely make out that there was somebody in it, and it occurred to her that the somebody might be herself, and then it also occurred to her that she was watching the room from almost the same position that the figure of her dreams had watched from, except that she was outside the room instead of inside.

She imagined that the television, now showing a scene from a drama in which headlights approached through the darkness of a storm, toppled in slow motion and in complete silence onto its front, and smoke drifted up from its metallic carcase to form strange geometric patterns which she felt she ought to recognise, but she couldn't quite grasp their meaning and she could feel their message slip away from her comprehension. The smoke was sucked up into the blades of an air conditioner high up on the living room wall which she had never seen before, and which was clearly not working properly because it gave out an uneven click.

Dorothy opened her eyes to semi-darkness and thought she heard a key in the front door, or the click of the latch as it closed. The television picture, now showing a documentary about something underground, seemed brighter. Dorothy was pleased that the television itself was still standing. 'Melanie?' she called out. 'Is that you?'

———●———

While Dorothy slept, Melanie and David ate lunch in a cafe situated on the corner of the main street, or rather David Wasson ate his lunch, consisting of a small piece of fish and a huge helping of chips, while Melanie picked at her open sandwich. They wandered over familiar ground, talking about family, films, childhood, books, swapping anecdotes from schooldays, pinpointing mutual friends and acquaintances. They had travelled there before, but now it represented safe territory for them both to navigate almost without thinking.

David Wasson's parents had left Ayr two years ago, in order to be closer to his grandparents, his father's parents, who lived in a small village outside Fort William, and who were becoming increasingly frail. He told Melanie the latest about the course he was taking in graphic design. He told her stories about his neighbours, all of whom appeared to be totally mad, especially the Welshman Frank who hung up his used teabags to dry—Melanie made an anticipatory grimace—because, he said, it halved the cost of a cup of tea, even if the second brewings, as he put it, were rather stewed. In the exact centre of his room was a pearly white skeleton that he had appropriated while studying for a qualification of some sort. Frank said the skeleton's name was Holy Joe. One morning he went out to the local shop, leaving his door open, and the girl who lived on the other side of David

Wasson's flat, Bethany Copwell, originally from London, glanced in as she went past and caught sight of Holy Joe standing there, gleaming innocently. She had fainted and, or so she told David Wasson afterwards, subsequently found it very difficult to explain to her employer that she was late that day because of being rendered unconscious by the sight of a ghostly skeleton. Melanie laughed dutifully.

After lunch they took a look at the weather, which was grey but dry, and decided to take a walk along the promenade, past a couple of hotels and the main residence of the local authority, past a wide expanse of grass sparsely populated by other walkers, mainly with dogs, and up towards a new pedestrian bridge built over a river. They didn't hold hands or link arms.

Once over the bridge they turned around and came back again, not talking very much, but comfortable with their silence. At one point he asked her if she was going to do anything about what had happened, and she shook her head. They steered their way past a group of excited late season tourists who were standing by a plaque and peering out at the horizon and were clearly perplexed at the apparent non-existence of the island of Arran, although both Melanie and David Wasson could have told them that it frequently vanished, even on days when the sun was shining, the sky was clear, and there was no obvious reason why it should have become invisible.

'It's over,' said Melanie Viviani. 'I'm never going to see the bastard again.'

They walked on up to the harbour, where they leaned on a wall and watched a ship flying an unfamiliar flag take on a load of coal, the giant blue diggers looming over both ship and coal like aliens strutting across a devastated, smoking battlefield. David Wasson absently wondered for how much longer it would be politically acceptable for coal to be loaded or unloaded—he wasn't sure which—at Ayr harbour, but kept the thought to himself. He didn't think Melanie would be interested.

A small boy was perched on the same wall a few yards away, his mother holding on to him with one distracted hand while the other aimed a bottle into the mouth of an even smaller child—it was impossible to tell whether it was male or female—strapped into a baby walker. The small boy had a tiny pair of binoculars through which he was watching the coal loading with great excitement, shrilling repetitive bulletins about what was happening to his mother, who didn't seem very interested. Another handful, he told her as the giant digger released more coal into the ship. Another handful, as the second digger did the same thing. And another one. His mother straightened briefly, not so much to watch the fascinating sight of a ship being loaded, but to stretch her aching back, but as soon as she did so the milk bottle disengaged from her younger child's face, and he or she promptly started to wail.

It was almost dark by the time they turned away from the harbour and wandered back to the main street and circled round to David Wasson's flat. They had another cup of tea. They had swapped places; Melanie now sat in the one chair. She looked quietly out of the window, at the railway and the taxis.

'You know,' said David Wasson, awkwardly, 'you're welcome to stay.'

Two things happened as he said this: streetlights came on outside, reminding Melanie of the way that had happened during the storm, when the cream coloured taxi had nosed into their cul-de-sac like a hesitant ghost; and her mind unexpectedly splintered and thought of several things at the same time.

Even though it was gloomy, Dorothy saw a shadow darken the doorway and then pass by it, lengthening into the living room.

It wasn't Melanie.

It was George.

He stood on the other side of the doorway, in the hall, holding something and smiling oddly. Dorothy noticed he wasn't wearing any shoes. Her first thought was that she was glad the last few weeks had, after all, been just a dream, and her meetings with Constable Sargent, James, the people at the funeral, Trudy, and even the weird visit of the taxi driver and the young man who had come with him, had all been contrivings of her imagination. Her first reaction was to jump up, to run over to George, fling her arms around him and tell him that she had had a terrible dream. She did jump up, or stand up; she was sure of it, though her muscles seemed strangely stiff and unmoving, and her body unresponsive; she was pretty sure of it because she thought she felt the television channel changer slide off her lap onto the floor, and she absently wondered whether the picture on the television would change yet again.

On reflection, George seemed to have a very strange expression on his face, something between embarrassment and anger, and on reflection the dream of the last few weeks had been very detailed, even down to all the cards and flowers she had received, and Melanie's reaction, and the phone call from Barker Associates regarding George's stories, so it suddenly occurred to her that perhaps it hadn't all been a dream at all, in which case the appearance of George in the hallway was perhaps more than just a surprise. She didn't say anything. He didn't say anything. He shifted from one bare foot to the other; his eyes stared at her and the expression on his face changed very slightly, admitting to a trace of sadness and longing.

Dorothy suddenly noticed that he wasn't wearing a tie either, though she was fairly certain that when he left that morning, he had been wearing one, a light blue and white design that matched his pale shirt and jacket, and of course she was quite sure that he had been wearing shoes and socks. Was it only that morning he had left, waving briefly and then disappearing from view, heading up to Glasgow and his meeting with Robert Barker? She felt an icy tremor. How did she know he had gone to meet with Robert Barker? George had never told her exactly who he was going to meet, only that he was popping up to Glasgow to talk to someone about his stories, something he did every few months with a conspicuous lack of success, so much so that he had given up telling her chapter and verse on who exactly his latest hopes rested on.

Dorothy realised that something was very wrong. She couldn't possibly have known about Robert Barker of Barker Associates unless he had telephoned and introduced himself to her, and if he had rung her then the last few weeks hadn't been a dream, and in any case why wasn't George wearing anything on his feet? When she opened her mouth to speak, or stutter, or scream she noticed that her breath plumed in the air and she really, really hoped that the central heating hadn't broken down again, with winter just around the corner.

In the few seconds it took for the streetlights to steady and begin to shine more brightly, in the way of modern ecologically sound lighting, Melanie's thoughts jumped in different directions. She thought that in some ways she would like to stay longer with David Wasson, but she couldn't, even though there was an unspoken understanding between them that if she did stay, she would be perfectly safe. One reason why she couldn't stay was that at some stage she would have to take off her pink jumper, revealing her upper arms, and she had already decided not to tell David Wasson about her little box containing razor blades and ointments.

She was worried about her mother, that was another reason why she couldn't stay.

Into her mind flashed a series of images, each one slightly different from the time before, rather like images shot by an animator. In each image, she was sitting in the same position at her desk in her university room, in front of a mirror she had fixed up on the wall. In the first image she was wearing a black blouse and the box was not in sight; then in each subsequent image she was wearing something different, and it seemed as if she was jerking slightly because the chair wasn't in exactly the same position; the tiny box put in an appearance and scooted up and down the length of the desk because she never put it in exactly the same place, and jagged red scars bloomed on her upper arms, visible in the mirror, or sometimes it was her face visible, her expression a study of concentration.

She couldn't tell David Wasson any of this. She might have told her father. Her father. She would never see her father again. She was worried about her mother after the events of that morning. She might have told her father about her sordid secret, but she could never tell her mother because— well, she just couldn't; and there was nobody else she could tell or wanted to tell, only her father. She missed her father. She needed her father. She didn't know what he would have said, when she told him what had happened to her and what she had been doing to herself, but she was quite certain he would have not only known what to say, but he would have known exactly what to do about it, and with a few masterful words and actions, he would have put her life back on an even keel.

Only a few seconds had passed since David Wasson had made his offer. She shook her head, trying to hold back tears, and failing. He put his arms around her, but didn't say that everything would be all right. He said she knew where he was if she needed him, but he knew she would not be back.

She pulled away, rubbed at her eyes.

'Thank you,' she said. 'I mean, really, thank you.'

She kissed him.

He mumbled something and helped her on with her coat. She smiled at him once before she left, stepping out into semi-darkness where people were locking up shops, queuing for buses, scurrying towards the railway station. Almost furtively, she made her way back down the main street to the other end of town, and plunged into side turnings.

The streetlight was on outside the house, outside her bedroom window, but her heart pounded uncomfortably as she saw that no light was on inside the house, only the garish flicker of the television brightening the uncurtained windows of the living room one moment, and plunging them back into darkness the next. No lights, the windows uncurtained, and as she hurried closer she saw that the front door was standing ajar.

She pushed in, her shadow cast by the streetlight stretching in front of her, and closed the door behind her. The house was freezing. A huge bouquet of flowers was standing on the table at the foot of the stairs. She was about to call out, then changed her mind and went swiftly and quietly into the living room. Dorothy was standing in the middle of the room, looking confused.

'Melanie?'

'I'm here, Mum. What's the matter?'

Dorothy swayed, and Melanie went forward to steady her. She saw that Dorothy was holding something in her hands, and Dorothy appeared to notice the same thing at the same time. She held out her hands, trembling.

It was a tulip.

'He was here. Your father was here. I saw him.'

Chapter 9

'But the front door was open.'

'Like the window was open this morning. You must've opened it in your sleep.'

'But the tulip!'

They investigated the bouquet of flowers, with inconclusive results. There were no other tulips in the bouquet, but on the other hand, there were single instances of other flowers.

'He was here. I saw him.'

'Oh, Mum.'

'I've never walked in my sleep,' protested Dorothy.

Melanie forbore from pointing out that she had never lost her husband, either. They sat, side by side, on the sofa. Melanie had closed the curtains and switched on the lights. Dorothy had put the tulip—perhaps *replaced* the tulip—in the bouquet in the hall, and on the way back in she had picked up the television remote control and muted what appeared to be a documentary about making a documentary. She had told Melanie about the towel, and Melanie just shrugged. A towel. She told Melanie about the door swinging shut, and Melanie just shrugged again.

'Doors do that. My wardrobe door is always opening.'

'Really?' said Dorothy, greatly interested. 'I never knew that.' She supposed that getting out two mugs from the cupboard, and putting pickle in her sandwich, were just symptoms of grief and years of habit. She sighed eventually.

'I must have imagined it; I suppose I must have been dreaming. It just seemed so real. I wonder why he wasn't wearing socks and shoes?'

Years ago, when she had been a tiny girl of not much more than four or five, Melanie had taken to running into her parents' room because she was terrified, not of ghosts, but of dolls and puppets. Dorothy and George never got to the bottom of exactly what dolls and puppets crawled into their daughter's imagination and sent her screaming along the corridor night after night, although they did establish that the dolls were completely different from the dolls scattered about her bedroom and a diligent search revealed that she didn't own any puppets.

That had all happened in another house, long before they moved to Ayr. Dorothy couldn't remember everything about the house, which had been in Reading, but she remembered with absolute clarity the short stretch of upstairs corridor and the gate George had made to fit across the top of the stairs specifically in case Melanie took a wrong turn as she ran in terror through the darkness, from her bed to theirs.

All this came into her mind because after dinner and after trying to talk to Melanie about nothing in particular for a while, she came to the realisation that she didn't want to go to bed in her own room. She didn't want to sleep alone. She briefly entertained the notion of running along the upstairs corridor of this house, running through the darkness with her nightdress billowing out behind, fumbling open the door to Melanie's bedroom and, once inside, closing the door and leaning breathlessly against it. But that just seemed too melodramatic and rather silly, so instead she just asked Melanie if she could share her bed for that night. Fortunately it was a double bed.

Melanie had reached out to put her hand over Dorothy's, but had hesitated before saying that of course it was all right. She hesitated because she had needed a moment to consider whether she had night clothes which concealed her upper arms.

In bed, they giggled like a pair of silly girls and with the lights out, surrounded by darkness relieved only by orange streetlight glow seeping around the edges of the curtains, they chattered more than they had in weeks. Eventually Dorothy said she would have to get some sleep, as she was going to Glasgow the next day, to meet up with Robert Barker of Barker Associates. That night she slept deeply and, as far as she could tell, without any dreams.

Melanie lay awake for a long time, thinking about her conversation with David Wasson and how she felt a lot better afterwards, but not completely better, and how talking with David Wasson had somehow brought sharply into focus how much she missed her father. When she finally slept, she dreamed of a gigantic blue digger scooping up piles of jumpers and blouses, all of them horrifically bloodstained, and worse still, she was certain, in the way of dreams, that some of the garments still contained severed body parts, but she couldn't tell which of the clothes were empty and which weren't, something which in the dream she desperately wanted to know, and the reason why she couldn't tell was simply because she was too far away, drifting further away, as if she was afloat on something and the current was taking her far out to sea.

———◆———

That same evening, Tully said to Harry McCabe: 'Flowers. You said he had flowers.'

'Yeah. Tulips.'

'I wonder where he got them?'

'From the flower shop.'

'What?'

'I picked him up just outside a flower shop. I expect that's where he got them.'

Tully, exasperated: 'Why didn't you tell me?'

Harry McCabe, calm as you like: 'Because you never asked.'

Tully sighed theatrically, pinched the bridge of his nose, and asked Harry McCabe whether he could possibly, just possibly, find time in his crowded appointments diary to take him to the aforementioned flower shop.

Harry McCabe, immune to theatrics, said he could probably be persuaded to undertake this task at some time before lunch the following day, provided that Tully had managed to get up.

Was there anything else, Tully asked, that Harry McCabe had neglected to tell him?

Harry McCabe thought back to that day, which already seemed months ago. He visualised first seeing the figure of a man hailing the taxi, then seeing the features of George Viviani as he drew closer, then being distracted by a woman walking past, and then finally seeing George Viviani topple into the back of the taxi. He remembered thinking that George must have just tripped and fallen, and how he had come to the slow, icy realisation that George was not, in fact, going to sit up, dust himself down, and tell Harry where he wanted to go. He informed Tully that the only thing he could think of was that when he first saw George Viviani he had been grinning like someone who had lost a pound and found a fiver.

'He looked happy?'

'Yeah. That important?'

'Don't know. Tomorrow at ten? Ten thirty?'

'Okay,' grunted Harry McCabe.

Earlier, while David Wasson and Melanie Viviani strolled along the promenade, Claire and Caroline entertained a man called Pete Mayer, although he told the girls that his name was Stuart. Even earlier, the young man across the road had seen Claire arrive and ring the buzzer to number eleven. He expected to see Caroline, who he knew as Jade, emerge from the block of flats some time after Claire had gone in, as the two of them swapped places; and he expected that either Claire on the way in or Jade on the way out would pause long enough to fiddle open the plastic covering the cards by the buzzers, and turn over the one pertaining to number eleven so that it said *Claire* rather than *Jade*. Claire had pushed open the plywood door and gone in all right, but then rather unexpectedly both girls had come back out again, and had walked together up Laburnum Crescent towards Bedford Road, chattering and laughing, their body language vibrant.

The young man had watched until they were out of sight, and then gone into the back room where he had almost finished his painting of Claire. He was adjusting the texture on the bark of the trees, something which he always found difficult, harder even than the texture of human skin, which was hard enough with its subtle mixtures of colour.

He lost track of time.

Eventually he felt hungry enough to go and open up a tin of beans, which he scooped directly from the tin. He sat down by the window while he was eating them, watching desultory traffic, a cat which sprinted across the road so quickly that it was no more than a brown-and-white blur streaked like a brush stroke temporarily across the tarmac, and a few pedestrians, two of them carrying plastic bags from the local supermarket, and one walking an aged dog which had to sit down every ten yards or so, where it would sit panting heavily, giving the impression that it would much rather be at home curled up in front of a fire.

The young man was just polishing off a cup of tea and a bar of chocolate when he saw Claire and Jade returning from wherever they had been, still chattering, although Claire in particular didn't look quite so vibrant, and the young man thought that in fact she seemed distinctly nervous. Rather to his surprise, both of them went back into the block of flats and stayed there. Neither one came out. The young man watched and waited for a while, but when nothing much happened he finally gave up, raising his eyebrows and shaking his head in a manner which indicated he didn't quite know what was happening, but probably it didn't matter much, and then he went into his bedroom to get ready for one of the classes he attended at Bedford College.

Pete Mayer, *aka* Stuart, was in his mid-thirties, vigorous and enthusiastic. As soon as he came through the door he stopped, looked around, shivered and said, 'Jesus, it's like a fridge in here, you-all had the windows open? Gonna take me an hour or so to warm up, but I 'spect you-all will help me out there, won't you girls? Hiya Jade, I guess this must be Claire, pleased to meet you-all. I guess this is what you're waiting for, huh?' He reached into his breast pocket, produced an envelope, and passed it to Jade. She put it to one side, on the dressing table next to the big new television, without opening it. This was a regular client.

It was hard to tell whether his American accent was genuine. He was dark-haired, stocky and strong, and he kept talking whenever he was in a position to do so.

'Nice to see you-all again, Jade, you're looking good, looks like you got a bit of a tan from somewhere, sure as hell weren't from here, was it? heh,' and Claire smiled inwardly, knowing that Caroline frequented a sunbed parlour not all that far away, despite all the government exhortations that it wasn't safe.

Pete Mayer went on to tell a joke about the weather, and Claire giggled, causing Pete to moan appreciatively. He told her that he was young and single but admitted that he wasn't entirely footloose as he had a girlfriend who he might marry 'in a year or two, but hell, I ain't tied no knot yet, and I sure as hell ain't over the hill yet', whereupon he went on to tell another convoluted joke, broken into several segments by the various actions they were undertaking, about an old man whose memory was going but who still felt the urge to jump into bed with women, and during part of this story Caroline caught Claire's eye and made an expression which informed Claire that she had heard most if not all of these jokes before.

Claire giggled some more, to the accompaniment of more appreciative moans, and in this way, with orchestrated movements, jokes and monologues from Pete Mayer and the odd admiring remark from Claire or Caroline, time passed without any great difficulties for any of the three parties involved. It is possible that the flat did, in fact, warm up, although none of Claire, Caroline or Pete Mayer would have been able to say for certain because they had all warmed up anyway as a result of their tripartite activities.

Afterwards, as he was dressing, Pete admired the big television and without pause for breath went on to discuss several programmes he was currently following, mainly serialised dramas but also a documentary series about economics because, he said, he had never been able to follow economics, and he still couldn't understand it worth a damn but, he confided, he fancied the presenter like mad, a pig-tailed woman who looked like she was just out of school, and Pete was about to give a lurid description of this sexually alluring economics presenter when he stopped short.

'What the fuck?' he said.

He was mostly dressed, but his socks and shoes eluded him; he searched around and finally discovered them by the wall half way to the door of the flat, where he hopped awkwardly in place, pulling them on under Caroline's amused gaze.

Claire knew nothing of the incident, as she was in the shower: when she came out, coyly pulling on her towelling robe, Pete Mayer was already dressed and ready to leave. He gave each of them a chaste kiss on the cheek, and was gone, his footsteps clattering down the stairs, it seemed, almost before the door had latched shut behind him.

Claire and Caroline exchanged a look and burst out laughing.

'H-how long you known him?' managed Claire eventually.

'About a year. He's all right.'

Caroline opened up the envelope and shared its contents.

'Whoo-hoo, this is all right too.'

'Half the work, twice the money.'

'Wonder what his girlfriend's like?'

'Must have the patience of a saint.'

'Or be stone deaf.'

'His real name's not Stuart, it's Pete.'

'Oh? How d'you know?'

'His mobile went off once, and he answered it...' Caroline assumed both stance and accent '... Pete, uh, I mean, yeah, hello?'

Peals of laughter; Claire, wiping her eyes, remarked that clients were always so keen to hide their identities that it never occurred to them that the girls might want to do the same. Caroline looked out of the window and noted that the rain had held off but that it was getting dark already. She suggested having a meal in an Indian restaurant about ten minutes' walk away.

Much later, Claire walked, slightly unsteadily, back up Laburnum Crescent. She was on her own. After the meal, at which they had had several glasses of wine, they had gone on to a local pub where they had sat squashed in a corner, watching a large, boisterous and generally good-humoured crowd as it milled restlessly, eddying frequently to the bar and back again, shouting, laughing, the occasional vehement argument drowned out by protesting voices; most faces in the crowd glowing with perspiration, shining, turned up towards a local derby being shown on a television screen easily three times the size of the one in the Laburnum Crescent flat.

Caroline had jumped into a taxi straight afterwards. She would be back in three days, possibly. Or next Tuesday, she said.

Claire's thoughts were as unsteady as her legs. She couldn't remember who was booked in on the next day, Thursday, but she was sure there was somebody. She wondered whether the flat really was cold. Caroline had said nothing had happened to her over the last couple of nights but then, Caroline had never known George.

It was freezing cold outside, that was for sure.

Claire wrapped her arms around herself, shivering inside her inadequate coat, as she went unsteadily up Laburnum Crescent, tottering slightly from side to side. She shouldn't have had the wine, never mind the shandies afterwards. She wasn't much of a drinker. Her dad would be proud of her. She giggled. She glanced at the houses opposite the block of flats, but the window where the young man lived was dark. What was the number he had told her? As she fumbled the key into the lock she cast her mind back, saw him pause at the door to regard her with his calm eyes. Seven B, that was it. Seven B.

She didn't really want to go upstairs, she realised, as she hauled herself up the stairs. She didn't really want to return to the flat. She realised that she had been hoping to see the young man watching her from across the street, so she could have veered off, still tottering, and pretended to visit him when all the time what she was really doing was putting off the moment when she went back to the flat on her own. This moment. This flat. She stood in the doorway and looked in, like an animal suspecting a trap.

They had forgotten to make the bed. The curtains were still open, as it had not been all that dark when they had left. The discarded, crumpled envelope shone whitely by the side of the television. The flat looked just as it always did, and Claire stumbled forwards. She shut the door, closed the curtains, turned the television on and found a programme which played cheerful music; tried to dance to it as she undressed but got hopelessly tangled and fell, laughing hysterically, to the floor. There she writhed out of her underwear, wondering what Stuart *aka* Pete would say if he could see her now, and thinking that he would surely find something to say, a thought which only made her laugh even more hysterically. Then she wriggled into her nightdress and fell into bed and, because she was half drunk and very tired

162

after a day initially full of tension and nerves and then full of physical activity, she was asleep at once.

She was on a bus. She seemed to remember dreaming about being on a bus before. No, it wasn't a bus, it was a plane. She was jetting off somewhere with Caroline to get a tan. Only something was wrong with the plane. It was buffeting from side to side, and the lights were flickering, and something was banging and crashing. A window exploded outwards and she was instantly sucked to a place where a wind was blowing, garish light danced on walls and distorted a ceiling, and the banging continued, underscored by a terrible low-pitched roar. The door was shaking, flexing as if in the grip of frenzied power.

She sat up, stone cold sober and looked around bemusedly. One of the windows must have come open and now a chill wind made the curtains flap and tugged at her sheets. The television, which she must have forgotten to turn off, was channel-hopping at a terrific rate. The door was shuddering; she was sure it was shaking and bending; it wasn't just an effect of the jumpy television light. Someone, something was pounding on the door. Someone, something, *was trying to get in.*

The last vestiges of sleep left her and in growing panic she reached out for her light, although she hadn't thought through how that might help, given that she could already see in the frantic, dancing brightness cast by the television. Her flailing hand knocked the light and her panic escalated as she imagined it falling to the floor, its tiny crash unheard in the cacophony barrelling around the room, but she caught it, steadied it. Breath sobbing in her throat, she turned it on.

The roaring stopped; it must have been the television— now she could hear an individual voice almost submerged in a hissing crackle, or voices—was that from another room?—a throaty chuckle.

She screamed.

The pounding noise changed; it was just somebody banging on the door. Voices. Lucy, Lucy shouting and so was someone else. It was still cold and the curtains still moved. She ran quickly, barefoot on the icy tiles; opened the door.

'Are you all right?'

'Was it you?'

'What?'

Bailin, the tiny Chinese girl, hovered anxiously behind Lucy. A man peered out of Lucy's door but ducked back inside when Claire caught sight of him.

'The banging. Banging.'

'You were shouting, it sounded like... Jesus, the television's on.'

Bailin, having ascertained that Claire was alive and well, disappeared into her own flat.

'You heard the television?'

'I don't know, Claire.'

'What about the wind?' said Claire desperately. 'You feel the wind?' But it had dropped, perhaps sucked out of existence by the opening of the door. The curtains rippled in heat generated by the television, which had settled on a repeat showing of a football match. Claire looked at the screen without seeing what it was showing.

'Well, you're all right.'

'I'm not staying here.'

'Well, you can't come in with me, not tonight.'

'I saw.'

Claire started pulling on clothes, not bothering to remove her nightdress first.

'Where are you...?' Realisation dawned. 'Jesus, Claire, you're going over the road, you can't do that, you hardly know the guy.'

Claire hunted around in her handbag, found the newspaper clipping that Caroline had given her and thrust it at Lucy. 'Read that. Tell me you didn't hear footsteps. Tell me you didn't hear the banging on the door. Listen, it was like there was a window open in here, only there wasn't, and the television was going mad.'

'Mad?'

Claire gestured. 'Flickering, jumping. I'm not staying here, Lucy, I can't.'

'I remember this guy.'

Claire shrugged into her coat, picked up her bag. 'Number seven B,' she told Lucy.

'You don't believe this, do you?' said Lucy, handing back the cutting. 'Hey, I thought you said the window wasn't open?'

Claire paused. Her mouth tasted sour and her stomach ached. Had she opened the window and forgotten about it? She didn't think so, but anyway she didn't care one way or the other. She hadn't said anything about the chuckle she thought she had heard; she never did tell anyone about it—she wasn't sure now whether she had really heard it, and if she had, whether it had just been a noise from the television, or whether it had been in her mind. 'I don't know,' she said. It wasn't clear whether she meant the window or whether she believed something strange was happening. 'I don't know.'

She and Lucy stared at each other.

'A fucking ghost?' said Lucy, her voice a curious mixture of scorn, amusement, surprise and, thought Claire, unease.

'I don't know,' insisted Claire. 'You heard the banging, didn't you? Didn't you?'

Lucy wouldn't meet her gaze. 'There was some noise,' she admitted.

'And you told me about hearing footsteps, didn't you?'

'Oh,' said Lucy dismissively. 'Footsteps.'

'It doesn't matter, I'm not staying here tonight,' said Claire. She went out into the hall, Lucy following slowly; locked the door. 'Seven B,' she reminded Lucy; turned, passed beneath a single, exhausted light bulb giving out a feeble pool of aged, yellow light, and plunged into the darkness of the stairwell.

There was no movement outside. It was so still that Claire fancied she could see the orange glow from streetlights painting the air, which was itself motionless, frozen in place. No cars. No people. No moon; the sky was blacked out. No stars; it was hard to tell if they were obscured by cloud or whether they just hadn't bothered to come out. No wind. No wind to stir curtains through half-opened windows, Claire thought.

She fled across the silent street, her breath coming in hurried gasps, the sound of her footsteps swallowed by the night. She wondered if she had been awake, and now she was asleep and dreaming. It occurred to her that she had no idea of the time. She must have collapsed into bed at ten, maybe half past ten, but she had no idea how long she had lain asleep. Thank God, the numbers on the houses opposite were easy to follow, because everything looked different in darkness and she couldn't be quite sure of the young man's window. She hastened past a ragged hedge. Behind her, the street was unchanged, silent, still, unmarked by her passing.

The buzzer for 7B was clearly marked and she pressed it, tilted her head as she tried to hear the sound of a bell or buzzer; failed, so pressed again, and again. The door was solid, apart from a letter flap which for some reason was about six inches off the ground, so she couldn't peer through it to see what was happening on the other side, but eventually she noticed light escaping from around its edges and she tried not to think how that reminded her of the same thing happening back at the flat, as she lay in her bed. That was how it had all started, with the strips of light, two vertical, two horizontal, slowly changing from white to angry red, but she tried to ignore the memory, standing there at the door to the house on the other side of the road, cold seeping through her motley selection of clothes.

A rattle; a key turning. The door opened and the young man stood there, wearing a dark red dressing gown and his hair tousled. He didn't look surprised to see her. He didn't make any meaningless exclamations, or ask pointless questions. He didn't say anything at all; merely stood back, opening the door wider.

Claire went in. There was no hall, just a small space at the bottom of a flight of carpeted stairs. For a disorienting moment she thought she was five years old again, visiting her grandmother, because her grandmother's flat had been laid out in the same way—small space, stairs, and the colour scheme of the walls and carpet was nearly the same. She almost expected her grandmother to appear at the top of the stairs, lean smiling around the banister and say in her thin, old voice: *Come on, Sam, up you come.* Wouldn't that be great, she thought, two ghosts in one night. The young man followed her up and when they reached the first floor he touched her shoulder, guiding her into a room which contained a curious mixture of furniture. He said she felt cold, and suggested a hot chocolate.

She turned towards him, nodded. 'That would be nice.'

A single bed stood against the far wall, its sheets rumpled and turned back, and a bedside light on a small cabinet was shining brightly. In the middle of the room was a black leather sofa, but there was no corresponding armchair. A large flat-screen television was attached to a wall, but it didn't face either sofa or bed. Underneath it was a cheap-looking bookcase stacked with DVDs and large hardback books. A straight-backed wooden chair and a green-topped card table stood by the curtained windows. Something odd. Claire had a sudden urge to know what the time was, but when she looked again around the room, she saw that there was no clock. She noticed a watch on the bedside table; she walked over and discovered that it was 1:47a.m.

At the window she peered out between the curtains and was unsurprised to find that it looked out over Laburnum Crescent and across to the block of flats. She imagined the young man sitting here, in the straight-backed chair, making notes of the comings and goings at Block 1 on the other side of the road. She imagined seeing herself arriving from further up Laburnum Crescent, putting a key to the plywood door and going inside. She imagined Caroline arriving. She imagined Pete bouncing up the street and pushing enthusiastically at the buzzer to number ten, talking and laughing to himself all the while. Inexorably, or so it seemed, she imagined George arriving, shoes clicking and clacking on the pavement, saw him bend forwards to talk into the intercom and, before he went into the dark entrance, she imagined him glancing up, across the street, to where she stood looking through the parted curtains.

She fell back.

She noticed that the room was very clean, very tidy, not as if the young man had cleaned and tidied in a frenzy of activity but more as if it had never been allowed to become dirty or untidy in the first place. There were no letters, no newspapers, no discarded wrappers, opened books, used crockery; in fact, Claire noticed, there wasn't even a waste paper basket. For the first time she saw a door at the foot of the bed and supposed it must be a wardrobe.

She sat down on the sofa, pressed her hands together and pushed them between her knees. She felt as if she was in a waiting room, waiting for bad news that she already knew, or waiting for an interview where she wouldn't know any answers to any questions. Nothing felt real. She supposed this was a consequence of being awake in the middle of the night in unfamiliar surroundings, and also because of the bizarre nature of the events which led to her awakening, not to mention those that followed. Still, she could not help thinking that if only she could open her eyes, force herself awake, then she would find herself tucked cosily in bed back at the flat or, better still, back at home.

The young man padded back into the room and proffered her a mug of hot chocolate. She took it and held its warmth between her palms.

'Sorry about this,' she said. He didn't respond, but cast around for somewhere to put down his own mug. Finally he balanced it on top of the bookcase and went out of the room, returning a moment later with a small table which he placed carefully in front of Claire. He lifted the straight-backed chair from beside the sofa and put that down on the other side of the table. As he retrieved his mug of hot chocolate and sat down in the chair, Claire thought that even here, in his own flat and in the middle of the night, the young man was too nervous or awkward to sit down on the same sofa that she was sitting on. But that didn't matter. It didn't matter. He put his mug on the small table, and then, rather unnervingly, pressed his right ear flat and leaned his head against his left shoulder and for a few moments looked up at her from this awkward position. Claire understood him easily enough. He had told his story: now it was time for hers.

He sat up again and regarded her with his calm gaze, expectantly.

Chapter 10

Next morning they slept late. Claire had slept in the single bed, feeling a curious sense of intimacy as she slid between sheets still warm from his body heat. He had collected a sleeping bag and blanket from somewhere and stretched out on the sofa. At half past nine the doorbell rang and he scrambled out of the sleeping bag, pulled on his dressing gown and disappeared out of the door, returning a few minutes later looking slightly amused, with Lucy in tow.

'Oh, Lucy!' Claire sat up in bed, yawned and rubbed at her eyes. She felt an unexpected surge of gratitude, that Lucy would take the trouble to make sure she hadn't come to any harm. The young man pulled the curtains, and light flooded the room. Lucy was looking around; she gave an arch smile, almost a wink at Claire, meaning that she thought Claire had done all right, that she had landed on her feet. Claire blinked and wondered if that could be true. Her night fears were almost banished by the sunlight—almost, but not quite. She could not quite convince herself that everything had been her imagination. Lucy, as if she could read Claire's thoughts, drily remarked that it had been a lot quieter in the flats after she had left, and the young man asked both girls if they wanted a cup of tea.

———◆———

Dorothy was on the train to Glasgow, feeling absurdly nervous, like a young girl on her way to her first date or first interview. She looked out of the window as the sea and sparsely populated golf courses slid by. Her first date had been with a boy called Terry Wilson, known to most of his friends as Tez, who had inadvertently knocked her over with his bicycle when she had stepped out from an alleyway partly blocked by a telephone kiosk. They went to the cinema a few times, Dorothy remembered, but then either he had moved away or she had; it was hard to remember now. He hadn't kissed her. The first person to kiss her had been another boy, Johnny Travers, who had done it to win a bet from his friends.

She looked at the reflection of her face in the window as the train clattered through a tiny station without stopping.

She couldn't remember her first interview any more, though she recalled applying unsuccessfully for some secretarial jobs before ending up with the local authority. Now she was on her way to meet with Mr Robert Barker of Barker Associates, about the publication of stories written by her dead husband, and it occurred to her that at no time in the past while she was going out on first dates and looking for a job could she possibly have imagined that her life would take such a bizarre turn.

She carried a copy of the stories in a briefcase—it was actually Melanie's case, because Dorothy couldn't bear the thought of using George's—along with a map annotated with notes of how to get from Central Station to Stableside, which Melanie calculated to be less than fifteen minutes' walk and hardly worth a taxi fare unless it was raining.

The train started to ease away from the coast, heading further inland. Dorothy leaned back and closed her eyes. The train was on time. She had plenty of time to walk to the offices of Barker Associates. She wasn't a writer, she couldn't be expected to do anything with the stories themselves, and anyway Robert Barker had been the one to contact her, not the other way around. There was no reason for her to feel nervous. Excited, perhaps, but not nervous.

On the inside of her eyelids she saw George standing in the hallway, smiling crookedly, holding something in his hands which she now knew must have been a tulip. She had told Melanie that she must have been dreaming, that the other things that had happened were just tiny coincidences blown up out of all proportion by her stressed state, and when she had said as much to Melanie, she had believed all of it. But doubt had crept back and grown with the passage of time. There was something not quite right with the house ever since... ever since... with a shock, she realised that nothing had been right ever since the visit of the taxi driver and that tall man dressed in black, whatever his name was, she couldn't remember it now, but she did remember what he said: *Now that we have been here, you may need to contact me*; and she suddenly remembered what it had said on his card: *Ghosthunter*.

Something wasn't right, and here she was on a train to Glasgow leaving Melanie behind, alone in the house. Her eyes snapped open and she fumbled in her handbag. The man sitting opposite watched her out of the corner of his eye, pretending that he wasn't. Dorothy wondered what he thought of her, smart briefcase in one hand, handbag in the other, pressing buttons on a mobile in something of a panic; perhaps the man was wondering whether she had suddenly remembered that she had left the gas on, or suddenly remembered something about an important business meeting. There was not the slightest chance, Dorothy thought, that he would guess what she had actually suddenly remembered.

Melanie didn't answer the phone. She had said that she might go out for a while, stroll up the High Street, have lunch somewhere. Dorothy dropped the mobile back into her bag and looked up as the train started to slow. A female voice announced that they were approaching Paisley Gilmour Street and that anybody disembarking should please mind the gap. Glasgow Central, informed the woman, was the next stop, where the train would terminate. Terminate. Dorothy always thought that an odd choice of word and now, less than an hour away from her meeting with Robert Barker which had thrown her into such a schoolgirl panic, it resonated and twined with something in her own mind and she almost cried out at the terrible idea that George had taken this same trip before, to meet up with the same Mr Barker, and the even more terrible idea that if all the tiny coincidences weren't tiny coincidences, then perhaps he was somewhere with her, on the train.

Melanie was luxuriating in blue bubble bath and trying to decide if she should quit her part-time job when the telephone rang. She struggled upright, hopped out of the bath, grabbed a towel, and ran along the hall, leaving a trail of wet footprints. The phone stopped ringing just before she picked it up. She had known that it would. The damn thing rang precisely seven times—she had counted it often enough over the years—and no matter how quickly she reacted and how quickly she scrambled out of the bath and ran along the hall, she could never quite get there in time. Nine rings, easy. Eight rings, probably most of the time. Seven rings— no chance, except once when she had just been putting her foot into the bathwater so it didn't really count, because she hadn't really been *in* the bath.

One four seven one told her that a mobile number had tried to reach her. She couldn't think whose it was, so she wandered into her bedroom to check her list, and discovered it was her mother's. She dialled back, but Dorothy's mobile had been turned off. It was odd, she thought, that she recognised any number of mobile phone numbers that belonged to friends, but she didn't recognise her mother's. Then she thought that perhaps it wasn't so odd. After all, how often had Dorothy tried to contact her from a mobile? Melanie racked her brains. She couldn't remember it ever happening before. She glanced at her bedside clock before heading back to the bathroom. Nine forty-five. Dorothy must be nearly in Glasgow by now.

In the bathroom she was surprised to find a towel draped over the edge of the bath, one corner drooping into the water itself. It was a green towel. Melanie tried to recall whether it had been on the towel rail when she had grabbed at the one currently wrapped around her body. Perhaps it had been. It must have been. But could she have dislodged it with sufficient violence that it had ended up here, partly in the bath, on the other side of the bathroom from the towel rail? It didn't seem very likely, but perhaps she had. She must have done. She was uncomfortably aware of her mother's story, of how she had found a towel where, apparently, her father had been prone to leave one lying around.

No, it meant nothing. Melanie picked up the green towel, wrung out its sodden corner, placed it on the towel rail, unwrapped herself from her own pink towel and placed that on the rail as well, and with a slight frown at both towels which sat there innocently enough, looking like two towels on a towel rail, no more and no less, she slipped back into the bath.

She imagined her mother getting off the train at Glasgow Central, probably looking a little lost and out of place because she hadn't made the trip to Glasgow for ages, not by train anyway, and wondered why she had tried to call. She couldn't really have left anything important behind; she had a copy of the stories (although Melanie secretly thought she didn't need them for this meeting), and a map showing the way to Stableside (although she didn't really need that either, because she could always jump into a taxi and ask to be taken there), and she knew the address she was going to, because she had input that into her mobile that very morning over breakfast, and she obviously had her mobile with her because she had just tried to call. Well, no matter. If it was important she would try again, and if it wasn't she could explain all about it when she got back.

The stories.

Melanie allowed herself to slip further into the hot water, wincing slightly as it covered her more recent scars. Daddy's stories. She remembered them all, remembered him reading to her at Halloween or Christmas in front of the log fire, spooky stories which often kept her awake far into the night, thinking, as she turned this way and that and tried to close her eyes, that she would never again listen to him reading about ghosts, or inexplicable events, or about strange twists in time, but was then unable to resist listening again a year later, or a few months later, at Halloween or Christmas. She loved the stories. They were part of her childhood. How happy her father would have been to know that they were to be published, but now...

It suddenly occurred to her that he had known, hadn't he? He had been to see Robert Barker on the day he had died, Dorothy had said that Robert Barker told her so, in fact Robert Barker had said he might have been one of the last people to see her father alive. Melanie couldn't work out if this was a strange thing to say. She supposed it depended on how it was said, in what tone of voice, and whether it was meant as a sort of condolence. Anyway, her father had known about the possible publishing deal; he had been to Stableside and he must have been so happy.

Melanie frowned again as something tried to make itself known to her, some odd fact or anomaly, but whatever it was slipped away from her consciousness at just about the time a shadow moved across the water and across the wall next to the bath. Abruptly she felt cold, and she turned, thinking that someone had come into the bathroom even though she knew there was nobody else in the house, and curiously it didn't occur to her until after she had turned and discovered that nobody was coming in that the pounding of her heart and sudden chill signified that she had been frightened that her father had been coming in, not that this was his bathroom, but he had used it sometimes when he wanted a bath rather than a shower.

What she saw was the door slowly swinging shut (she must have left it open, she supposed, when she came back from failing to answer the phone to discover the green towel on the edge of the bath); she remembered saying *doors do that* to her mother, somewhat dismissively, but here was this bathroom door swinging shut, not as if it had been blown by a sudden gust of wind but slowly, remorselessly, and in fact as she watched, it closed completely with a small snick which meant it had closed with enough force to engage the latching mechanism, a small silver ball-shaped thing which her father had filched from an old cabinet when the original door handle broke.

Dorothy consulted her map and turned between two big buildings which might both have been banks. She had plenty of time. It wasn't raining. She decided to find out precisely where the offices of Barker Associates were and then retrace her steps for five minutes or so, back to where she had passed a coffee shop. She crossed one road, turned into the next, so narrow it was more of a lane than a street, and finally found Stableside, so small that it was more of a passageway than a lane, fenced off from traffic by three black posts, its entrance marked by an archway spanning the gap between a pub on one side, and a small hotel on the other.

Dorothy found number eight in a matter of seconds, and discovered that Barker Associates shared an old building that had been converted into offices with two other companies, Arand Developments Ltd and Graham, Graham & Hay & Sons, neither of which gave any clue to the exact nature of their business on the signs fixed to the front of the building. Neither did Barker Associates, if it came to that.

Dorothy looked around and decided that Stableside seemed to have been caught in a time warp. It looked as though it had scarcely changed since the nineteenth century, and she half expected to see men wearing top hats and old-fashioned suits and waistcoats, sporting beards or mutton chop whiskers, or both, come out of the various small office buildings scattered along the street. She checked her watch again. Yes, she did have time for a cup of coffee. She headed back out under the archway, feeling that she crossed a time barrier and jumped forwards a hundred years or so, to where cars inched past, their drivers looking in vain for somewhere to park. She wondered if George had felt the same thing when he had paid his visit to Barker Associates, and then had to stop and wipe at her eyes at an unexpected wash of sadness, as she realised that she would never know.

There was nothing in the hallway. Melanie stood, trembling slightly, with the same pink towel wrapped around her again and this time, because it was already wet, it felt cold and clammy instead of warm and fluffy. The door had opened easily enough and showed no sign of trying to close again. Melanie had a momentary vision of doors all over the house slowly opening or slowly closing, depending on whether they had been closed or open to start with.

'Daddy!' she shrieked, hoping there would be no reply and feeling disappointed when there wasn't. Tears were streaming down her face, dripping downwards, adding to the wetness of the towel. She sniffed and shuffled into her bedroom, where she sat down at her dressing table and regarded herself in the mirror. She saw red eyes, nicely set off by the dark lines beneath them, her nose shiny and most of her wet hair, looking several shades darker than usual, lying flat and unprepossessing against her skull.

Movement, something glimpsed in the mirror, behind her. She whirled, thinking that this time, this time, he would be sitting on the end of her bed, smiling, ready to hear what she had to say and put everything in her world to rights, shoes and socks or no shoes and socks. A curtain flapped again, wearily; her heart jumped and then she remembered opening the window earlier, to air the room. She turned back again and this time saw the bottom two inches of the curtain intrude into the reflection before falling back out of sight.

She leaned forward, covering her face with her hands.

'You gonna be all right?'

'Yes,' said Claire. 'No. I don't know,' she said irritably. She had just spent half an hour telling Lucy everything she had already told the young man several hours ago and Caroline on the previous day. She couldn't make up her mind whether recounting for the third time the events which led up to her running, terrified, from her room in the middle of a cold night made those events seem more real or less.

The young man asked if anyone wanted more toast. It was hard to tell if he was being humorous. The original cup of tea had become cup of tea with some cereal, which had led on, naturally enough, to toast and coffee, and now the small table was overflowing with cups, pots, bowls and a giant egg-timer-shaped coffee maker of some sort which the girls had never seen the like of before, but which appeared to produce endless cups of coffee. Claire recalled how spotlessly clean and almost obsessively tidy the surroundings had been when she had arrived in the middle of the night, and felt a stab of guilt. She jumped up and started to stack crockery. Lucy caught the mood and helped. The kitchen was two doors away along a short hallway and on the way back for a second load, while the young man filled a dishwasher, Claire saw Lucy peer out from one of the doorways and beckon vigorously. She was grinning.

The room had been set out as an art studio. Almost exactly in the middle, its back to the door but facing the windows on the other side of the room, was a large painting on an easel which Lucy, hand on hips, was regarding critically. Claire moved round to join her. Many other paintings, drawings and sketches were stacked round the room; landscapes, seascapes; a few portraits; flowers in pots; two nudes, one male and one female, both rendered in what looked like charcoal. The big painting on the easel was of Claire peeping out from behind a tree which almost bisected the painting; her red hair was the highlight on the left hand side, offset by a red shoe on the end of her leg, stretched out to maintain her balance, on the right-hand side.

'It's you,' said Lucy unnecessarily. The young man appeared in the doorway and Lucy had the grace to look slightly abashed. 'It's good,' she said. She looked around the room. 'Uh, they're all good.'

As Claire looked at the painting, and in particular as she looked at the trees, each of them tall and thin, and all of them placed far apart so that the natural space resembled the inside of a cathedral, particularly as the entire scene was only dimly lit by sunlight filtering through a high, invisible canopy, she suddenly remembered the memory which had unexpectedly surfaced during her appointment with Brian (except she had decided that it wasn't really a memory) of being in a place just like this. Perhaps what had come into her mind that day had not come from the past at all. Perhaps she had somehow seen into the future, to this instant in time.

This notion was so strange but so powerfully persuasive that she had to close her eyes for a moment. When she opened them again it was to see the young man regarding her with a sardonic look; she understood immediately that his expression wasn't referring to the big painting, but to Lucy's remark that all the paintings and sketches scattered around the room were good. His look clearly told her that he knew perfectly well they weren't all good, that he had no doubt that Lucy knew that they weren't all good, and that he was sure that she, Claire, was also under no illusion that all the pictures were good, but that she at least would not feel obliged to say that they were.

She caught sight of a framed pen-and-ink drawing on the wall not far from the doorway. A tag attached to the bottom of the frame announced that it was called 'The Observer'; a scrawled set of initials on the bottom right of the drawing looked something like SMC or possibly SNE. The drawing itself was an astonishingly accurate depiction of the young man currently standing in the doorway. In the picture he was sitting at a window, chin resting on a cupped hand. His profile was slightly turned away from the viewer, but his calm gaze looked back out of the picture as it was reflected in the glass of the window.

He told Claire that one of his friends had drawn it.

'It's amazing,' said Claire.

Diffidently, he indicated the easel in the middle of the room and asked Claire what she thought of the painting. Claire met his eyes and told him honestly that she did like it. He got the idea, he explained, when he saw her in the doorway.

'Look,' said Lucy. 'Thanks for the breakfast, but I've got to get back.'

'So have I,' said Claire, suddenly remembering that she had an appointment sometime that day. She hoped it was for some time in the afternoon, as the morning was already half gone.

The young man said he would come with them.

'Why?' asked Claire bluntly.

He spread his hands and explained that he had to go to the shops to stock up on bread and milk, as he always did on a Thursday. Lucy and Claire exchanged a look, and Lucy shrugged.

'Okay, whatever,' said Claire.

Less than half an hour later, having parted company with Lucy and Claire, the young man turned the corner from Laburnum Crescent into Bedford Road. As he did so, a cream taxi pulled up outside the flower shop; in fact, it stopped twice because having pulled up initially it started up its engine and jerked forward a matter of three or four feet, then stopped again. He watched incuriously as a tall man dressed in black emerged from the passenger seat at the back, and the driver—a bulky, bald, older man—climbed out of the driver's seat to join him. They appeared to be arguing, but the young man was too far away to be able to make out what they were saying, and in any case he wasn't particularly interested in discovering what their argument was about, and he forgot all about them a few seconds later as he pushed through the door to the tiny grocery store.

Round the corner in Laburnum Crescent, Lucy and Claire had negotiated the plywood door to Block 1 and climbed the stairs. Having unlocked and opened the door to her flat, Claire hesitated before going in.

'You gonna be all right?' asked Lucy again.

Up until this juncture, Claire had thought she was going to be all right. It was daylight and even if she had not explicitly thought about it, she had an inbuilt belief that fears of the night would be banished by sunlight. But as she stepped carefully through the doorway, her shoes clicking on the uncarpeted floor, she felt disoriented. It didn't make sense; she was coming back to the familiar from the unfamiliar, but there it was—the confines and configuration of the flat seemed strange, almost dizzying, especially when she saw the television just exactly where she knew it would be, casting the same shadow that it always did at this time of the morning, and she saw the unmade bed with its covers thrown back just as she had left them when she had run to the door after the noise, and the cold, and the pounding... everything familiar, expected, and in its place but still the sense of disorientation grew, and the flat was very cold.

She stumbled. Lucy put out a steadying hand, and both of them jumped as Claire's mobile phone shrilled. A car horn blared from somewhere close outside, Goliath answering David. Claire tugged the mobile from her coat pocket, looked at its display. Colour drained from her face and she tottered forward to sit on the edge of the bed.

Lucy looked on helplessly.

Claire lifted the phone to her lips and shrieked: 'Leave me alone! Leave me alone! Why won't you leave me alone?'

———•———

When Annabel Clancy had started up Mae's Flower Shop almost twenty years ago, she used the name Mae rather than Annabel for two reasons: partly because she opened the shop not long after her favourite grandmother, Mae, had died, but mainly because Mae had only three letters in it rather than seven, which meant that it was possible to use bigger letters on the shop sign, making it easier to read from further away.

Whether this shrewd move contributed to the success of the shop was hard to say, but the fact remained that the shop was a success, so much so that Annabel was able to open two other flower shops. One was in Paisley, not much more than twenty miles away, and the other was in Ayr. Mae's Flower Shop was not the only flower shop in Ayr, but even so it was extremely likely that some of the bouquets and wreaths brought along to the funeral of George Viviani had been ordered from there, a coincidence that bordered on the obscene given that George himself had bought a bunch of tulips from Mae's Flower Shop, Bedford Road just minutes before he died.

Annabel Clancy no longer worked personally in any of the shops, although she occasionally called in to each one to chat to the staff who did (and to keep an eye on whether the flower stock looked fresh, and whether any customers who happened to be there at the same time as she was were being properly attended to, and so forth). The manager at the Bedford Road branch was Janine Hamilton, married, with two small boys aged seven and nine, and she was thinking about her two boys—or, more precisely, she was wondering who she could get to child-mind on Saturday, as she and her husband Mark had been invited out to an evening meal—when the door to the shop jangled open to admit two men, one wearing black clothes and an older, stockier man who, as he followed his companion through the doorway, rubbed his hand over his bald head in an exasperated fashion.

'Yeah, but you said you never could tell.'

'Exactly,' said the black-clothed man, a response which left the bald man looking baffled but resigned, rather as if, thought Janine, he was used to being baffled by remarks made by the younger man. She wiped her hands on her apron.

'Can I help you?'

'I hope so,' said the younger man. He took out his wallet from a breast pocket, opened it and plucked out a business card. Janine noticed that the bald man craned his neck, trying to look at the business card as she took it and turned it in her fingers. It was mainly white. The letters on it, designed to look as if they had been typed on an old-style typewriter, read *Colin Taylor: freelance reporter.*

'I work for several different papers, on and off,' said Taylor.

'Oh yes?' said Janine, handing back the card.

'And occasionally magazines,' said Taylor.

'Oh yes?'

'Sometimes I do obituaries,' said Taylor. 'Not often, but as it happens a friend of a friend has asked me to do one for LAA.' Janine looked puzzled, and Taylor explained: 'Local Authority Accounting.' Janine pursed her lips and raised her eyebrows, and clearly had never heard of LAA, which was hardly surprising as Taylor had only just that moment invented it. Immediately afterwards, her expression cleared as she realised where the conversation was leading.

'George Viviani,' she said. Harry McCabe admired the way in which Taylor managed to convey that he thought this an unusually perspicacious remark, even though he only gravely nodded and pursed *his* lips. 'Do you know,' said Janine, 'that for days after the article in the *Post*, people kept coming in here to buy flowers. Well, we only sell flowers. Well, you know what I mean.' Her voice transmitted indignation.

'I'm afraid I'm not surprised, Mrs...?'

'I'm Janine Hamilton.'

'I see it all the time,' said Taylor glumly, as if he saw no real hope for the entire human race. He noticed Janine Hamilton glance curiously at Harry McCabe. 'Oh, this is Harry. He's... uh, a taxi driver...' He waited for the penny to drop, which it did almost instantly.

'*The* taxi driver?'

'It was my cab,' said Harry McCabe, nodding. 'Colin here, he tracked me down too. Not that I could tell him much,' he added, 'because by the time I... er, met Mr Viviani, it was, er, too late for me to meet him, if you see what I mean.' He didn't like to actually say that George Viviani was dead before he got to speak with him, in case Janine Hamilton became upset.

'You mean, he was dead,' said Janine.

So much for the sensitive approach, thought Harry.

'You never even got to speak to him?' inquired Janine.

Harry McCabe shook his head, thinking that Janine, accidentally or deliberately, had turned the tables and was asking more questions than they were. Perhaps Taylor thought the same thing, because he leaned forward and asked: 'Were you here that day, Mrs Hamilton?'

'Oh yes,' said Janine.

'I just wonder, you know, did he say anything? Can you remember?'

'Well, I would've remembered all right,' said Janine, 'because the policeman, he came in and asked the same thing.'

'The policeman?'

'Constable Kirkwood,' said Harry McCabe. 'Like I said before, I called for an ambulance and the police, and the police that came was Constable Kirkwood.' He shrugged. 'I remember names, like place names, and names that sound like places.'

'Oh yes,' said Janine. 'There's a Kirkwood Avenue over by the expressway, isn't there?'

'And Kirksland,' said Harry McCabe. 'Out towards Govan; and Kirkmichael down the west coast...'

'You'll remember my name, then, won't you?' said Janine Hamilton with a smile.

'Janine?' said Harry McCabe, deadpan.

'All right, all right,' Taylor interrupted irritably. 'So Constable Kirkwood came in to ask you if George had said anything?'

'He did,' said Janine Hamilton, 'and he hadn't.'

'Nothing?'

'No,' said Janine. 'Oh well, he asked for a bunch of tulips, and I think he might have said something about the weather.'

'What was the weather like that day?'

'It was sunny, but cold. Oh.' Janine Hamilton fell silent for a moment.

'What?'

'It's probably nothing,' she said slowly. 'I just remembered, he seemed hot. You know, a bit shiny, a bit sweaty. Like he'd been running.'

The two men looked at her, and Harry McCabe, disdaining the gentle approach this time, said: 'Perhaps that was him starting his heart attack.'

'Oh yes.' Janine Hamilton's expression cleared again, as if she was relieved at finding an explanation for this small anomaly. 'Yes, that'll be it.'

'How did he seem?' asked Taylor. 'Happy, sad, anxious, what?'

It struck Harry McCabe that these questions almost certainly went beyond what would normally be asked for the purposes of an obituary, but fortunately this either didn't occur to Janine Hamilton, or if it did occur to her, she decided to ignore it because she enjoyed being the centre of attention.

'Happy,' she said, without pausing for thought. 'He couldn't stop smiling.'

'I saw him smiling,' said Harry McCabe.

'Yes, yes, you said,' said Taylor. 'I wonder why he was so happy? Any idea?'

Janine shook her head.

'He really didn't say anything?'

She shook her head again.

'Had you seen him before? Had he bought flowers here before?'

The door jangled again, and two elderly women came in. Janine Hamilton looked across at them, sized them up as genuine customers and not people who wanted to engage her in conversation without actually buying anything, and instantly started to fidget.

'Last question,' said Taylor reassuringly.

'I want to buy some flowers,' said Harry McCabe.

'What?'

'Flowers,' said Harry. 'Bunch of. A.' He waved his hands vaguely. 'Shop.'

'Yes, but why?' asked Taylor.

'That's my business,' said Harry McCabe, and although he said it aggressively, he also blushed. Taylor was fascinated to see that the top of his head blushed as well as the rest of his face, and could not help wondering if that happened to everybody when they blushed, but it was usually impossible to tell through a head of hair, or whether it was something peculiar to Harry McCabe. While he was thinking this, he was also remembering Harry's insistence that this trip to the flower shop took place before lunchtime, and he was unable to resist drawing certain conclusions.

'Not that I remember,' said Janine Hamilton.

Taylor blinked at her, trying to recall what question she was answering.

'Of course, I'm not here all the time. But I asked Angie, she's here on the days when I'm not, well, we were talking about it the other day, anyway she said she didn't recognise him.'

'Okay, right, thank you,' said Taylor. 'Thank you very much.'

Harry McCabe moved towards a bouquet of roses that he'd noticed almost as soon as they had come into the shop; Taylor wandered out while Janine Hamilton parcelled up the bouquet and accepted payment.

After dropping Tully back at his house, Harry dressed up and went to an internet-arranged date at an Italian restaurant two minutes' walk from Central Station, where he sat for half an hour, and then three-quarters of an hour, waiting for Gabriella, 39, slim red-haired beauty looking for true love, speaks perfect English (not that Harry had been bothered about how well she spoke English), broken heart needs mending, genuine gentlemen only need reply, singles only, age and looks not important—and then after more than an hour he had left the restaurant feeling distinctly strange as he had spent most of his time there sipping strong coffee and feeling nervous, then anxious, then angry, then finally despondent. He dumped the roses in a large black industrial wheelie bin on the way back to his taxi and never told Tully or anybody else anything about it, although Tully must surely have guessed that something untowards had happened, to account for his surly mood for the rest of that afternoon.

Before this failed date, Harry McCabe came out of the flower shop with his newly purchased roses to find Tully standing more or less exactly where George Viviani had stood when he had wrenched open the door of the taxi and plunged inside. Tully was looking round, wondering if the large glass windows in a building not far away might flash and dazzle in the autumn sunlight, not something that would happen today as it was grey and cloudy.

He climbed back into the taxi with Harry and was unable to resist a snigger, which was nothing to do with the roses, but was a reference to their earlier argument, arising when Harry had insisted on not parking exactly where he had parked before, in case the ghost of George Viviani lurched out of time and back into the taxi, and Tully had told him not to be so bloody silly, for various reasons, not least that if the ghost of George Viviani did put in a second appearance (which, Tully remarked, was extremely unlikely), then what was to stop it veering off course a few feet and falling or climbing into the taxi in its new location?

That evening, Dorothy Viviani called.

Chapter 11

Robert Barker turned out to be so completely different from the Robert Barker of her imagination that Dorothy almost said she would rather speak to his father, the man who had made the phone call, rather than this Robert Barker. On the basis of the telephone call, she had imagined him to be elderly, maybe a little frail, but energetic in an enthusiastic, jerky way, perhaps wearing slightly old-fashioned clothes, probably surrounded by books and tomes, ledgers and loose-leaf manuscripts, illuminated by an anglepoise lamp in an otherwise darkened office.

On reflection Dorothy realised this was perhaps an idealised picture based on watching too many films rooted in the Dickensian period—but still: Robert Barker turned out to be a young man, blond, quite beefy, sitting in a wheelchair surrounded by—well, it was true, there were some books and papers strewn across the office, but there was also a desktop computer, a laptop, and several small printers. Robert Barker's voice didn't match his overweight frame; no doubt this was something to do with whatever illness or disability kept him in a wheelchair, but as soon as she heard it, Dorothy recognised it immediately.

'Mrs Viviani.'

'Mr Barker?'

'Please sit down. Allow me to offer my condolences.'

The meeting went well. A young woman wearing a skirt which in Dorothy's opinion was so short that it was hardly worth the bother of putting on brought in coffee and biscuits. In one respect Robert Barker did match her imagination: he did not much go in for small talk, generalities or platitudes. He told her which company was interested in George's collection of stories and outlined the deal. They talked about illustrations, timescales, a dedication (Robert Barker diffidently suggested that the book could be dedicated to George himself; it would be a little unusual, he said, for a book to be dedicated to its author, but scarcely unique. Dorothy said she would think about it), royalties, rights and delicate financial details regarding agents which, Robert Barker pointed out, was the capacity in which Barker Associates had been acting.

There were no difficulties in any part of the discussion, although Dorothy did ask if she could see any proposed changes to the text once an editor had been through it, a request to which Robert Barker readily agreed. After a little more than an hour, the conversation coasted to a natural conclusion. Dorothy thanked Robert Barker, gathered up her papers—the number of which was considerably swollen as a result of the meeting—and said she had better be going. Robert Barker made some remark to the effect that he hoped she wouldn't be offended if he didn't get up to see her off. The tone in which he made the remark made it clear that it was something he said dozens if not hundreds of times each week, that he really meant nothing by it because it was obvious that Dorothy (or anyone else) could not conceivably take offence, but it was a neat contrivance which drew an end to any meeting or conversation.

'Safe journey, Mrs Viviani.'

'Thank you, Mr Barker.'

Afterwards, weeks or even just days later, Dorothy could not remember much about what happened immediately after leaving the premises of Barker Associates, although whether this was because of what happened when she got home and over the next few days, or whether it was a continuation of the memory lapses which had assailed her, with decreasing frequency, since the visit of Constable Sargent and her dreadful news, was hard to say.

She treated herself to lunch somewhere, vaguely recalled thinking about a film which featured a figure in red which was forever disappearing around corners, at the edge of vision, probably prompted by something she saw out of the restaurant or cafe window, though she couldn't remember what that might have been. She thought she must have tried to call Melanie again, but could not bring to mind a picture of her mobile phone in her hand, or of her fingers pressing buttons, or of hearing the telephone at home ringing its routine seven rings before a recorded message kicked in, which is what she must have heard, because Melanie afterwards said she never received a call from her mother that day. Obviously she must have found her way back to Central Station and caught a train, but she remembered none of it. Perhaps she slept.

When she arrived home Melanie flew down the stairs and into her bewildered arms. Dorothy made comforting noises, somehow elbowed the front door shut behind her and managed to deposit handbag and briefcase onto the hallway table without knocking over the vase of flowers or letting go of her daughter. Melanie wailed that she had been wrong and Dorothy had been right. Dorothy started to mix questioning noises with the comforting noises as she disengaged herself from Melanie and guided her towards the kitchen. Melanie rubbed at her eyes and wiped her nose and in a choked voice told Dorothy about the bathroom door closing, and the towel appearing at the edge of the bath, and Dorothy nodded encouragingly as if she was listening to a promising student finally beginning to understand something which she, Dorothy, had known for quite a while. She put on the kettle, got two mugs out of a cupboard, and introduced encouraging noises into the combination of sounds she had been making ever since coming through the front door.

Calming down, Melanie explained that she went out into town for a while after her bath, wandering up and down the High Street and into a couple of shopping malls, and found herself close to the train station, not all that far from where David Wasson lived, although the existence of David Wasson never entered her thoughts. (The reverse was most definitely not the case. David Wasson had been in a black humour ever since her visit and their walk of the previous day. He had sat up most of the night and laboriously crafted:

Time is my own invention.
I made it up when you,
Smiling slightly,
Shook your head and turned away.
All this is in the distant past,
The faintest trace of remote memory:
The sudden pain has gone.
Echoing through all eternity,
I can still hear
Your fading footsteps.

while his thoughts would not let go of his vision of a future in which Melanie Viviani played no part, not even a small part, and the name *Dr Graham Rowbotham* burrowed even deeper into his memory, especially as it occurred to him that, but for the treacherous activities of the mathematics tutor, Melanie Viviani might have proved more receptive of his, David Wasson's advances. He didn't see Melanie walk past his flat that morning, but at one point he did give in to the impulse that he had resisted earlier, and slammed his fist into the plasterboard wall, an action which resulted in blood pouring from two lacerated knuckles, an unsightly bloody dent in the thin plasterboard wall, and no noticeable reduction in the bleakness of his mood.)

Outside, unobserved by David Wasson, Melanie had seen the row of taxis parked outside the railway station, and had suddenly remembered the taxi which had driven to their front door at the height of the storm, a *Glasgow taxi*, she said significantly to her mother, and paused.

What she didn't tell Dorothy was that, when she saw the row of taxis, she also thought of two other things. She thought of what she had said to Dorothy only that morning, that Stableside was only a hop, skip and a jump from Central Station, not worth a taxi fare unless it was raining. But, she thought, her father had loved to walk. He used to put on boots and walk along the beach. He never took the car unless he had to. Melanie was suddenly, overwhelmingly sure that her father would never have bothered to get a taxi to get from Central Station to Stableside. Rain or no rain, he would have walked.

And hard upon that thought came a second, disconcerting thought, which was that her father had not died in the back of a taxi either at Central Station or anywhere near Stableside, but in Bedford Road, which she vaguely remembered was on the north side of the city, some way out from the centre. Certainly not anywhere near Barker Associates. So what, thought Melanie, standing motionless on the pavement much to the annoyance of several passing pedestrians, had her father been doing in Bedford Road?

Dorothy paused in the act of making the tea. 'A Glasgow taxi,' she whispered. 'You don't mean...?' She stared at

Melanie, who raised both shaking hands to her mouth. 'A Glasgow taxi,' repeated Dorothy wonderingly. She made the tea and passed one of the mugs to Melanie. 'Let's go and sit down.'

'Not in the sitting room,' whispered Melanie.

Dorothy looked at her, didn't say anything, didn't ask any questions, but merely made her way to the dining room and sat down at the big oval table. Melanie joined her.

'Hang on,' said Dorothy, disappearing briefly into the kitchen and then reappearing with a packet of biscuits. She opened them and they took one each.

Melanie sighed.

A little while after she had got back home, she had settled down to watch some television in the sitting room. She didn't watch television very often, but sometimes she liked to see some sport, the news, occasionally programmes about dancing or makeovers. She was nervous. She admitted it: the events of the morning had unsettled her (and so had the events immediately after she got back home, although she kept those to herself).

As she sat on the sofa she had the distinct impression that somebody was standing behind her but when she turned, there was nobody and nothing to be seen. At any rate there was nothing inside the room. Outside the room, just on the other side of the windows, which were hard to see through because of their small panes and the fact that net curtains were permanently in place—Melanie said that outside the windows, she thought she saw something going past, blurring past with incredible speed, not a car further away on the road, she said, but something close up by the side of the house, passing by the windows.

She kept watching for a little while, but nothing further happened until she turned back towards the television, which had been bleating away behind her, talking about the best way to make a soufflé which wouldn't fall flat as soon as you looked at it; as she turned away, the blurring happened again, in the same direction, as if whatever it was had circled round the entire house or block of houses and just happened to be speeding past again as she turned away. Startled and fearful, she knelt up on the sofa to look more closely, banging her knee on something and absently noticing that the tenor of the sounds made by the television changed. Still nothing. It was very cold. She got up and went over to the radiator, finding that it was warm if not particularly hot.

As soon as she started to turn again, this time to make the short journey back to the sofa, she caught out of the corner of her eye something going past the window, just the same as before, in the same direction, with the same blurring effect as if reality just outside the windows was becoming unsteady and refused to transmit normal light rays quite as reliably as before. Melanie's heart pounded uncomfortably; was this going to happen every time she turned her head? Was something waiting for her to turn her head, watching for her attention to stray so that as soon as she was looking elsewhere—as soon as she started looking elsewhere—it could rush past the windows, for what purpose she couldn't possibly imagine?

Then her attention was captured by the television, now showing the replay of a football match—she knew it was a replay because it had a big red R displayed up in the corner of the screen—and casting back frantically in her mind she did remember kneeling on something hard, and that might well have been the remote control for the television.

Dorothy was nodding; yes, George had liked to watch football; yes, the same thing had happened to her; was it likely that this had happened by chance, after all there was a lot of football shown on television these days?

Something else Melanie didn't tell her mother was that when she got back to the house the first thing she did was to go into the study. She wanted to make sure that Bedford Road was where she thought it was, and she couldn't be bothered to switch on her computer and check it out that way, and she knew that Dorothy had taken the map from the kitchen, but she also knew that there was another map—in fact, several maps—piled up in one corner of the study.

She found a Glasgow map in a matter of moments, spread it out on the desk, and after squinting at the unfeasibly small print for a while she discovered that Bedford Road was indeed in the north-west of the city, nowhere near Central Station or the offices of Barker Associates, but having confirmed this puzzling fact, she still had not the faintest idea of why her father might have gone there.

Her glance fell on a clear plastic bag on the corner of the desk. In it she could see some keys, some small change, pieces of paper folded small, sundry other objects which she could not quite make out... and a mobile phone. Melanie drew a shaky breath as she realised that she was looking at her father's possessions, presumably taken out of the various pockets of his clothing at some stage after he died, perhaps at the hospital, perhaps at the undertakers; how was she supposed to know?

An idea jumped into her head, and she reached out for the bag, paused to look around to make sure nobody was observing her, laughed shakily at her own stupidity. She took the phone out of the bag and turned it on. She had never used the phone before, but it wasn't particularly modern and she had no difficulty in deciphering its logic. Within seconds she knew that approximately two hours before he died, her father had sent a text to somebody called Claire which read simply *On my way*. Before she could change her mind, she called the number and nearly dropped the phone when a female voice screamed at her.

'Leave me alone! Leave me alone! Why won't you leave me alone?'

In Glasgow, Lucy took Claire's mobile from her unresisting hand. She noticed that its display was showing some number and then the name *George*. She frowned and put the phone to her ear.

'Hello?'

Melanie somehow managed to catch her father's phone in mid-air. She gave it a puzzled look, as if the reason why somebody would scream at her would be apologetically displayed on its small screen, then lifted it to her ear again.

'Hello? Is that Claire?'

'No.'

Melanie realised that this voice was different from the one that had screamed at her.

'But she answered the phone, right?'

'Who is this?'

'Can I speak to Claire, please?'

Lucy hesitated. 'She's not feeling so good.'

'Please. I need to speak to her.'

Lucy hesitated again. Claire had collapsed sideways on the bed and curled into a ball, but Lucy could tell that she was listening.

'Please,' said Melanie desperately. 'I really need to talk to her and find out what she knows about... about my father.'

'Your father?'

'Yes.'

'George was your father?'

'Yes.'

'Jesus. Claire had a fit when she saw the number calling because... uh...'

'My father is dead,' said Melanie. Suddenly she appreciated the black humour of the situation. 'Yes, I can see that it might have had that effect,' she added.

Another pause. Melanie sensed that the phone at the other end—presumably Claire's phone—was being moved. She heard faint sounds, a handful of words, though she couldn't make them out. Then another voice:

'Hello?'

It was the first voice, clearer, perhaps younger, but also more hesitant.

'Is that Claire?'

'Yes. Who's speaking?'

'I'm Melanie. I believe you... knew my father?'

Even now, Melanie realised, she found it difficult to use the past tense.

'His name was George?'

'Yes.'

'He had curly hair?'

Melanie thought this rather an odd question, but she acknowledged that yes, her father had had curly hair. 'You knew him?' she persisted.

'Yes,' said Claire.

'Oh,' said Melanie. 'It's just that, well, I think you might have been the last person to see him alive.'

'Maybe.'

'Do you work for a publisher's?'

For the first time Claire sounded amused. 'No.'

'Well, it's just that... well, my father was in Glasgow to meet with a publisher.'

'Yes,' said Claire. 'He told me. Ghost stories, he told me.'

'Well, I just wondered, you know, why he went to see you? You did see him, didn't you?'

'Yes, I saw him,' said Claire, but didn't say anything more, and after a few moments had passed while neither of them said anything, Melanie felt too embarrassed to ask a second time *why* her father had gone to meet Claire. Instead she blurted:

'Can I come to see you?'

An even longer pause.

'Wait a minute.'

In Glasgow, Claire put her hand over the mobile and looked up at Lucy, who was leaning against the wall with a faintly amused look on her face.

'She wants to come and see me.'

'You can't blame her.'

'She wants to know why her dad came to see me.'

'Then she might be in for a bit of a surprise.' Lucy chewed her lip. 'How old is she?'

Claire uncovered the mobile and said: 'How old are you?'

'What?' came Melanie's voice. 'Oh, well, I'm nineteen.'

Claire covered up the phone again. 'Nineteen,' she said.

Lucy shrugged. 'She's old enough. What's she going to think when she finds out what her dear old dad's been up to?'

'How should I know?'

'I wasn't asking,' said Lucy. 'It's up to you.'

Claire thought for a few moments. She put the phone back to her ear.

'Okay. But you might not like what you hear.'

'Thanks,' came Melanie's voice. 'Maybe. Maybe not.'

Rather to her surprise, Claire detected a hint of steel in the girl's voice that she hadn't noticed before. 'Okay,' she said again.

'Where are you? When shall I come?'

Claire told Melanie her address in Laburnum Crescent, and they arranged to meet at eleven on the following day, Friday.

They disconnected. In Ayr, Melanie carefully transferred Claire's number to her own mobile before deleting it from her father's. She also deleted the corresponding text. She already had more than an inkling of just who Claire was and why her father had gone to visit her, if only because Claire had asked her that odd question about her age, and if she was only half right, the last thing she wanted was for her mother to find out. Before leaving the study, she opened up the map of Glasgow again and discovered, not entirely to her surprise, that Laburnum Crescent was a turning off Bedford Road.

In Glasgow, Lucy remarked that she hoped Claire knew what she was doing. Claire made an expression so vague that even she was unsure of its meaning, and murmured something about not having much choice, and did it really matter? She was eyeing her phone, thinking that she really ought to delete the details pertaining to George, and promising herself that she would do just that, as soon as she had met up with this daughter of his. Who would have thought that she would end up arranging to meet with George's daughter? She felt an unexpected thrill of anticipation, and could not decide if it was because she was looking forward to the meeting, or whether she couldn't wait for the whole episode to be finished.

———●———

It was growing dark in the dining room, but neither Melanie nor Dorothy moved to turn on the lights. Melanie, calm now, had finished telling her mother about the events in the sitting room and her mind had moved back, to the first words Claire had screamed at her. *Why won't you leave me alone?* At that stage Claire had not known that Melanie was making the call. She had jumped to the conclusion that the man with the curly hair, who she knew as George, was making the call, but Melanie was beginning to realise that this didn't make a lot of sense.

'There's something not right,' said Dorothy. Melanie started, thinking for a moment that her mother must have read her mind, or that she had unknowingly spoken aloud. Then she saw that Dorothy's gaze had turned inwards and that it was entirely possible that she was the one who had unknowingly spoken aloud. 'About the house,' said Dorothy softly. 'About anything.' She fell silent again while the room darkened still further.

Seeing that her mother wasn't looking for any immediate answers, Melanie went back to wondering about Claire's outburst. If Claire hadn't known that George had died, then her shouted words might have meant that George had been stalking her or pestering her, not that Melanie could imagine her father doing any such thing. But Claire *had* known. That was why the phone call had come as such a shock to her. So, if she knew that George was dead, why would she scream at him to leave her alone? Unless, unless... Melanie's blood turned cold. *Unless he had been bothering her after he had died.* This thought was so logical but so outrageous that she almost burst into hysterical, frightened laughter but stopped herself just in time and instead emitted a high-pitched squeak.

'What?' Dorothy looked up and saw that Melanie had clapped both hands over her mouth. 'Well, I don't want to go into my own bedroom, my own bathroom.' Without moving her hands, Melanie nodded. 'And you don't want to go into the sitting room, or the main bathroom.' Melanie nodded again. 'There's something not right,' Dorothy repeated. 'Is it something to do with your father?' she added calmly. 'I don't know.' Melanie shook her head, not in disagreement, but to indicate that she didn't know either. Although, now she came to think about it, perhaps she did know. Not that it was something she could tell her mother.

'Have another biscuit,' said Dorothy.

Melanie emitted another squeak, then moved her hands, wiping her lips.

'Has it occurred to you,' said Dorothy conversationally, 'that all these things that have been happening, me dreaming or seeing a figure, the bathrooms, something outside the window, television...' She paused, pursed her lips and raised her eyebrows, as if listing the events of the last few days made her realise just how many of them there had been. 'Yes, all these things, I don't know if you realise it, but they've all happened since those two men came.'

Melanie hadn't thought of that. She nodded slowly.

'What was it the young one said? Something about needing to contact him, now that they had visited?'

'Something like that,' said Melanie.

'And it was a Glasgow taxi,' said Dorothy. 'You just told me that.'

'Yes,' said Melanie.

The room was almost dark.

'It's a ridiculous idea,' said Dorothy firmly.

'Ridiculous,' agreed Melanie.

A long pause. It struck Melanie that the room wasn't just dark, it was cold. The unpleasant notion crept over her that the whole house was cold and dark; it was no longer the warm, loving house in which she had grown up. Fleetingly she remembered her vision of—was it only that morning?— all the doors slowly opening and closing of their own accord.

'I don't think I can keep on like this, Mel.'

Tears came to Melanie's eyes. She could hardly remember the last time her mother had called her Mel, and she was sure she had never heard her mother sound so desolate and lost, not even in the days after her father had died. She rubbed the back of her hand across her eyes, glad of the darkness.

'Shall we tell Uncle James?'

Dorothy thought about this; shook her head slowly. Melanie understood. James was good at practical things, like keeping on top of paperwork or arranging to get appliances fixed if they broke down, but he would be bewildered and out of his depth if Dorothy and Melanie asked him what to do about the strangeness creeping over their lives.

'Then we better call whatever his name was, shall we?'

'I think I threw away the card.'

'I've still got the one from the driver, somewhere. Harry. Anyway, we can always look him up on the internet.'

Dorothy got up and turned on the light. She stood for long moments, her back to Melanie, staring out into the hall. She was remembering when she stirred from sleep and looked out into the hall from the sitting room, into the same hall albeit from a different angle, to see George standing, barefoot, grinning at her with an expression on his face which she had never seen before and which she could not quite work out, not even now as she replayed the expression in her mind. If the conversation with Melanie had contained any elements of truth, did that mean that George really had been there, hopping from one foot to the other—in what form precisely she didn't know and she wasn't even sure that she wanted to know—but did it mean that he had been there? Dorothy shivered and felt a surge of horror.

———◆———

Harry McCabe logged on to the internet and, unaware that it would be the last time he would ever do so, navigated to *eharmony.co.uk*. He signed in, banging the keys angrily, and saw without any surprise that there were no emails in his inbox. No new emails and no apologetic emails either. Gabriella, he wrote. I waited for over an hour. Where were you? No, forget it.

In quick succession he signed in to *match.com*, *tinder. com*, and *zoosk.com* and was equally unsurprised to find no emails waiting for him at any of those locations, either. He was beginning to think that these sites were a waste of time, effort and money but one of his few remaining friends from his schoolboy days, Hugh McLellan, who now worked in Aberdeen for an oil company (though not, Hugh insisted, in any particularly glamorous role, but as some sort of book-keeper) had met his wife through one of these dating sites, and they had been happily married for several years, producing two sons and a daughter into the bargain. The particular site that had introduced Hugh to the future Mrs

McLellan had wound up some time ago, but Hugh told Harry that internet dating sites were rapidly becoming an accepted and acceptable way of meeting members of the opposite sex (or even the same sex, Harry remembered Hugh joking).

Two years ago Harry had met up with a woman called Sandra who, it turned out, weighed half as much again as Harry did and smoked like a chimney, in no way resembling the photograph of the super-fit badminton-playing woman on the dating site. That had been a major disappointment.

Over a period of four or five weeks he had gone out with a woman called Katherine, an attractive slightly plump redhead who actually did look like her internet photograph, and who really was looking for a serious relationship, but who turned out to have absolutely nothing in common with Harry, so that on their half a dozen dates they had spent most of the time sitting around wondering what to say to each other, and even on the one occasion they had gone to bed together, they discovered that their individual notions of what constituted a good time were not the same. He had met another woman, Olga, about a year ago. She was vibrant, not unattractive and appeared to like Harry as much as Harry liked her, but as soon as he mentioned that he had a son who lived at home, she vanished.

Harry surveyed his empty email boxes gloomily. Perhaps the problem was that he was no longer as young as he had been; maybe the idea of being with a taxi driver didn't drum up as much feminine excitement as being with, say, an ex-SAS officer or an executive who spent most of the year flying business class to various exotic locations around the globe (both these characters appeared on more than one of the dating sites, and Harry imagined that *their* inboxes were always filled with dozens of messages from swooning, adoring, attractive, sexy women; although it did occur to

Harry to wonder why an ex-SAS officer and executive who etc etc needed to register on a dating site in the first place).

The phone rang. Harry picked it up and somewhat brusquely gave his number.

'Hello? Is that Mr McCabe? Harry McCabe?'

It was a female voice and for a confused moment Harry thought that Gabriella had somehow got hold of his number and was ringing to explain why she hadn't turned up. That was nonsense, of course; anyway he vaguely recognised the voice.

'Yes.'

'Oh, it's Dorothy Viviani here, from down in Ayr. I don't know if you remember me?'

Harry's heartbeat quickened. He sat up straighter.

'Yes, Mrs Viviani. I remember very well.'

'I was wondering, well, I wanted to contact the other man who came down with you that day. I'm afraid I can't remember his name...'

'Cheyne Tully,' said Harry McCabe.

'... oh yes, how could I have forgotten a name like that?'

Harry and Dorothy chuckled politely at each other.

'Anyway I lost his card but luckily my daughter kept yours, and I was just wondering if you knew how to contact him?'

Harry reported that Cheyne Tully was actually staying with him at the moment. Dorothy Viviani exclaimed that this was good news, and asked if she could have a word with him, but Harry informed her that Tully had gone out for a while, but should be back in—oh, probably less than an hour. He didn't inform her that Tully had in fact stormed out, slamming the door, because, as he said in no uncertain terms, he was damned if he was going to sit around with such a miserable grumpy self-pitying bastard as Harry McCabe any longer. Instead Harry asked for Dorothy Viviani's telephone number, noted it down, and said that he would get Tully to call back just as soon as he returned.

'Mr McCabe?'

'Just Harry, please.'

'My husband died in the back of a taxi in Glasgow. I was just wondering if, well...'

Harry pinched the bridge of his nose.

'... if, well, I was wondering if it was actually your taxi.'

Harry closed his eyes, sighed silently, and opened them again. 'Yes. Yes, I'm afraid it was. I'm sorry, Mrs Viviani.' It struck him that this sounded as if he was apologising for positioning his taxi in the exact spot at the exact time to take advantage of George Viviani's dying moments, when what he really meant was that he was sorry that George had died. Fortunately Dorothy Viviani didn't seem to notice the ambiguous nature of his words.

'Thank you, Mr—Harry. I take it, then, that it wasn't a coincidence that it was you who drove Mr Tully down to Ayr the other day?'

'No,' said Harry McCabe. 'No, it wasn't a coincidence.' He wondered how he was going to explain why he had contacted Tully and why the two of them had made the trip to Ayr. Or perhaps it hadn't been the two of them, his mind insisted on correcting, but the three of them. The computer screen in front of him flickered, blanked out, and then displayed a mass of stars all moving past at terrific speed.

'Hello?'

Harry realised that several seconds had passed.

'Sorry,' he said. 'Sorry. I was just thinking. I think it would be better if Mr Tully explained everything to you. I'm not sure I understand it myself.'

A large orange blob appeared in the middle of the screensaver and travelled diagonally downwards, towards the lower right hand corner of the screen, moving much more slowly than the mass of white dots.

'But I take it that you contacted Mr Tully? At some time after my husband died?'

'Yes.'

'So, I imagine that you contacted him for similar reasons... I mean, for similar reasons why I'm contacting him?'

Dorothy Viviani's voice had become quite faint, almost breathless.

'I imagine so,' said Harry McCabe cautiously as the orange blob eased out of existence.

'Oh,' said Dorothy Viviani. Harry thought that she sounded as if she had known this was going to be the case, but was surprised nonetheless. 'Well, I'd be grateful if you'd pass on my message to Mr Tully when he gets back.'

'Of course, shouldn't be long,' said Harry McCabe.

They both said goodbye and they both hung up. In Ayr, Dorothy Viviani turned a white face towards Melanie, nodded, and whispered that Melanie had been right, but Melanie had already gleaned as much from hearing Dorothy's side of the telephone conversation, and her hands had already started to tremble. In Glasgow, Harry McCabe moodily exited the dating sites, closed down his computer and went to stand by the front window, wondering where the hell Cheyne Tully had got to.

Chapter 12

This time the weather was quiet as the taxi nosed into Ayr. Neither of them said very much. At one point Harry McCabe asked whether Tully had learned anything from the woman in the flower shop. For a few moments Harry couldn't remember her name, then he remembered Hamilton, and shortly afterwards he remembered their humorous exchange about her first name being Janine. Not really, Tully admitted. He said he had been hoping to find out why George Viviani had seemed so happy—he had obviously been happy about something, Tully said, and whatever it was, it had equally obviously been rudely interrupted by the heart attack, and being interrupted in the middle of something was often the reason why someone refused to accept the fact of their death. But Janine Hamilton didn't seem to have any idea why George had been so happy, which was a pity, remarked Tully, as in his opinion the reason, whatever it was, lay at the bottom of everything.

Just outside Ayr, Harry asked whether Dorothy Viviani had asked any questions about why they had gone down to Ayr the first time; not only driven down to Ayr but done so in the very taxi in which George had expired. Tully said yes, but added that he had told her that he would explain everything when they arrived.

———●———

As the taxi swung around the remains of an old tower and angled towards some tennis courts, almost at the end of its journey, some forty miles away Claire bundled nightclothes and wash bag together. She had decided that she couldn't stay in the flat, at least not that night. Lucy had offered space in her bed, but rather to her own surprise Claire found that she preferred the idea of going across the road to impose on the young man again.

This time, as she slipped out through the plywood door into the street, she could hear traffic from the direction of Bedford Road; many buildings were showing lights; a woman wearing a long headscarf glanced at her incuriously as she walked past. She could hear voices but could not make out if they were coming from a radio or whether some people were actually talking somewhere nearby. It was all very different from the last occasion on which she had made this journey, panicked and jittery, in the small hours of the previous night.

For the first time, apart from once when she had gone down with flu, she had missed an appointment. She had given it to Lucy, who had met the client at the outside door, on Laburnum Crescent, to explain that she, Claire, wasn't very well and would she, Lucy, be acceptable as a substitute? Lucy had dressed herself up in what Claire thought of as her fire-engine ensemble, and apparently the client had been unable to take his eyes off her, particularly when Lucy preceded him up the narrow stairs in her short skirt. She took him into Claire's room because, for some reason that they afterwards realised wasn't very logical, the client was originally Claire's, so they arranged that he should be taken into her room rather than Lucy's.

Meanwhile, Claire closed the curtains in Lucy's room, flung herself down on Lucy's bed and put an arm tiredly across her eyes. She heard movement next door, the occasional giggle, creaks. It felt odd to lie on Lucy's bed, not because it was Lucy's bed (she had done that before, most recently when Pete aka Stuart had paid them a visit), but because the shape of Lucy's room was a mirror image of her own. When she lay on her right side in her own bed she would have her back to the door and her face to the wall; to achieve the same effect in Lucy's room she had to lie on her left side and even with her arm across her eyes or with her eyes closed she felt disoriented.

Lucy had spread garish red and yellow rugs over her floor. Claire wondered if Lucy and her clients ever used the floor instead of the bed. She would normally have summoned up a smile at this thought, but she felt depressed. She felt as though something heavy was pressing down on her life, squeezing out all colour and leaving nothing but a dull uniform grey. At least she felt safe enough to curl up, back to the room, not fearing that she would hear sudden footsteps, or see strange rectangular lights, or feel a buffeting wind. She did feel the ordinary Glaswegian cold, though. She tugged a blanket over her shoulders even though she was fully dressed. Something banged on the wall and she imagined it must be an outflung foot or knee. She had been shivering, but slowly she warmed under the blanket.

She slept. Afterwards Lucy told her that the client had been a young man in his twenties, with long hair and a spotty face, but even as Claire started to grimace at this description, she hastened to add that he was perfectly clean, and slim; apparently he did a lot of running which kept him fit. He had been nervous, Lucy said, but she had soon put him at ease and they had had a grand time. She apologetically told Claire that she had given him her number, but Claire just shrugged. They went on to hold the conversation about Claire not wanting to stay in her own room, and Lucy offering to share hers, and while she shook her head, Claire had been unable to meet Lucy's knowing eyes.

Across the road, then, to watch the door of 7B swing open as if in a dream. The young man bobbed his head and gave what might have been a smile of welcome when he saw her. She didn't have to explain why she was there or ask if she could stay. She could see in his eyes that he already knew the explanation and understood the question; by way of answer he squeezed back against the wall in the tiny hallway, pulling the door open still further. He nodded again as Claire entered and, clutching her clothes and bags, climbed the already familiar stairs.

———————●———————

'It was like this,' said Tully. 'Your husband—your father—dies in the back of Harry's taxi. Then a bit later, two weeks later, maybe less, the back of the taxi starts to get cold. At first Harry doesn't think anything of it; cold in Glasgow? What can you expect? But it keeps getting colder, to the point where passengers ask him to turn up the heater. At one point he takes the taxi in to a garage, but they say it's nothing to do with the heater. I think it's fair to say Harry was perplexed, and more than a little worried, since if passengers stop getting into his taxi because it's too cold... well, there wouldn't be any passengers, and no fares either.

'One evening he moans about all this down at the local pub—if there's one thing I've learned about Harry it's that he likes a good moan—and it so happens that some guy there has heard of me. Doesn't matter how.' Tully waved his arms vaguely to demonstrate how much it didn't matter. 'But after he hears Harry's tale, he suggests that Harry contacts me. Which he did. Thank you.'

Tully took a cup of tea, and Harry took another one, as Dorothy poured them out. 'Have you got a cat, by the way?'

Dorothy Viviani looked startled. 'A cat? No. Why?'

Disconcertingly, Tully's gaze seemed to be focussed to the right of where Melanie Viviani was sitting.

'Because there's one sitting on the arm of the chair right there,' said Tully. 'But you're all ignoring it.'

Melanie glanced sideways, shivered, and shifted along the sofa slightly.

'You're kidding, right?' said Harry McCabe.

'No,' said Tully, switching his gaze to Harry. 'Why would I do that?'

'Uh, no reason.'

'It's a small cat,' said Tully. 'Stripey. Black and white—I mean, like out of a photograph, so I can't tell what colour it is. Was.' He brooded for a moment. 'Looks like something has chewed on one of its ears.' He glanced enquiringly at Dorothy and Melanie, but both shook their heads. Both of them looked distinctly nervous.

'It's gone now,' said Tully.

'Can you see—uh, anything else?' asked Harry McCabe.

'If you mean can I see George,' said Tully, 'don't you think I would have mentioned it?' Harry McCabe managed to look chastened and irritated at the same time. Tully put down his cup.

'Anyway, Harry decides to contact me and by the time I turn up, the back of the taxi is like a fridge. He doesn't tell me what's going on, but it's pretty obvious what had happened, especially when I find a business card slipped down between the seats. George's business card. That's how we knew to come here, that first time—knew the address—mind you we could have found out easily enough by following through from the newspaper reports. So we came down,' said Tully, 'and that solved the problem with the taxi. But I guess you've got problems here now.'

Tully raised an eyebrow at Dorothy Viviani, who nodded.

'Mrs Viviani, we know George was happy just before he died. We know this because both Harry and the lady in the flower shop where he bought tulips saw him and said he couldn't stop grinning, couldn't stop smiling about something. You wouldn't by any chance know what it might have been?' As he asked this question, Tully noticed that the girl Melanie looked up sharply, and then turned away with a thoughtful expression on her face.

'Yes,' said Dorothy. 'But wait a minute. When you came down the last time. In the storm. What happened?'

Tully looked at her steadily.

'I mean—I mean, *did* anything happen?'

Tully sighed. 'Things were different after we came, yes? The house was a certain way before our visit, and then it was a different way after our visit? So something must have happened during the visit to cause the change, yes?'

Dorothy looked confused. Harry McCabe felt sufficiently moved to lean forward and say: 'You told me that you felt him going in.'

Tully gestured impatiently. 'It doesn't matter what I feel; what I think; what I see. What matters is what Mrs Viviani and her daughter feel; what they believe. Mrs Viviani?'

Dorothy looked up.

'Why was George so happy, Mrs Viviani?'

'Oh, that'll be because of his stories. A publisher had agreed to take them.'

'Stories?'

'Yes, that was why he had travelled up to Glasgow, you see. To talk to a publisher.'

'What sort of stories, Mrs Viviani?'

'Oh, they were mostly stories he wrote for Melanie. They were...' She stopped suddenly and her eyes widened.

'... ghost stories,' whispered Melanie.

A long pause developed during which everyone reflected, in their various ways, on the curious fact that George, who appeared to be having trouble accepting that he had died, had himself written a number of ghost stories. Dorothy wondered how she could have entirely overlooked the bizarre coincidence. Harry wondered if any of the stories were about the haunting of the back of a taxi, or car, or any sort of vehicle. Melanie had a sudden, vivid image of her father, laughing in firelight at her reaction to one of the stories; she also wondered if his success with the publisher had been the only reason why he had been so happy on the day that he died.

Tully was considering whether the whole thing *was* a coincidence. Wouldn't George have been just as excited, just as keen to buy flowers and go home to celebrate his success with Dorothy, if he had published, say, a textbook on local authority accounting? It wasn't clear to Tully that there was necessarily a connection, but he asked Dorothy if he could see a copy of the stories nonetheless. He had learned long ago that it paid to be thorough in this sort of investigation. There was no telling what apparently insignificant detail would turn out to be pivotal to a case, rather like (as he was fond of explaining to both friends and clients) the tiny details which turn out to be so important in a well-constructed murder mystery.

Dorothy nodded, thought for a moment, and then asked Melanie if she would fetch George's briefcase from where it had been lying in the study ever since somebody that she could not bring to mind had returned it to the house. She explained that there would be a full set of the stories in the briefcase.

While Melanie went to search it out (though of course she knew exactly where it was, as her father's mobile phone which she had noticed earlier had been sitting right on top of it; she opened it and looked quickly through its contents before taking it back to Tully, in case there was anything in there she would rather he didn't get to see but, she was glad to discover, there wasn't)—while they waited for Melanie, Dorothy suddenly realised that she could offer to put up Tully for the night, assuming he wanted to stay for a while, but she had no room for Harry McCabe. She added that if Harry didn't want to drive all the way back up to Glasgow, then her next door neighbour would be able to put him up. At a cost, she added, as it was a bed and breakfast establishment, although she could probably negotiate a discount.

Harry McCabe thanked her. Tully said he would like to stay for a couple of nights; he said he would probably need to speak with both Dorothy and Melanie individually. Melanie, arriving back in time to hear this last comment, said that she would not be around for much of the following day because she would be going up to Glasgow to meet a friend for lunch.

'Thank you,' said Tully, accepting the briefcase from Melanie.

'Give you a lift,' grunted Harry McCabe.

Tully didn't open the briefcase, but placed it carefully on the floor by the side of his chair. Then he looked back up at Dorothy Viviani.

'So,' he said. 'Your turn. What's been going on?'

Later, while Melanie showed Tully up to the third floor and the guest room, Dorothy slipped on a coat and escorted Harry McCabe next door to the Seashore Guest House. Harry fetched his small overnight bag from the taxi and followed her without any sense that anything extraordinary was about to happen. Dorothy rang the doorbell. Light sieved through the glass in the door, failing to illuminate the path or pick out the silhouettes of Dorothy or Harry. The sky was black, stars hidden above clouds. It was drizzling. Harry was trying to work out what to say to Dorothy Viviani, to cement the few moments they had spent together, walking from one house to the next. A blurred figure became visible through the glass, approaching. The door opened.

Harry knew that Dorothy said something; he wasn't sure what—something banal like *hello Trudy, this is Harry* (he knew the woman who appeared in the doorway was called Trudy, because Dorothy had mentioned it on their way between houses); he was aware that Trudy responded in some fashion, at least until he moved closer, into the light, and she caught sight of him. But for long seconds he hung back, shrouded by darkness.

The woman who opened the door wasn't very tall. The curious thought struck him that she probably wouldn't reach to Tully's shoulder, although why he should have thought of Tully at that precise moment was difficult to understand. She would reach to Harry's shoulder, and a little further. Her hair was thick and dark and much of it was tied back in a practical pigtail. She wasn't slim, in fact she was slightly plump, but her figure, thought Harry McCabe, definitely went in and came out at all the right places. All things considered, Harry also thought, she looked about as different from Dorothy Viviani as it was possible to be and still belong to the same sex of the same species. Harry wasn't very good at guessing how old people were, especially women, but he gained the impression that she was younger than he was, but not much younger.

It was amazing how much thinking he could cram into a few seconds.

He remembered keying preferences into dating websites, not that he was overly prescriptive as he couldn't afford to be, but he had a distinct predilection for taller, slim, blonde women which was what Annette had been, and he supposed now that he must have been searching for her ever since; that was why he had been so taken with Dorothy Viviani (although she now looked pale, insubstantial, and not very desirable standing next to the woman in the doorway). It even struck him that it would probably not have been a good thing to have found an Annette look-alike because he would have been reminded of Annette every minute, every second that he looked at her, and now he realised what a torture that would have been.

It was remarkable the shock he had experienced when the door to the Seashore Guesthouse opened and Trudy appeared; what sort of a name was Seashore Guesthouse, Harry found himself thinking; the establishment was nowhere near the sea. When he stepped forward, he discovered that his breathing was uneven, his legs were unsteady, and he wished he was wearing something more presentable.

Only a few seconds had passed.

Dorothy had said something about *overnight*, and something else about *rooms* and *Glasgow*. The woman who had delivered such an unexpected shock to Harry McCabe's nervous system peered past Dorothy Viviani, behind her, into the darkness. When Harry came forward into the light, her eyes widened. She had been about to say something, but the words died on her lips which, Harry couldn't help but notice, remained parted slightly. Trudy? asked Dorothy, at first concerned, then amused. Harry McCabe heard her this time but it was clear that Trudy didn't.

As more seconds crawled past, Harry at first suspected, then hoped, and then became certain that Trudy was experiencing the same sort of shock that he had just experienced. What he was thinking must have crept into his eyes (he could no more prevent his eyes betraying his thoughts than he could prevent the Earth revolving around the sun), because he saw confusion mirrored in hers. Dorothy Viviani ceased to exist. He edged around the space where some subconscious part of him recognised that she was still standing, and crossed the threshold into the guesthouse. Having also forgotten that Dorothy Viviani existed, Trudy pushed the glass door shut.

A smile played across Dorothy's lips when she got back to her own house, and her step was lighter.

'Mum?' asked Melanie.

'You should've seen the pair of them,' Dorothy told her. 'Harry and Trudy. They hit it off like nobody's business. I could see it in their eyes.'

Melanie smiled, a little uncertainly. Dorothy suddenly folded her arms around her body and shivered, thinking that she felt cold, even though she was indoors now and was still wearing her coat. Was this the same cold that had invaded Harry McCabe's taxi, or was it just plain cold from outside? The light was on in the upstairs hall, and in the sitting room, but not in the downstairs hall where she was standing with Melanie. It was full of shadow.

Dorothy realised that she felt like a stranger in her own house. The exuberance she had felt after seeing Trudy and Harry take to each other was abruptly gone, snuffed out. She felt instead as if a crushing weight was making it difficult for her to breathe or think straight; was making it hard for her even to properly exist, standing there in the dark hall, face to face with her daughter, while the darkness coiling at the door in no way matched the darkness gradually filling what for so many years had been a happy family home.

Footsteps. Top stairs, upper hallway, lower stairs. Cheyne Tully appeared and even though he was dressed in unrelieved black, Dorothy felt the atmosphere lighten. From the expression on Melanie's face, she did too.

'Mrs Viviani?'

'Yes, Mr Tully?'

'Could I beg a sandwich or something? I've been staying with Harry for almost a week and he's not the greatest cook in the world.'

'Of course. Would you like some soup? We can do both.'

'Will you be sleeping in your own room tonight?' asked Tully.

'I was planning to try,' said Dorothy.

'Soup would be good,' said Tully. 'Anything but lentil. It disagrees with me.'

'Do you know what's happening?' asked Dorothy.

'I shall want to spend one night at least in your bedroom,' said Tully.

It occurred to Melanie that this was what happened when two Olympic-standard butterfly thinkers engaged in conversation.

'As to what's happening, I shan't know until I've spoken to you both. Maybe not even then. When will you be back?'

Melanie blinked. 'Er, sometime in the afternoon, I suppose.'

'Oh, I forgot you were going out,' said Dorothy. 'Who are you going to see?'

'Er—a friend—Claire.'

'And the stories,' decided Tully. 'I'd better check them out too.'

Dorothy shrugged off her coat. 'Well, we'd better not stand around in this hallway all night. I'll do a sandwich. Come to think of it, I fancy a sandwich too. What about you, Mel? Your room all right, Mr Tully?' Tully descended the last few steps, and the three of them headed towards the kitchen.

———●———

Next door, Trudy laid out some tea, biscuits and cake and watched with obvious pleasure as Harry McCabe tucked in. Her heart was pounding in a pleasurable, excited fashion. Once Harry had stepped into the house and she had pushed the door closed, they had stood staring into each other's eyes for what seemed like an eternity but was probably only a few seconds. Trudy remembered reading somewhere that only young children and lovers were supposed to be able to do that. Then she had turned away and led Harry further into the house, past the photographs and various certificates up on the wall, past the small counter where she had set up a computer and telephone, into the room which she thought of as her drawing room.

Harry said he liked the furniture and the decoration; clearly he didn't know quite what to say but he felt he ought to say something. Trudy sat him on the big old-fashioned settee, told him she was going to make a cup of tea, and bustled out to the kitchen.

Once there, she put the kettle on and then smoothed her hair and straightened her clothes, stood for a moment thinking and then reached back and unpinned her hair so that it fell around her shoulders.

Harry looked up and scrambled awkwardly to his feet when she came back in but she told him not to be so stupid and to sit right back down again; if he was going to stand up every time she came back into a room she was going to get an attack of vertigo even if he didn't. She saw him looking at her hair, so she pushed at it casually. When she met his gaze she saw a look which was unmistakeable, even after all the years since Gordon had died. All things come to those who wait, she thought to herself.

Harry asked whether she had many lodgers at the moment. She looked at him directly and said no, it was the wrong time of the year, there was nobody in the guesthouse at the moment although she was expecting a party of Germans next Monday, so that meant, she told Harry, that he could pick whichever room he wanted. It was perfectly clear what she meant, and a few moments later she was wondering if the top of everybody's head turned red when they blushed, or whether it was something that happened only to Harry McCabe.

During their long talk that first evening she told Harry about her Canadian roots, about the young man who had brought her to London but had dumped her (at which point Harry, without realising it, shook his head in disbelief), and about the short but happy time she had spent with Gordon. While she talked, Harry's gaze wandered over some photographs, making some sense out of them as she told her story. He asked her whether she had any children. She said she didn't and enquired whether Harry did. Harry knew this marked an important point in their conversation and he started to tell her about Tommy and why he was a little more difficult to understand than most eighteen-year-olds, but he trailed off into silence, not watching to see how Trudy would react to this information, but instead focussing on a photograph fixed to the wall—one of a set of four showing a younger Trudy on the arm of a tall dark-haired man Harry assumed must be Gordon.

Trudy started to tell a story about a couple that stayed with her some years ago, whose son had suffered some form of autism. She was in the process of explaining that the son, who she remembered very clearly, had been in the habit of watching shadows move across the walls, evincing great excitement every time a shadow crept across a picture or piece of furniture, as if he thought they were actually being swallowed up by the creeping darkness, and she was explaining that she had got on very well with the boy, whose name had been Martin, so much so that the parents had left him with her on at least two occasions while they went out to dinner, or to the cinema, something which they were never normally able to do. Halfway through this explanation she noticed the direction of Harry's gaze and confirmed that the set of photographs showed her with Gordon—taken, she said somewhat sadly, after his tumour had been diagnosed and they had known that he did not have very much time.

A little to her surprise Harry didn't appear to notice her sadness. Instead, he leaned closer to one of the photographs and unexpectedly asked her whether the cat in the picture had been hers. Yes, she said, that was Cosmic who had wandered into the guesthouse one day even before Trudy had arrived, and decided to stay. They never did find out where he had come from. Harry asked if Cosmic had been the sort of cat prone to getting into fights. She said no, as a matter of fact he hadn't, although once he had had a terrific battle with the dog from next door and almost lost an ear as a result. She watched curiously as Harry paled and swallowed. Why? she asked, and when he told her in a long rambling fashion, beginning with Tully's comments about the cat next door then, naturally enough, moving backwards into the past to explain why he and Tully were in Ayr, and then still further back to explain why he had found it necessary to contact Tully in the first place, she sat motionless for a very long time.

At first she was trying to work out if there was any way Tully could have known about Cosmic. For instance, did the picture which had so taken Harry's interest appear on her website? Or some other, similar, picture? She didn't think so. Anyway, why would Tully have checked out her website? How would he even have known that she was next door to Mrs Viviani? Thinking about Mrs Viviani set her thinking about George Viviani, a man who she had liked even though she had not known him very well. She looked at Harry, who had stopped telling his long convoluted story and was looking back at her. How odd, thought Trudy, that George's death and the events which followed had brought such misery and horror to the house next door, but looked like bringing an end to loneliness for two other people.

Over the next few weeks Harry drove down to Ayr on Friday evenings and back up to Glasgow on Sundays. He was relieved to discover that Trudy and Tommy got on just fine. Tommy liked walking along the beach. On some mornings when business at the guesthouse was slack and Harry slept late, Trudy and Tommy went walking together, enjoying the views across to Arran and the clear, cold air. Raucous seagulls hunted crabs at the water's edge until the last possible moment, flinging themselves up into the air as the intruding humans approached.

'I like it here,' said Tommy once.

'Good,' said Trudy.

'I think my dad likes it here too.'

'I think he does.'

'My mum died when I was born, but I think Dad still misses her.'

Trudy had learned not to be surprised by sudden changes in conversational direction. 'I think so too,' she said. 'I don't think your dad realises you know that.'

'I don't mind being on my own,' said Tommy. 'But Dad does.'

'He's not on his own,' said Trudy. 'He's got you.'

'It's not the same. He hasn't got Mum. You know what I mean.'

'Yes.'

They stopped at the harbour to watch a rusty cargo ship carefully manoeuvre into place alongside a pier where a huge pile of coal and giant blue diggers awaited. Trudy was thinking that Harry would have a fit if he knew just how much Tommy understood about their situation.

'Is it possible,' Tommy said, with the exaggerated care of a child, 'that we could live here?'

Trudy put an arm around his shoulder, hugged briefly, and dropped her arm back to her side.

'It's possible,' she said, equally carefully.

Four months later, in the new year, Harry McCabe put his house on the market and moved down to Ayr. He brought his taxi with him and applied for a job with a local taxi company, but after another four months he and Trudy discovered that having a registered taxi was a huge advantage for her guesthouse business, and he became self-employed. They married in late summer. Harry briefly considered asking Tully to be his best man, but in the end decided against it. After all, he had only known him for a matter of days, and they had lost contact after the curious events of the house next door. In the end he asked Hugh McLellan, who he had known for more than twenty-five years, and didn't invite Tully to the wedding at all.

He and Trudy McCabe ran the guesthouse and taxi service business for many years, and afterwards Tommy lived there on his own because, as he had once told his stepmother, he was perfectly happy being on his own and saw no need to be with anybody else.

He discovered that he had a talent for painting sunsets over Arran and the intervening sea. Some of his pictures were grey and cloudy; some were cloudy but filled with orange light underlining the clouds as they swept in from the sea; most were clear-skied, a blaze of colour, with seagulls tracing great circles high above placid waves. He sold a number of the paintings locally, and for a long time afterwards they could be seen in the waiting rooms of doctors or dentists, or above reception counters in businesses throughout Ayrshire.

Tommy McCabe lived alone in the house for many more years, and whether it was because of the nature of his character or for some other reason, he was never troubled by any ghosts, not even those of Harry and Trudy.

Chapter 13

As far as Tully could see, there were twenty-five stories, fifteen written for children and ten for adults. All were laid out in the same way, in 12 point Bookman Old Style font, not justified, and double-spaced (apart from one story called 'The Flapping Curtain' which was keyed in Times New Roman). Tully knew this because during the evening, while the three of them consumed soup and sandwiches in the kitchen, Melanie asked whether he had a laptop with him, and when he had said yes, she said she thought so, she thought she remembered him carrying one up to the third floor, and that being the case, wouldn't he prefer to have the stories in electronic form rather than have to sort through piles of printed paper?

> Jim stood beside his son. Outside, Claire walked slowly along the beach, from right to left. Her head was down, and she did not look at the sunset.

> "How did she know?" whispered Greg, for of course he had seen Claire's famous picture, and now here it was come to life, only it was Claire herself walking in front of the sunset, and how could she possibly have seen that?

> Jim knew. It was the same – it was all the same – as he had seen with Claire all those years ago. A white-haired lady walking across the beach at sunset, with a small dog running at her heels.

"Look at that," said Jim softly, his eyes filling with tears. "Under her coat! It's a wonder she doesn't trip!" He raised a hand to wipe away his tears, and as he did so the sun dropped behind the sea, and all the world turned dark.

'Well done, George,' muttered Tully. The story, 'Sunset', had turned on the idea that the ghost was a vision of the future so only those alive at that time in the future would be able to see it. This was a clever notion, but it wasn't what Tully was looking for, not that he was entirely sure what he was looking for. 'Halloween Stories' appeared to be about some children temporarily staying at an old house in the country, and it appeared to be about something ghostly riding a rocking horse in the middle of the night. But, as Tully was coming to expect with George's stories, there was a twist.

Mum paused for a minute, there in the darkest of dark rooms, with the Halloween wind howling. "So you see," she said softly, "there was a ghost in the old house that night. But it wasn't something riding the rocking horse. It was the rocking horse itself. And I have heard that in later years visitors to the house often heard a faint *creek-crok*, *creek-crok* from that room, even though nobody ever saw the horse again."

'Nice one,' muttered Tully. This story turned on the sound that the rocking horse made, but again, this was not what he was looking for. Sound did not seem to play any part in whatever was happening at the Viviani house, although he could recall other cases where it had.

He was sitting downstairs, in front of the fire which Dorothy Viviani had made up for him when he had announced his intention of staying up to look through the collection of stories. It struck him that he was reading them in similar circumstances to when they had originally been read out by George to his daughter and to Dorothy—in front of a log fire, with the lights turned down low. The thought didn't unnerve him in any way: he didn't know quite what was going on with George and his apparent return to the old Edwardian house, but whatever it was, it didn't involve him. It involved Dorothy Viviani and, he was increasingly coming to believe, it especially involved the daughter, Melanie Viviani.

Near the end of 'The Flatulent Ghost', which had clearly not been written for children, he read:

> "So there was Carole Morton, yelling and screaming in the middle of the road in the middle of the night wearing just a towel, just like I told you. And, so Harry says, she never went back into the house again.
>
> "That's it, guv. Weird, eh? Something to tell at the club, eh? Whassat? Yeah – Berwick Crescent. Like I say, I dunno the number but it's got a yeller garage and I reckon there was a merc parked outside. Maybe the place has been sold again. Maybe someone else's going to be farted out of house and home. What d'you think, guv? I mean, was it really a ghost? Hell, how can anyone know?"

Tully grinned, amused at the idea of a ghost with flatulence, particularly as it was not something he had encountered during his career as a ghost hunter. It was also nice to know that George had possessed a sense of humour, because Tully felt that this haunting—assuming that it was a genuine haunting—contained no elements of humour at all. He felt a sense of repressed violence, fuelled by something like anger, or fear. But everything he had learned so far indicated that George had been an even-tempered, good-natured man; and now Tully could see for himself that he had had a sense of humour. So where was all the anger and fear coming from?

Reading about Harry in the humorous ghost story made him think of Harry McCabe and Dorothy Viviani's comment that he had hit it off with the woman next door. 'Go for it, Harry,' murmured Tully, thinking of Harry's attempts to find a partner on the internet, and remembering the slightly faded photographs of a slim, blonde woman in various places around his house in Glasgow.

He leaned forward, poked at the fire, and put on another couple of logs, which started to crackle and burn with blue flames. That was the salt, Dorothy had explained earlier. One of her neighbours regularly collected driftwood from the beach, sawed it up, and brought her some of the proceeds from time to time. Tully recalled when he had climbed into Harry's taxi for the first time, and thought he had seen the internal light turn blue. A memory popped into his head of going to the library with his mother, and seeing the fluorescent lighting flicker with strands of blue. Salt or spectres, he thought. Take your choice.

> Dad nodded. "We were all sitting there on the bed, opening presents, when Mum suddenly gripped my arm and said, 'What's that?' When I listened, I could hear footsteps." He shrugged. "That's what they were. *I could say something that sounded like footsteps*, or I could say I *thought I heard something that sounded like footsteps*. But it wouldn't be true. Your mum and I sat

on the bed, and we listened to footsteps. There was no doubt in our minds. Upstairs, someone was walking across your bedroom towards the stairs."

Footsteps, mused Tully. His cases often featured footsteps. Heavy footsteps, slow deliberate footsteps, rapid footsteps pattering overhead in a deserted roof space. But there were no footsteps in this case—nothing significant, anyway. Mrs Viviani mentioned that she thought she had heard somebody go upstairs at the same time as Melanie had opened the front door to Harry and himself, but she had also said that she wasn't really sure about it, and neither she nor Melanie had heard any footsteps at any other time. Tully was inclined to write off the one instance as incidental imagination, but to be on the safe side he copied the paragraph into a file of his own making, called *George*.

I sat up in the bed, thinking 'but didn't I open the curtains?' I was sure that I had. Then I remembered that grandmother Mae had come to tuck me in, so I thought that perhaps she had closed them.

Anyway, I slid out of bed and pulled them open again. I could feel a draught of cold air from the window and then I suddenly saw a misty patch on the window. You can imagine what came into my mind! But really I knew that it was just condensation on the window. It was an old-style wooden window, and it was a cold day.

I rubbed at the misty patch, and at the same time I heard a footstep behind me. My mind stopped. I tell you, for a few seconds I could not think of anything at all. The misty patch was on the outside of the window, not the inside! Just like what happened to Harry's friend in the story that my old schoolteacher had told. The only thing was, this wasn't a story. It was real. It was real, but I couldn't believe it.

I stepped back from the window, and then remembered that grandmother had come to get me up. I turned round, and there was nobody there! I know, I know, you will say that I imagined the footstep – but I tell you I didn't. And there is one more strange twist. I ran in terror from the haunted room. I ran out, and found grandmother downstairs having her breakfast, and after she managed to calm me down, I told her the whole story. I remember how she looked at me.

"I can't get up those bendy stairs to the tower room any more, Janine," she told me. "My maid who comes in from the village made up the bed for you some time ago. Do you understand what I'm saying?" I must have looked blank. My brain had stopped working again. Grandmother leaned back in her chair and smiled a little sadly. "I don't know who came to help you, and tucked you in, my dear," she said in a gentle voice. "But it wasn't me. I haven't been inside the tower for more than three years."

There was Harry again. George obviously liked to use the same names; maybe he liked them, or maybe he just couldn't be bothered to think of new ones. Tully's brow creased. Janine? Wasn't that the name of the woman in the flower shop? Yes, he was sure of it; he could almost hear Harry McCabe deadpanning 'Janine?' Well, that was an odd coincidence, to be sure. More footsteps; odd marks on the window. Nothing really relevant, but he copied the paragraphs into his own file anyway and was about to turn to the next story when something snagged at his memory. There was something... he was sure there was something... He looked back through the passage he had just copied, and when he spotted what his subconscious must already have noticed, he sat for long moments staring into space. Then he grabbed his mobile phone.

'Unnh?'

'Harry?'

'Unnh. What?'

'Listen, you—'

'Tully?'

'Yes. Listen, you remember—'

'Jesus, Tully, what time d'you call this?'

In the background, a sleepy female voice.

'Yeah, right. It's half past one. Sorry about that. But listen—'

'Urgh. What is it? Can't it wait?'

'I'm trying to ask you a question, Harry!'

Silence.

'Listen, you remember the woman Janine, in the flower shop?'

'Yeah.'

'What was the name of the flower shop?'

'What was the...? Jesus, Tully!'

'It might be important.'

The female voice again, and Harry's muffled voice responding.

'Come on, Harry. If you can't remember, you might still have that receipt.'

'I remember all right, don't need a receipt.'

Silence. Tully wondered if Harry was going to deliberately withhold the name out of a fit of pique at being woken. Or maybe not woken, he suddenly thought, but disturbed. He had to hold back a bark of laughter.

'Come on, Harry.'

'It was Mae's Flowershop. Tully...'

'Yes?'

'You'd better have a good explanation for this tomorrow. Or...'

'Or what?'

'I'll think of something,' said Harry McCabe, and disconnected.

Tully started. The stripy cat with a chewed ear was sitting on the arm of the sofa again, exactly as it had been earlier. Tully stared at it curiously. As he watched, the cat lifted a paw, licked it delicately, turned its head sideways slightly so that it could wash behind its good ear, but before it could get a good paw-rubbing cleaning session going, it caught sight of Tully. He almost recoiled as the cat's eyes focussed on him. The cat *did* recoil; it opened its mouth in a soundless yowl and leaped down from the sofa, and either merged into the shadows beyond the firelight or disappeared into thin air, because Tully could see it no longer.

He was shaken. He imagined somebody sitting where he was sitting, a long time ago; imagined that person watching the cat, which had suddenly stared into space as if it could see something that cats could see but humans couldn't; imagined the same somebody raise an eyebrow as the cat yowled with fear and leaped out of the room, scampering out of sight, whereupon the person sitting in the selfsame place where Tully was now sitting would either think to himself (or herself), or turn to another occupant of the room—in either case, to make the observation that cats were strange animals. Cats *were* strange animals, thought Tully. This one had clearly seen him sitting there, a ghost not of the past but of the future, like the little dog in 'Sunset'.

Tully supposed that George Viviani might have been to the flower shop on some other occasion and remembered its name; he supposed that he might have known that the woman who worked inside was called Janine (although it was difficult to know how), or that somebody he knew was called Janine; and he supposed it was possible that George knew somebody else called Harry. It was all a lot of supposing, thought Tully, but it was just possible that the conjunction of all three names in one of George's stories might have come about by such a three-fold coincidence, rather than because the three names had all been present, more or less, at the scene of his death. There was, of course, no way of telling. There never was, thought Tully tiredly. He massaged his temples with the tips of his fingers, then opened up a new document and called it *Names*.

Upstairs, Dorothy Viviani lay with the bedside light on, alternately closing her eyes and almost drifting off to sleep, then jerking them open in sudden panic in case something happened while she had them closed.

Once, she was sure she had opened her eyes, swung her legs out of bed and gone over to the window to pull aside the curtains and look out over the back yard where she saw that, as expected, the back gate was shut, the yard was half-lit by light emitted by neighbouring windows but, not as expected, the dark lump of somebody standing underneath her own window interrupted the light and threw a huge shadow across the gate. It was unmoving, but carried the sense that it was *about to move*, and Dorothy was much more frightened by the shadow than she was by the small lump of a figure. She bared her teeth and prepared to scream defiance (but also prepared to draw the curtains violently closed, to shut out the disturbing view), whereupon she opened her eyes and was instantly back in bed, looking fearfully around the room, which looked just as it always did.

This had happened to her before, even before George had died, the dream of waking, and then the true waking, sometimes the dream followed by another dream, and sometimes by yet another, and each time she thought she awoke, only to find that the blackness in which she thought she opened her eyes was in her own mind, again, and again, until she finally awoke coated in a sheen of sweat, convinced that she had been locked rigid, unable to move, for hours. But on those occasions she had never really known what she had been frightened of, beyond the depth of darkness, and now she knew that what she was frightened of was George, her own husband, the man with whom she had shared her life for more than twenty years.

Tears welled in her eyes. How had it come to this, lying afraid to sleep in her lighted room, a stranger in the house reading through George's stories? She suddenly remembered seeing Melanie's bleak face reflected in the window. What was the matter with Melanie? She had forgotten to talk to her. What sort of mother would forget to talk to her own daughter?

She heard Tully's voice downstairs, though she could not make out his words. He spoke for less than a minute. Stopped. Who could he possibly be calling at this time of night? She rubbed at her eyes and closed them again, trying to sleep. Then she jerked them open yet again, and yet again the room looked just as it always did, perhaps just a little colder, a little less inviting than normal, in the bright electric stillness of the night.

———●———

I had no more occasion to take the last train out of Glasgow, although I am sure that it still waits, slumbering, until the last possible minute before grumbling off into the darkness. I am fairly sure George White still starts at the front end of the train and works slowly towards the rear. But I have no idea whether Hamish Rackham still appears in the corner seat of the third carriage just before the railway tunnel. Why don't you take the trip and see?

Remember – corner seat of the third carriage. As you come away from the beach and swing down towards the tunnel, scant minutes before arriving at Ayr, be sure to be looking out of the window.

Tully added George and Hamish to his list, along with Frances and (for the second time), Jim. This from 'The Ticket Collector', which featured the appearance of a spectre in one particular seat of the last train from Glasgow to Ayr, a few days before every Christmas. But even though George had used his own name in the story, and even though the strange events of the story took place in a vehicle, Tully didn't feel that there was any real connection between the imaginative world of 'The Ticket Collector', and the grim reality of Harry's taxi and the Viviani household after George's death.

He quickly scanned through 'The Thirteenth Bookshelf', which told the story of a man who built bookshelves in his house, and afterwards discovered that the thirteenth shelf in one particular old room never seemed to contain the books that he thought he had put there, but a weird collection of mythical and semi-mythical volumes (at this point Tully glanced up at the bookshelves ranged across two walls of the sitting room, unable to resist counting them; from top to bottom, there were only eleven); two more children's stories—one called 'Teddies', in which a girl called Claire had a strange and scary experience when her teddies came to life and turned out not to be very pleasant, and the other titled 'The Scariest Moment'.

> Bradley wrote: 'The light was on, but it was the only light on in the whole school, and the streetlight outside was broken. In the silence, while old Cobbers caught his breath and I said nothing, we heard a faint noise, coming closer, up the dark corridor outside the room.
>
> It sounded like *click-scrape, click-scrape*.
>
> I'm sure you remember that noise. Do you? It was the noise Bobby Wilson used to make when he walked along! And old Cobbers at first frowned at me, probably thinking it was some prank of mine, and then his red face turned white as he saw that I was terrified.
>
> "It isn't me," I screamed at him. "It isn't me!"
>
> We listened for a few moments more. *Click-scrape, click-scrape*, coming steadily up the corridor, sounding exactly like it did when Bobby Wilson came in late in the morning.

"Come on, lad," whispered old Cobbers, and he grabbed me by the shoulder and shoved me out of the classroom, and followed close behind, and as soon as we were in the corridor we took off like a pair of champion racehorses.'

There was Bobby again, or Bob, and there was another story which turned on a sound, this time the limping sound made by a young boy in school corridors. Something stirred in Tully's memory as Cobbers stared at young Bradley and Bradley screamed, 'It isn't me! It isn't me!', and he grinned. 'You old rascal,' he told George reprovingly.

'What?' Tully jumped. Dorothy Viviani had come down the stairs, barefoot, wrapped in a blanket. 'Oh, sorry. Didn't mean to make you jump.'

'Is everything all right?'

'Oh yes, I just couldn't sleep. You know.' She indicated the laptop. 'How're you getting on?'

'Fine, fine.'

'What did you mean, "you old rascal"?'

Tully shifted uncomfortably. 'Nothing really. Just one of the stories—er, the plot isn't completely original, that's all.'

Dorothy yawned and sat in the sofa opposite Tully, on the other side of the fire. She didn't seem too concerned. 'Oh, there's only so many stories, aren't there? So many plots?'

Tully made an indeterminate noise.

'Don't let me interrupt you,' yawned Dorothy. She laid her head back against the sofa and closed her eyes.

> The car ran smoothly every day, but he was forced to agree that Dorothy was right. The car was cold. It never seemed to get warm.

Tully perked up.

The car became colder. At first it was just whoever was in the back that noticed, but after a while both the front passenger and the driver started to shiver too. It was most peculiar. Melanie said that the car, being white, box-like and cold, was actually a fridge on wheels. "Yes, and behind the seats is the ice-box," said Claire. "It's really cold back there."

This was 'Trouble with Gus', a story about a dog which refused to sit in the back of a family car; and the car was growing colder because (as the main character in the story eventually found out) the dog of the previous car-owner had died, but had clearly decided to stay in the back of the car despite this inconvenience.

> ... and then, he left the ground and was sailing out over the sea. Higher. Higher. The blue sea caught the sun and turned white, then became curiously flat. It wasn't the sea any more. It was a piece of glass, made white by frost, and he was looking out of it towards a house. His house. For some reason he felt immensely sad, and tears trickled from his eyes.

'You remember 'Trouble with Gus'?'

Dorothy opened her eyes. 'Trouble with Gus? Yes, I remember. Oh, I see. You're thinking of the taxi. That's clever. I would never have thought of that. Is there a connection, Mr Tully?'

'I'm not sure, Mrs Viviani.'

> He made sure nobody else was watching, then went to the back of the car and opened it up. A blast of cold air came out. He held out the

second lead, made a sort of unclipping motion with it, and stood back.

"Come on Shu," he whispered. "Good dog. You can come out now."

More names to add to the list. Tully sorted and counted the results:

Harry	6
Claire	6
Melanie	5
Bob/Bobby	4
Dorothy	3
George	3
Jim	2

No other name appeared more than once, but for completeness Tully also highlighted:

Mae	1
Janine	1

He scratched his head. Was coincidence at work, or was it not? He could understand George using his own name, and those of Melanie and Dorothy, but Harry, Mae and Janine all appeared in a single story, and if that was not a coincidence, who was Claire, and who was Bobby?

'Mrs Viviani?'

But Dorothy had rested her head on folded arms and gone to sleep.

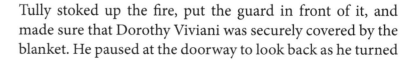

Tully stoked up the fire, put the guard in front of it, and made sure that Dorothy Viviani was securely covered by the blanket. He paused at the doorway to look back as he turned off the light. She didn't stir. With the lights out, shadows from the fire danced crazily across the walls.

Upstairs he paused again at the door to Dorothy's bedroom. Its light was still on. He stood looking at the rumpled bed, at the curtains hanging motionless, at the door to the en suite bathroom. There was nothing out of place, and yet he was uneasy. He would not have been surprised to see the curtains jerk apart, or the bathroom door swing open, or a depression appear in the shape of the bedclothes and hear the bed itself creak as if it was taking some weight. As far as he could tell, it wasn't particularly cold, although because the heating was off and it was the middle of the night—Tully glanced at his watch and corrected himself—because it was the early hours of the morning, neither was it particularly warm. He reached inside the doorway to turn off the light and continued up the second flight of stairs to the guest room.

Downstairs, Dorothy dreamed that she was in a car driving towards the sunset. First she dreamed that she was driving; she wasn't sure who she was, but her hands were strong and masculine on the steering wheel, not that she needed to do much steering as the road was wider than any road she had ever seen before, and straighter, and there was no other traffic. As she guided the car towards the sunset she knew, without consciously thinking about it, that there was somebody with her in the passenger seat, and somebody else sitting behind. It was warm and peaceful; the sun didn't blind her but whether that was because it wasn't very strong sunlight or because she was wearing sunglasses, it was difficult to tell.

Then she dreamed that she was sitting in the passenger seat of the same car, leaning her head back against the headrest, listening to something, either tyre noise or music, she couldn't tell which. It was comfortable; the minimal movement and sway of the car easing her towards sleep, and she saw the lids of her eyes slide down, saw the shape of the windscreen superimposed on the inside of her lids, which were swimming with red motes transfixed by the setting sun.

Finally she dreamed that she was sitting in the back of the car. She was very young and the figures in front of her, the driver and the other passenger, were much older, and bigger. She watched the hands of the driver, relaxed on the steering wheel, occasionally making some small adjustment. She saw the silhouette of the other passenger slip sideways, sleeping. When she turned her head she saw white asphalt blurring past, uninterrupted by marks or intersections or by other traffic, and she understood that this was a trip that would never end because they were chasing the sun as it set, chasing it across the curve of the world forever, and she was happy, because the inside of the car was warm and comfortable and nothing from outside could ever touch her or hurt her or influence her in any way.

Just before he went to sleep, at nearly three o'clock in the morning, the restless brain of Cheyne Tully reminded him that the girl Melanie was planning to go up to Glasgow later that day, to meet up with somebody called Claire.

Chapter 14

At five past eleven Melanie got out of a taxi in front of the Laburnum Crescent apartments—not Harry McCabe's taxi; he had telephoned early in the morning to apologise, but he had decided not to go back to Glasgow immediately, a piece of news which had Dorothy chuckling to herself as she fixed breakfast for Melanie and herself (not for Cheyne Tully, who had yet to stir). In any case, even if Melanie had gone up in Harry's taxi, she had planned to have him drop her off at a random spot some way distant from Laburnum Crescent, because the last thing she wanted was for him to start wondering why she wanted to be taken just round the corner from the spot where her father had died.

She had tried to doze on the Glasgow train but found herself too keyed up by the prospect of meeting Claire, whoever she was exactly. Outside Glasgow Central she had got into a plain black taxi and her heart had jumped and pounded when, about ten minutes later, it turned into Bedford Road, and about two minutes after that it turned right into Laburnum Crescent, and she saw out of the left window a flower shop sandwiched between a newsagent and a Chinese takeaway. They swung round the corner too quickly for her to make out names, bumping past a convenience store with a green facade sitting on the corner, but she felt certain that it was Mae's Flower Shop, and if it was, then that spot on the pavement which she had seen slide past, just there, was where her father had died.

It had been all very well to think about it on the train, to refer in her mind to *just round the corner from the spot where her father had died*, but it was altogether different to actually see the place where he had spent his last moments, toppling into the back of Harry McCabe's taxi. She felt dizzy getting out of her own taxi and staggered slightly (she thought how bizarre it was, that she was getting out of a taxi at more or less the same spot where her father had spent his dying moments getting into one).

The taxi driver, a young coloured man wearing a strange sort of flat turban, asked if she was all right. She thanked him and paid him, and the taxi roared off without bothering to turn around, heading for the alternative exit from Laburnum Crescent into Bedford Road.

In Ayr, Tully finally got up and came downstairs, yawning. Dorothy Viviani enquired if he had slept well, and asked what he would like for breakfast. Tully replied that he had indeed been very comfortable; he requested just tea and toast, claiming that was what he always had for breakfast, and asked whether Melanie had left.

'Ages ago,' said Dorothy. 'Not with your taxi driver friend, though. He's still next door.'

'Oh,' said Tully. He accepted a cup of tea from Dorothy, stirred in one teaspoon of sugar thoughtfully. 'That sounds like... good news.' He met Dorothy's gaze and they shared a moment of understanding.

'And you?' asked Tully. 'How did you sleep?' He nodded his head towards the next room, the sitting room, and Dorothy gave a slightly embarrassed laugh.

At about the same time, Melanie turned around on the pavement outside the Laburnum block of flats. She saw windows mostly with curtains or blinds drawn shut, a few windows boarded up completely, black and red graffiti sprayed on grey concrete walls; she noticed that two of the doors leading out into the street were boarded up, one of them had been sprayed with random paint, an erect penis had been depicted by somebody on the other one, using bright red curves and a laudable effort at shading.

As she stood there hesitantly, unaware that she was being watched by the young man across the road, she wondered if there had been some kind of mistake. Would her father have visited a place like this? Then she thought, well, she had spoken to Claire using the number on her father's phone, and Claire had confirmed that they had met, and given this address; furthermore, she was damned if she was going to travel all the way up to Glasgow only to turn around and go back again without some attempt to discover what had happened on the day her father had died.

She stepped forward, found #11 *Claire*, just as Claire had said she would, and pressed the buzzer.

'Yes?'

'Er, it's Melanie. I've come to see Claire?'

A pause. Then the door buzzed and clicked and the disembodied voice said: 'First floor.' Melanie pushed the door open, and as she disappeared into the gloomy interior the young man across the road turned away from the window. He knew that the girl with blonde, shoulder-length curly hair was called Melanie, the daughter of a man Claire used to meet, because Claire had told him of her impending visit over breakfast. She had asked what he thought about it, and he had said that it might not be a good idea, which he thought at the time was more committal than saying it might be a good idea, leaning as it did towards a negative opinion, and in any case was better than a completely non-committal shrug, or an answer that consisted of vague words indicating not so much an opinion, but more that he didn't know, or didn't want to express an opinion at all.

He sat down on the sofa, facing away from the window, picked up a copy of *The Revivalist*, and waited.

Tully said: 'Have you got a few minutes, Mrs Viviani?' and added, when she looked at him questioningly, 'You've told me all about the strange stuff that's been happening. Now I want to ask you about the ordinary stuff. I need to fill in a background. All these weird things don't mean anything unless I can put them into some sort of context, some sort of frame of reference.'

'Oh.' Dorothy shrugged slightly and sat down opposite Tully at the big oval table in the dining room. It crossed her mind that the last time she had sat down at the table, it had been with Melanie, in the near darkness, when they talked about a taxi driving down from Glasgow. 'Oh, well, what do you want to know?'

'Tell me where you met, you and your husband.'

'In an office in a local authority,' said Dorothy promptly. She sighed. 'I've always remembered the first time we met, and so did George, but I've been thinking about it these last few... for a while.'

'I'm sure you have,' said Tully.

'He came into the wrong office, actually. But we met up, and we went out and... well.'

'Where did you go on your first anniversary?'

'Nowhere,' said Dorothy. 'We couldn't afford it.' She held up her fingers and started counting. 'Second anniversary—nowhere—I was pregnant with Melanie. Third anniversary—nowhere—Melanie was a few months old. Fourth anniversary—nowhere—George just got a new job and it wouldn't have been a good idea to take holiday. Fifth anniversary—nowhere, although we had planned to go to Jersey. George hurt himself and was laid up in bed.'

'Oh?'

'He was making shelves—not here, we hadn't moved up here yet—anyway he fell off a ladder and landed with the small of his back on the arm of a chair.'

Tully winced.

'He was in bed for almost three weeks. He wrote one of his stories then, I don't know if you read it, 'The Thirteenth Bookshelf'?'

'I read it,' said Tully.

'Anyway,' said Dorothy with an air of having said the same thing many times before, 'it wasn't until we had been married for six years that we managed to get away for an anniversary. Malta. We left Melanie with James and Helen—they were still married, then—and went to Malta.'

'James?' asked Tully.

'George's brother,' explained Dorothy.

'Do you ever call him Jim?' asked Tully.

'Not usually,' said Dorothy Viviani.

'When did you move up here?'

'When Melanie was ten, just before she started secondary school—academy. George got another job, and we moved up to be close to his mother, who was very ill. She died two years later.'

'Tell me about tulips.'

'George was allergic to roses.'

'He bring them often?'

'Oh, well, yes. Every birthday. Every Valentine's Day.'

'Every time he went to Glasgow?'

'Oh, well, no. Just sometimes.'

The telephone shrilled. Dorothy jumped, then went to answer it. While he was temporarily alone, Tully took the opportunity to butter more toast and pour another cup of rapidly cooling tea.

<hr />

As she climbed up the steps, Melanie wondered why there had been a slight pause before the door had clicked open and the voice had said *first floor*. Presumably the voice belonged to Claire. Perhaps she paused because she was thinking about having second thoughts, about not meeting up at all. It didn't really matter, thought Melanie, as she emerged into a dingy first-floor vestibule, lit only by an ancient yellow light bulb. It didn't matter because whatever had gone before, here she was crossing towards the door marked number eleven, and even as she did so, the door was starting to open. It didn't matter because, whether or not either of them had had second thoughts about meeting up, here they were about to meet up.

'You're Melanie?'

'Yes. Claire?'

The girl was shorter than Melanie. She had bright red hair into which she had interlaced a handful of green ribbons. She was wearing some sort of green wrap-around, bangles on her left arm, a tiny black mini-skirt, and black boots. Her appearance, although Melanie couldn't possibly know it, was quite different from her usual appearance. Earlier, Lucy had taken one look at her and burst into peals of laughter. 'What do you look like?' she had asked, and then—realising the answer to the question almost before she had finished asking it—she burst into laughter again.

Claire didn't quite know why she had dressed up in the manner which, curiously, hardly any of her clients liked. Perhaps she was trying to scare Melanie away, not that that made much sense. Perhaps she was trying to make herself look contemptible to Melanie, not that she could think of a reason why she would want to do that either. She just didn't know. A long time afterwards it occurred to her that the way she had dressed might have affected what Melanie thought of her father; Melanie might have looked at her through George's eyes, and wondered exactly what it was George had seen in her.

'You better come in,' she said.

She tottered backwards, unused to the boots, and Melanie followed. While Melanie closed the door and looked round the tiny flat (Claire noticed that her eyes lingered on the double bed), she rummaged in her bag and found the clipping Caroline had given her.

'Here.' She passed it over. 'Better make sure. That's him, yes?'

Melanie glanced at the photograph, nodded.

'I called him George,' said Claire.

'I called him... father,' whispered Melanie.

For the first time it occurred to Claire that passing over the photograph within the confines of the tawdry flat might not have been a very sensitive thing to do. She made a vague gesture and said, 'You better sit down. You all right?' She sat down in the wicker chair and watched as Melanie perched on one corner of the bed, putting a hand down first and then lowering herself tentatively, as if worried that the coverlet and duvet might be red hot.

'But why did he come here?' asked Melanie, her voice barely audible.

'I think you know why.'

'Yes, but why here?'

'Oh, that.' Claire shrugged. 'I don't know. I advertise on the internet.'

'Yes, yes, of course,' said Melanie, as if that made sense of everything.

'I liked him,' said Claire.

Was Claire good-looking? Melanie found it hard to decide. She certainly looked very striking. She wasn't unpleasantly fat, in fact she was possibly the wrong side of slim, and as Melanie gazed at her a different sort of Claire seemed to emerge; the same Claire, dressed in the same clothes with the same flaming red hair, but when Melanie tried to ignore these obvious features and look more closely for the real Claire, she saw a young woman whose eyes were tired, whose hands clasped nervously, who tried to give the appearance of regarding her, Melanie, with an older, world-weary look, but Melanie suddenly saw that the assurance was eggshell thin. As the silence stretched, it was Claire who became discomfited, turning away to rummage in her bag again.

'Look,' she said, producing a week-to-view diary and shifting slightly so that Melanie could see the names inside. Stuart. Grafter. Adrian. George. Pieterson. Brian. Adonis. More than twenty names, perhaps as many as thirty, spread out across the pages as she turned them. Most were first names (Claire said she guessed about half of them were genuine); some were surnames (she guessed none of them were genuine); a very few were fictional names. Every name had a number by it. 'See,' said Claire. 'Ten means someone I like, someone I trust. Five means someone I'm not sure of. One means a bastard.'

'You give them scores?'

Claire rubbed at her chin, slightly embarrassed. 'It's easy to get them muddled up.'

'My dad?'

'He gets a ten. See?'

'Adonis gets a two,' remarked Melanie.

Claire remembered Adonis all right. There was no chance of her forgetting him. There was no chance of him visiting her again, either.

'How often...? My dad...?'

'I thought you might ask that. Five. Five times over the last eighteen months.'

They sat together, Melanie on the bed, Claire twisted slightly on the wicker chair so that she could show Melanie the diary. An observer might have taken them for two friends poring over a glossy magazine.

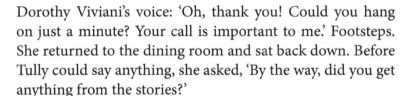

Dorothy Viviani's voice: 'Oh, thank you! Could you hang on just a minute? Your call is important to me.' Footsteps. She returned to the dining room and sat back down. Before Tully could say anything, she asked, 'By the way, did you get anything from the stories?'

'Not sure. D'you know anyone called Claire?'

'Claire? No... no, I don't think so. Did you enjoy them?'

'Yes, I did. Bob, or Bobby? '

'Why do you ask?'

Tully explained the tenuous links he had discovered, and showed Dorothy the list of names. Dorothy frowned.

'George may have called James Jim, when they were alone together. I could ask him. Maybe George knew a Claire or a Bobby at work. I don't know. I suppose I could find out.'

'How has your daughter been?'

Dorothy didn't answer, but locked her hands between her knees.

'Was she happy at school?'

'Yes, yes.'

'She's nineteen, I think you said last night?'

'Yes.'

'She wasn't bullied?'

'Oh, no.'

'Did she do well at school?'

'Yes, yes, she did.'

'Has she got a boyfriend?'

'I think—I don't... Why do you ask, Mr Tully?'

'You'd be surprised,' said Tully, 'at how often something happens or seems to happen, when there's a young person involved. Especially if they're aged between, oh, about fourteen and twenty.' He had lost count of the number of times he had made this remark. Dorothy stared at him.

'But,' she said, and stopped. Tully waited patiently. Dorothy tried again. 'You think that Melanie... has something to do with... well, with what's been happening?'

'It's possible.'

'But... but what about your friend's taxi? How could Melanie have anything to do with that?'

'We don't exactly know what was happening with Harry's taxi. Yes, it's very unlikely that Melanie had anything to do with it, whatever it was. In fact, it's entirely possible that whatever is happening here has nothing at all to do with

Harry's taxi. Yes, I know.' Tully held up a hand as Dorothy started to protest. 'You and I think that's very unlikely, too. But take it from me, a sceptical outsider will not believe that anything was really wrong with the taxi, beyond something mechanical, and therefore will not accept that driving to this house—this house specifically—had anything to do with the problem going away. A sceptical outsider will not believe that anything unusual is happening at this house, either, and that being the case, how can any link be made to the taxi? Link what to what? Nothing to nothing? You see what I mean, Mrs Viviani?'

Dorothy nodded slowly.

'But let's say the sceptical outsider is wrong. Let's say that there is a link, something to do with your husband; after all that's why you contacted me in the first place. Driving the taxi to Ayr has solved the problems with the taxi, but why has it created more problems? Let me put it another way. Harry is happy with his taxi now, but all is not happy with the house, is it, Mrs Viviani?'

Dorothy shook her head.

Tully leaned forward.

'Well, why isn't it? This was a happy house, a happy family. Everything you've told me and everything I can see with my own eyes tells me that. George was happy here. He's found a way home. He's found his way back to his family. So why, Mrs Viviani, isn't he happy?'

Dorothy stared at him, mesmerised.

'There's anger here; there's fear, I think. There's darkness and repressed violence. There's no happiness, is there? So, I have to ask myself, do all these things emanate from George at all? You're not happy, of course you're not happy, but there's nothing unusual in that. Normal unhappiness doesn't generate—' Tully paused '—the things you've been telling me. You see the way my thoughts are going, Mrs Viviani? If it's not your husband and it's not yourself, then is it something to do with your daughter? Now, Mrs Viviani, do you see why I'm asking?'

Dorothy twisted her hands together. Her face was white. 'I should have spoken to her,' she whispered.

'What?'

'There's something the matter with her. I saw her face in the window, she looked so... oh, I don't know, but I should have spoken to her and I forgot.'

'You saw her face reflected in a window?'

Dorothy nodded.

'And she was, what? Upset? Distraught?'

'More than that. I don't know. Desperate. Forlorn. I don't know.' Dorothy was struck by a sudden thought. 'Are you telling me that if I had spoken to her, none of this might have happened?'

'No, Mrs Viviani, I can't tell you that. It's a possibility among many others, that's all.' Tully leaned forward. He was getting to the nub of it now. 'Tell me about George,' he said softly.

Dorothy looked at him helplessly; he knew what she was thinking. She was wondering how she could sum up her husband, who she had lived with for all those years; sum up the essence of a person who had been part of her life, package him up in a few words and deliver him to this stranger, this young man who she scarcely knew and about whose abilities (Tully thought) she was probably still sceptical. She opened her mouth to say something, but then closed it again and gave her head a tiny, frustrated shake. Her gaze fell on the plate and cup in front of Tully.

'More tea and toast?'

'Thank you.'

He knew that she asked to give herself time to think, but that was all right. He needed time to think too. He looked at his watch. Almost twelve o'clock. He needed to speak to Melanie, that was certain. He didn't see how she could be the root cause of what was happening. Mrs Viviani was right about that: events in the taxi could scarcely have been instigated by Melanie, particularly as when the events started she had no idea of which taxi her father had died in, and no idea where it was located. But perhaps once something had started, she somehow acted as a conduit or amplifier, pulling events in an unnatural direction because... because what? That was what he had to find out.

He glanced at his watch again and gave an irritated frown when he remembered that he had just done that. It crossed his mind that Melanie had gone to see somebody called Claire, but then dismissed the possibility of there being a connection between Claire (Melanie's friend in Glasgow) with Claire (George's story) as being wildly improbable.

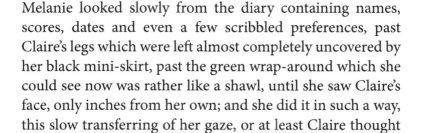

Melanie looked slowly from the diary containing names, scores, dates and even a few scribbled preferences, past Claire's legs which were left almost completely uncovered by her black mini-skirt, past the green wrap-around which she could see now was rather like a shawl, until she saw Claire's face, only inches from her own; and she did it in such a way, this slow transferring of her gaze, or at least Claire thought that she did it in such a way, that her thoughts were clear and her manner showed disdain verging on contempt.

'Don't!' she said, suddenly angry, her pale face suddenly flushed.

'What?'

'Don't judge me. Just don't!'

'What?'

'My mum left when I was eight. Do you think I want to do this? My dad's an alcoholic. Do you think I do this because I want to? My big sister stays with a gangster and my little sister's still at school. Who pays the bills? I do.' By now Claire was shouting. 'D'you think I can get a job to keep the whole family? D'you?'

Melanie gazed at her in bewilderment and dismay. Where was all this anger coming from?

'Just don't judge me, okay? Just don't pretend you're any better than me, okay?' Claire was breathing heavily, and before she could think any better of it, she added: 'Just look at what your own father got up to, all right?'

Melanie's face closed.

Claire made a gesture, pushed herself back in the wicker chair, snapped shut the diary in an abrupt fashion that indicated she wished that she had never shown it to Melanie. 'You just don't know,' she said. 'You don't know what it's like.'

'Oh, don't I?' whispered Melanie. This time she whispered not because she was nervous or overcome with sadness, but because of barely contained fury. 'You knew my dad, okay, you knew my dad, but you don't know me, okay? Keep my dad out of it, he's... he's not here, is he? I'm here.' Melanie gave a brittle laugh. 'I wasn't judging you. Listen, I'm not... I can't...I couldn't judge anybody. Look.' With an angry movement she shrugged off her coat, crossed her arms and pulled off her top. Claire's eyes widened as she saw the scars. Melanie laughed again, the brittle note tinged with hysteria. 'See? See what I think of myself? So how...? Don't tell me I don't know what it's like, okay?'

She glared wildly at Claire, whose own anger had turned to shock. Both of them felt their hearts race, felt the atmosphere in the tiny room crackle as if charged with electricity. Then the door shuddered and they heard a dull noise, a slow boom, if sounds can be said to be slow; Melanie and Claire exchanged a glance as the sound faded. They heard the blast of a car horn, and an engine roaring, almost immediately growing fainter and dying away. The two girls eyed each other uncertainly, their anger dissipated.

Melanie: 'What was that?'

Claire, dubiously: 'Someone left, banged the outside door?'

Melanie shivered and reached for her top. 'You've heard it before?'

Claire didn't answer. She jumped up, went to the door of the flat. She looked back once at Melanie, then steeled herself and yanked it open. There was nobody there. She closed the door again, gently. 'It happened once before,' she said. 'Maybe twice, I can't remember.' She went back to stand by Melanie as she struggled back into her top.

'Why would you do that?' she asked, her eyes indicating Melanie's upper arms, where the scars were now safely hidden from view. Melanie stood up and put her coat back on. She caught sight of Claire's diary perched on a corner of the dressing table; it flashed into her mind that there were thirty names in there, probably more if she looked back far enough. She snorted.

'What?'

'Adonis. I knew one. I bet he'd only score one on your scale. Zero.'

Claire looked at her curiously.

'But he was, like, just one. Just one. And he's in the past now.' Her mind cleared; she thought with distaste of the little box concealed in her own dressing table at home. She realised that she didn't need it any more and gave her head a tiny shake, the only outward evidence of inward amazement. She hadn't been at all sure what she would get out of this meeting with Claire, but whatever it was, she thought it would be something to do with her father, something to explain what had happened to him in the last minutes of his life; she certainly hadn't expected that meeting Claire would put her own problems into perspective.

'I'm not going to do it any more,' she said, suddenly certain of it.

'It wasn't anything to do with... you know, with your dad.'

'No.' Melanie blinked. Her father. She glanced across at the door to the flat, which was in shadow as Claire's room was long and thin and the door was at the opposite end to the narrow window. It didn't move. It looked like an ordinary door. There were no more strange sounds. 'When I called, you thought I was my dad, didn't you?'

Claire nodded.

'But you knew—I mean, you already knew he was dead, didn't you?'

'Yes.'

'Then why did you shout at me—at him—to leave you alone?'

Claire looked at Melanie helplessly for a moment, then leaned over to pick up her own coat from where it had been lying on the bed. 'I don't want to stay here,' she said. 'Shall we go and have lunch?'

Melanie trailed after her as she marched, slightly unsteadily in the seldom-used boots, to the door.

'I want to know. Why you said that.'

'All right, all right,' said Claire. 'Let's just get out of here first, all right?'

They went across the road to collect the young man, who bobbed his head awkwardly and smiled at Melanie but (Melanie could not help but notice) had eyes only for Claire. She wasn't sure how she felt about having a stranger join them for lunch, when they would talk about her father and her father's death, but then it occurred to her that Claire was really nothing more than a stranger despite the revelations they had already shared, and in any case she found the young man extraordinarily unobtrusive. Most of the time she barely noticed that he was there.

She was not entirely surprised when Claire told her what had been going on at the flat; she had deduced something of the sort after Claire had screamed at her on the phone. She was not surprised, but she was amazed and not a little fearful. At one point they were discussing the strange lights and Claire's feeling that someone or something was trying to get to her through the door, into her flat; Melanie shivered, but then thought to ask why her father, if it was her father, would be trying to do that, and Claire looked coy and suggested that she already knew the answer, at which point the young man made his presence felt by asking whether it was possible that events at Ayr, which Melanie had described in some detail, were triggered by fear—fear of being found out.

'He's been found out,' remarked Claire.

'Not by Mum,' said Melanie.

'Are you going to tell her?'

'Of course not.'

The young man observed in a diffident, offhand tone of voice that when people were afraid they often lashed out, flailed out, uncertain and terrified. At least they did when they were alive, he added. He went on to suggest that Melanie's father was not trying to reach Claire for the reasons Claire implied, but was in fact angry, furious with her because it was their unaccustomed activity (unaccustomed to him, at any rate) which had set off his heart attack shortly afterwards.

Claire giggled, but then fell silent as she remembered how frightened she had been, frightened at the intensity of what she thought had been happening.

'Perhaps,' she said, and fell into a reverie while she tried to work out whether she had been frightened before Caroline had showed her the newspaper clipping about George, and if she had, what it was exactly that had frightened her; but it was all a bit of a blur. She knew that after seeing the clipping, she had been frightened that George was somehow trying to come back to her, but she could not quite remember whether she had been frightened before seeing the clipping. She thought it weird, astonishing and frightening that something strangely similar had been going on down in Ayr; she also found it oddly reassuring. This thought prompted her to look at Melanie, who had fallen into a reverie of her own (she was trying to decide how she felt about her father seeing this girl, secretly, especially in light of an earlier part of her conversation with Claire:

'So, what do you think of your dad?'

'What do you mean?'

'Are you angry?'

'No.'

'Are you disgusted?'

After a pause: 'No.'

'Well, why not?'

'I don't know.'

'Most daughters would be ashamed, angry, disgusted. They would be ranting and raving at me.'

'I suppose so.'

'Is it because he's dead?'

'But if it wasn't you, it would have been someone else.'

'So what?'

'So I'm not angry at you. What would be the point?'

'But your dad?'

And the point was, Melanie could see it now—the point was that she would have ranted and raved at her father if only she had been able to; she would have felt angry, ashamed— perhaps disgusted was too strong a word—at his deceit and betrayal of her and especially of her mother; but the truth was that she rather liked Claire and her father was only human, and now that he was dead everything was different. It didn't seem to matter so much. If he had still been alive and she had found out about Claire, would she still have loved him? She knew that she would).

Meanwhile Claire, in her mind's eye, saw again the cuts on Melanie's arms; she looked over at the young man, and remembered the way he had said that his mother had killed his father, and how he had put his head on one side. She barely remembered her own mother. She sniffed suddenly, and when both Melanie and the young man looked at her, she said something which all of them would remember for the rest of their lives. She said: 'We've all got our ghosts, haven't we?' and both Melanie and the young man instantly grasped not only what she meant but the inherent truth of her words. Melanie even leaned forward to say to Claire:

'Yes, even my father,' and Claire nodded and looked down, picking non-existent fluff from her shawl, refusing to meet Melanie's eyes.

After lunch they went back to the young man's flat where Melanie admired his paintings, especially the one of Claire peeking out from behind a tree. Then they decided to go out to a coffee shop at the far end of Bedford Road, one that Melanie knew about because it was situated in an area cluttered by bookshops and so was frequented by students. In fact when they got there Melanie bumped into two friends, a blonde girl of her age studying to be a doctor, and her boyfriend, who was two years older and was taking a master's degree in some obscure subject related to archaeology. They ordered coffee and cakes, and the blonde girl's boyfriend kept looking at Claire, which both Claire and the blonde girl noticed; and Melanie smiled inwardly and wondered what her friends would say if they knew who Claire was, and at the same time she couldn't quite believe that she was sitting in the coffee shop, chatting away with the girl her father used to secretly visit.

Her own dark mood was dispelled, and she laughed, and suggested that they move on to another place which she knew, and they did, none of them noticing that the young man from Laburnum Crescent paid for everything and years later, that afternoon remained crystal clear in Melanie's memory, almost every word, every gesture, every surreptitious glance and the play of expressions across all their faces; but it was Claire that she remembered best, Claire's shining eyes, happy to be part of this impromptu group; her laugh; her outrageous clothing. It occurred to Melanie that Claire had made her father happy, and that they had been friends. As the afternoon wore on, she felt glad that her father had met Claire, even though at the same time she was sorry that he had met her; and so it was Claire that she best remembered afterwards, even though she met up with her friends on several subsequent occasions, but she never saw Claire again.

Chapter 15

Dorothy went out shopping in the afternoon and it wasn't until she was half way up the High Street that she realised she had gone out and left a perfect stranger alone in the house. She stopped for a moment to think about it; several pedestrians experienced moments of pavement rage as they had to swerve sharply to avoid a collision. Having thought about it, she shrugged. She found she had no fear whatsoever that Tully would bag the family jewels and make a run for it, not that the Viviani family had much in the way of family jewels. She went into Safeway and tried to remember what she had written on her shopping list which she had, as usual, left behind.

Almost as soon as Dorothy had left the house, Tully gathered up the paper copies of the stories from the briefcase Melanie had brought him, and went upstairs to Dorothy's bedroom. The house was very quiet. Tully knew that the High Street was a mere five minute walk away, and yet he could hear no traffic, no roadworks. He could hear nothing at all. He sat down in the single armchair in Dorothy's bedroom and closed his eyes.

───●───

Later, he went for a long walk along the beach, where he saw a few couples strolling hand in hand, a number of wellington-booted, anorak-wearing dog walkers with a variety of dogs ranging from a microscopic terrier of some sort which appeared to be out of its depth the moment it entered the water to an enormous creature which looked as though it was covered in wool rather than hair, and which bounded up to Tully, wagging its stumpy tail furiously. Its owner apologised to Tully as they passed each other further down the beach, saying that Leo was firmly convinced not only that everyone was his friend, but also that everyone carried dog biscuits around with them.

He stood for a long time watching giant blue diggers unloading something (which might have been coal, but it was hard to tell from the other side of the harbour) from an extremely rusty ship, swinging gigantic loads high through the air, watched not only by Tully but also by a small boy balanced on the wall at the end of the beach, his mother holding him safely in place with one hand. She was holding an even smaller child against her hip with the other hand, and Tully admired her dexterity, restraint and stamina.

He returned to the Viviani household and ate something that Dorothy Viviani had prepared for tea—long afterwards he couldn't remember what it was, but he fancied it might have been pizza—and he helped clear up the tea things, and also fetched in coal from the back yard when Dorothy decided to light the fire in the sitting room. And quite a long time after the sun had set, so that shadows were already crawling around the old Edwardian house, he and Dorothy Viviani sat in front of the television, ostensibly watching the news.

Melanie had called just after tea. Dorothy Viviani said: 'Hello? Oh, hello, dear. Where are you? Oh, I see. Did you? That was nice. Oh no, that's a pity. Yes, why don't you do that, we'll just... No, I'll leave it unlocked. Bye, dear, not the third carriage, remember.' She hung up. 'That's a family joke,' she told Tully.

'I understand.'

'You do? Oh, well, yes, I see.'

'Your daughter's still in Glasgow?'

'Yes. Apparently she had a great time, met up with friends. Then she missed a train by five minutes and the next one's cancelled.'

Tully made a sympathetic noise, although what he really felt was frustration. He felt that he really needed to speak to Melanie, because he felt that somehow she was the vortex of the tension coiling around the old house, but he wouldn't know until he could speak with her—something which she knew perfectly well, because he had told both Melanie and Dorothy yesterday that he would need to speak to them individually; and here she was staying away in Glasgow to all hours. He was irritated, not sympathetic.

'Anyway she's going to have something to eat and catch a later train.'

'I see,' said Tully.

The newsreader announced that a bomb had gone off in (here she made an unintelligible noise which Tully assumed must represent the name of the place where it had exploded, but he had never heard of it and was unlikely to remember such a complicated fusion of consonants); she went on to give some detail about the bomb, such as how many had been killed by it, and who was suspected of setting it off, but Tully wasn't listening. He was thinking about Dorothy Viviani's room upstairs, and he was thinking that although he had been shocked and surprised by the unexpected appearance of a face with bulging eyes, he hadn't felt especially threatened.

He leaned back and closed his eyes, trying to tune out the television, which was now showing a vociferous demonstration outside the Houses of Parliament. But the more he tried to tune it out, the more it intruded. He opened his eyes again in time to see two Members of Parliament arguing with each other and with a young female reporter who was beginning to look exasperated at not being able to get a straight answer from either of her interviewees, and reflected, as he often reflected when he saw the news, that if he could time-hop backwards a year or so, or even forwards into the future, then unless something particularly remarkable had happened—in other words, for the vast majority of days—the news would be almost identical.

He shivered suddenly and swung round. Dorothy Viviani asked what the matter was, but instead of answering he jumped up and went to the window. Outside was pitch darkness.

'The streetlight isn't working,' he said.

On the way back to the sofa he poked at the fire and the dancing shadows rose higher, doing battle with the flickering radiance from the television, on which an attractive pig-tailed girl, billed as an economics expert, was giving her opinion on what should be done to improve the economic lot of the country in general, and the unemployed in particular.

'That happened before?' asked Tully.

Dorothy thought for a moment. 'Not that I remember,' she said.

Before she went out shopping, Tully had suggested that she bought a tulip, or a bunch of tulips, and took them up to her bedroom that night. Fortunately she had remembered to get them. Tully had told her about a case of about three years ago when a woman who had gone out for her shopping had been knocked over and killed by a road sweeper ('Damned unlucky, that,' Tully had said. 'It was only travelling at about five miles an hour.'), and afterwards there had been a lot of trouble at the family home, some of it very similar to what was happening at the Viviani house, but also the lights kept going on and off, sometimes in one room, sometimes in another, sometimes in several rooms at the same time, or even all the lights of the house flicking on and off simultaneously ('The confirmed sceptic,' Tully had said, 'would point out that there was clearly something wrong with the wiring').

In desperation the husband, who was a self-employed tennis coach ('A surprising choice of careers,' Tully had remarked, 'in Scotland.') called in Tully, and after talking to everybody about exactly what had happened on the day the woman had been knocked over, he discovered that the main reason she had been going out to the shops was to buy a bulb for her bedside table light, something which ('for obvious reasons,' Tully said sombrely) the bereaved husband had never got round to doing. The point was, Tully had explained to Dorothy Viviani, that when he did buy a light bulb and fitted it into the bedside light, the problems stopped instantly, which just went to show that sometimes the simplest actions could solve apparently intractable problems and it was just possible, Tully further explained, that the problems in the Viviani household could be solved simply by providing Dorothy with tulips, just as George had wanted.

'Tulips?' Dorothy had said.

'Tulips,' Tully had confirmed.

'And by taking up some tulips, all these... everything, oh, you know what I mean, will stop?'

'I didn't say that,' Tully had said. 'It might. If it was the only thing to consider, it might. I need to talk to your daughter, though, because I'm not sure it is the only thing to consider. I think I'm missing something. Oh, Mrs Viviani?'

'Yes?'

'Take up a copy of your agreement with Barker Associates too. He would have wanted to share that with you.'

'Yes,' said Dorothy sadly. 'Yes, he would have.'

Now, Tully looked sideways at Mrs Viviani while the television news cycled back to the explosion in an unpronounceable city and proceeded to give an update which, as far as Tully could ascertain, was precisely the same as the previous update, apart from the fact that the number of casualties had increased slightly, and the newsreader's voice had correspondingly become even more grave, while the interviewer at the unpronounceable scene egged various officials into giving projections of still higher figures. Mrs Viviani had closed her eyes and Tully couldn't tell if she had fallen asleep.

The fire cracked and spat blue flames.

They were waiting for Melanie, thought Tully, but the longer they waited, the more he sensed they were actually waiting for something else. More than just shadows coiled in corners out of the reach of firelight, Tully thought fancifully. His heart jumped and pounded when he noticed that the television was showing football, but seconds later the screen switched to another sport, and he realised it was just the news sports summary.

He closed his eyes, feeling the warmth of the fire on his outstretched legs, seeing patterns on the inside of his eyelids, though whether they were caused by the firelight or by the television, or by both, he couldn't tell.

What had happened that afternoon? He had sat down in Mrs Viviani's bedroom and closed his eyes, just as he was closing them now, although he was closing them now because he was trying to recall the details of what happened at that time earlier in the day, whereas he had closed them then not because he was tired but because he was trying to tune in to the atmosphere of the old house now that, in theory at any rate, he was the only person inhabiting it. If he could sense anger, it would not be emanating from Melanie; if he could sense fear, it would not be coming from Dorothy; in fact, if he sensed anything at all then he would have to explain it either in terms of some residual feeling locked into or trapped by the old sandstone walls, or by… something else.

So he had closed his eyes and shifted uncomfortably in the chair, feeling the papers on his lap slip sideways, and discovered that his mind focussed not so much on the atmosphere in the house, but on the stories that George had written…

'Mr Tully?'

He jerked his eyes open. The warmth of the fire and droning television had almost lulled him into sleep.

'I'm going to go upstairs, have a bath, have an early night.'

'Right. Right.'

Dorothy levered herself to her feet. At the doorway into the hall she paused.

'Oh, Mr Tully?'

'Yes?'

'I'm going to use the main bathroom.'

'Right,' said Tully. 'Okay, thanks.'

It wasn't until Dorothy Viviani was half way up the stairs that he realised that she had not really been telling him that she was going to use the main bathroom in case he wanted to go in there; rather, she had been telling him that she was *not* going to use her en suite bathroom, and now he came to think about it, he had to admit he wasn't very surprised.

Melanie decided that she would treat herself to a proper meal rather than grab a fast food something and have to hang around the railway station for the best part of an hour. She bought a book (it was called *Secrets of the Ages*, and afterwards she wished she hadn't bought it, because it was poorly written, poorly researched, and sensationalist in the extreme), and headed out of the station towards one of her favourite restaurants.

She still felt absurdly happy, as if a black miasma that had been clinging to her ever since the business with Graham had finally been swept away and she was left—with grief, certainly; she still missed her father terribly—but it was clean, ordinary grief, untainted with any thoughts that she was worthless and so full of pent up disgust, anger and despair that—well, she wasn't quite sure what, but anyway it had all miraculously been swept away and now she felt, if not happy, then at least at peace with herself. She was going to be late home, but so what? What did that matter?

Dorothy watched as the bath gradually filled with hot, pink-bubbled water. She had locked the door with a slight sense of trepidation, remembering what had happened to Melanie—when was that, exactly? Yesterday? The day before? Dorothy shook her head tiredly. She couldn't remember. But the bath was filling normally enough, the towels were just where she expected them to be, and the door hadn't attempted anything untoward as she locked it. She wasn't quite sure how she would have reacted if the door had done something strange, or if the towels had piled themselves up in places they weren't supposed to be. She wasn't even sure she had the energy to react. She was just so tired. She slid into the hot water and felt it smooth away some of her aches and pains, but it didn't smooth away the tiredness.

The bathroom was almost dark; she had turned down the dimmer switch outside in the hall. George had fitted it himself. Turn it up when you want to read a book, he had said, and she had asked if anybody else even read books in the bath. Turn it down if you just want to soak, he had said. Now Dorothy wiggled her toes to make the hot water move against her skin. *I just want to soak, George*, she thought or she whispered, she wasn't sure which. *I just want to rest. Let me rest, George*. Scented steam drifted from the surface of the water, obscuring her view of most of the bathroom, although she could see the mirror on a cabinet already fogged over, and she could see the outline of the door into the hall, marked by two vertical and two horizontal strips of light in the shape of a rectangle. She must have left the light on in the hall.

She wiggled her toes again, luxuriating in the warmth, and closed her eyes. She heard a car go slowly past outside, no doubt one of the neighbours searching for somewhere to park. It popped into her mind that she had dreamed about being in a car, and almost immediately afterwards she remembered dozing in the car when she was a child. Before the time of seatbelts, she had once told Melanie.

She remembered that her father frequently made up the back seat into a bed so that she could sleep, or doze fitfully, while he drove through the night to London, or Brighton, or wherever it was they were driving, and the world was a grey streak outside the window, intermittently brightened by flashes of headlights of cars going in the opposite direction, and sometimes by rows of yellow streetlights as they wound their way through a small town or village, and whenever her mother spoke, which wasn't often, her voice failed to break the somnambulant sounds of the engine and the wheels on the road, and the wind rushing past the window, and her father's low answering voice merged with these sounds and vanished, and still they drove on.

Melanie wasn't in a car, she thought drowsily. She was on a train, or at least she should be by now. She tried to imagine being on a train, tried to imagine sitting next to Melanie, who normally sat in the leftmost corner of one of the carriage sections, facing forwards even though, as she had once told Dorothy, she knew perfectly well it was supposed to be safer facing the other way so that if the train crashed—well, Dorothy remembered Melanie laughing, if the train crashed it probably wouldn't matter much which way you were facing, despite what people said.

But she couldn't conjure up the right sort of train. Instead she found herself sitting in an old-fashioned carriage, with the wheels giving out a *clickety-clack clickety-clac*k in the way she remembered from her childhood, not that she went on the train very much as a child. It fleetingly crossed her mind to wonder why she kept thinking of her childhood, and even more fleetingly she wondered if it was because it represented a time when she had been happy—of course there had been other times when she had been happy, with George, but by then she had responsibilities which she couldn't even begin to imagine during her childhood—and then, on the old-fashioned train which might actually have been a steam train, she reached out to pull down a blind or unlatch the top of a window, and the hand and arm that reached out were a man's hand and arm, encased in a suit, with the cuffs of a white shirt protruding an inch or so, and the fingers on the hand were thick and sturdy.

She awoke, gasping.

Melanie climbed onto the train a good ten minutes before it was due to depart, hoping that it was the right train and that it wouldn't move off, either to an unexpected destination or, worse, to some obscure railway depot in the middle of nowhere. An elderly couple got on a few moments after she did and asked her if it was the Ayr train. She responded that she certainly hoped so, and the three of them sat for anxious minutes until the electric display came on at the end of the carriage and a voice said, rather musically, Melanie thought, 'This train is for Ayr. This train will call at' and proceeded to list an enormous number of stations, to which neither Melanie nor the elderly couple paid the slightest attention; they all sat back and relaxed, their earlier worries assuaged.

When the train did move off, Melanie looked desultorily through *Secrets of the Ages*, couldn't muster up the enthusiasm to read any more of it, resolved to leave it behind on the train. She couldn't doze. She was too wound up, too full of energy, too excited at how meeting Claire had opened her eyes. Instead she looked out of the window, past the reflection of her face, and watched house lights, streetlights, headlights and other lights she couldn't immediately put a name to, as they slid past and disappeared behind her into the darkness of night.

Dorothy shivered, even though the bath water was still warm against her heated skin. She had only been asleep for a few minutes. Pink bubbles still tickled her chin; steam still floated above the bath and thickened the atmosphere inside the bathroom. But she still shivered. In the corner of the third carriage. She didn't know how she knew, but the cloth of that jacket and the shape and style of that cuff were older still than the steam trains and diesels of her childhood. So what did that mean?

What did that mean?

She turned because she thought she heard something, a dull blow, perhaps a car door outside, perhaps Melanie had come in downstairs although it hadn't sounded like the front door, a sound she would normally recognise. Perhaps Tully was doing something or had dropped something. She didn't know, but the steam made it seem as if the door to the bathroom was shaking, as if in the aftermath of a heavy blow, which she knew was impossible, and the light around the door frame was no longer white but was a deep pink—could the steam from a pink bubble bath also be pink, she wondered—turning deeper even as she watched, until it became red. This time there was no doubt; a dull blow and the door shivering, shuddering. Abruptly the red strips of light vanished, to be replaced by ordinary white electric light.

'Mr Tully?' she called out.

The steam swirled, dissipating. A feeling of pressure vanished, a feeling of pressure which Dorothy hadn't even noticed until it faded away. She found herself sitting bolt upright in the bath, goose pimpled, waiting. Nothing happened. She was confused. She didn't know if she had really seen the door shivering, shuddering, or whether she had dozed off and it had been another dream within a dream. Nothing happened, but the sense of waiting did not go away.

Tully, she knew, was waiting for Melanie.

Something was waiting for *something*.

No, she thought. Not Melanie. Not Melanie.

She was shivering with cold. She climbed out of the bath, wrapped herself in a towel, and after taking an uncertain step towards the door, reached for the handle with a shaking hand.

———●———

Almost as soon as Mrs Viviani left the room, Tully turned the television down so that he could hear a background murmur of voices but couldn't make out what they were saying, leaned back and closed his eyes again. He swivelled his legs towards the warmth of the fire.

The stories.

No, he thought. Not the stories. He had sat down in Mrs Viviani's armchair in Mrs Viviani's bedroom and tried to tune in to the house. But he had started to think about the stories instead.

The stories.

Oh, all right, he thought. The stories, then. The names. The family car which became cold in the back, just like Harry's taxi. He had sat in the armchair, alone in the house, and mentally reviewed the stories which were actually sitting in a briefcase on his lap, just as now they were sitting on his lap in front of the fire, no longer in the briefcase because he had taken them out when he had sat down on the sofa, intending to look through them again, until the fire and the droning television had sent him to sleep.

In the armchair, he almost slept, or almost fell into a trance, the stories revolving through his mind, 'The Flatulent Ghost', 'The Flapping Curtain', 'The Scariest Moment', another one about an old woman who went upstairs when she heard something in the attic and found a mirror with a note on it which said *Don't look in the mirror*, only it was too late because she already had, and a series of horrific events that followed were all linked to the mirror and only came to an end when, unable to face the idea of going anywhere near the cursed mirror again, she set fire to her attic, only to find that the whole house went up in flames.

Tully couldn't remember what that one was called, but he remembered the mad ravings of the old woman almost word for word; at which point his head nodded violently and he woke up or came out of his trance, to find himself looking straight into a face inches from his own, a face with bulging eyes, with bulging cheeks, with fat red bulging lips, in fact the whole face was bulging, even its forehead, its eyes, its chin; another second and perhaps the entire bulging face would have exploded in a fine spray of blood and gristle, but Tully yelled not in fear (or so he told himself a moment later) but in shock and the vision, if it was a vision, vanished as his head cleared.

A thin, high note sounded. At first he had thought it was the sound of someone screaming far away, but when he went to investigate, he discovered the telephone receiver off its hook, warbling discontentedly to itself, and he remembered Dorothy Viviani saying *Your call is important to me*, before she went out to the High Street.

Subconsciously, while he remembered all this, almost asleep, he heard another sound, not a high sound but a thudding noise, and imagined a log falling sideways in the fireplace. He hadn't felt threatened by the face and he didn't know if it was anything to do with George, or whether it was some entirely unconnected phenomenon, maybe linked to the house, or even to himself. There was another sound and his eyelids flickered. A second bang and then a voice. He struggled to open his eyes and saw Melanie framed in the doorway, her hair writhing over her shoulders and across the wall. No, that was just an effect of the flames casting shadows.

'I couldn't...' She was swaying slightly. Tully looked to the shadows for an explanation but no, she really was swaying.

He heaved himself to his feet. 'Uh...'

'The door,' said Melanie. 'It wouldn't shut.' She reached a steadying arm to the doorframe, then appeared to notice Tully for the first time. She frowned. 'Where's Mum?'

'Uh, she went to have a bath...'

'She all right?'

'Yes. Why shouldn't she be?'

A little unsteadily, Melanie took off her coat and threw it onto a chair. She avoided looking at Tully.

'Sorry I'm so late. Train trouble.'

Tully didn't respond. Something about Melanie was different. Sure, her face was flushed and she'd obviously had too much to drink, but there was something else, something more fundamental. He shook his head, trying to clear the vestiges of sleep, trying to think. Melanie still refused to meet his gaze, looking at the television, glancing at the fire, even leaning backwards, staggering slightly, to look back along the hall, as if she was checking that she had actually managed to close the front door, or as if she had heard someone there. She was looking everywhere except at Tully.

'What is it?' he said.

Startled, she turned in his direction.

'There's something,' he said. 'There always was something you weren't telling me. Now there's something else.'

Her eyes flicked away again. 'Of course not,' she mumbled. 'Look, I've got to get changed.'

'Something's different after Glasgow,' said Tully. 'Have you found out something?'

Melanie didn't answer. She leaned tiredly against the doorframe.

'Why did you ask if your mother was all right?'

'Nothing's different,' said Melanie, pushing herself upright. 'I'll be down in a minute.'

She went out into the hall, into an unfamiliar darkness. Jigsaw pieces began to fit together in Tully's head.

... and the streetlight outside was broken...

Footsteps upstairs. Tully remembered hearing a sound earlier. Perhaps that had been Melanie trying to close the front door. But now footsteps, heavy footsteps. He knew before Melanie came back into the room that they weren't her footsteps; they were too heavy and she hadn't had time to reach the top of the stairs. Too heavy for Dorothy too, thought Tully. Too heavy; too heavy; was he really hearing footsteps?

> *I could say* something that sounded like footsteps, *or* I could say I thought I heard something that sounded like footsteps. *But it wouldn't be true.*

Melanie was ashen-faced. 'It isn't me,' she whispered.

Bradley: 'It isn't me! It isn't me!'

Tully started towards her, brushed past her, headed for the stairs. Melanie followed but stopped on the bottom step, her hand resting on the banister, unable to go any further. She was panting; the stairs ran from darkness into light, tilted; she grabbed at the banister with her other hand as the world began to slide sideways. Tully was a black-garbed spider

283

crawling across the wall; her hair streamed horizontally as she clung desperately to the banister with both hands, straining to prevent herself falling into the dark hallway, the mouth of a darker abyss. *No, no, Daddy,* she moaned. *I would never tell.* Nausea gripped her. She couldn't tell whether the wind she heard was real or inside her head.

As Tully ran upwards, he thought he heard a cry but he couldn't tell if it was in front of him or behind—perhaps both; perhaps there were two cries, and he also thought, although afterwards he could not be sure, that he heard a third voice, deeper, a throaty voice, but he might have just imagined it; and he heard another heavy sound, like something banging very, very far away, or like someone falling to a floor.

The papers which Tully had left on the arm of the sofa tilted and shifted, almost as if someone or something had nudged them. They slid slowly at first and then in a rush from the sofa to the floor, spreading out and fluttering to the ground. One sheet of paper, caught in a stray draught, looped a perfect airborne somersault, drifted over the hearth, and landed, face up, in the fire.

> *I am drawn by oblong city lights –*
> *The painful call of something lost;*
> *No-one, no place, no way to understand.*
>
> *Where does the future lie*
> *But in the night, rooted in night,*
> *Hidden in seas of endless night?*
>
> *I will not be alone.*

The edges of the paper, which represented an only copy, curled up, blackened, and burst into flames. Tully had never read it, because he had not noticed it tucked in at the back of the briefcase. Neither Dorothy nor Melanie had ever read it, because they had not known it existed. Nobody had ever read it and now, as the flames crawled inwards to meet at the centre of the sheet, destroying it utterly, nobody ever would.

Melanie's head appeared at floor level as she laboriously clambered the last few stairs. She found herself able to look along the length of the hall and make unexpected eye contact with her mother, who was lying on the floor just outside the bathroom.

'Mum!'

'I'm all right, dear.'

Tully bent over her.

'I slipped, that's all. Wait a minute, Mr Tully. Let me make sure I'm decent.'

Dorothy attempted to fold her towel around her upper body while lying prone on the floor. Melanie started giggling.

'You look like a snake.'

'You sure you're all right, Mrs Viviani?'

'I'm fine. I'm... a bit shook up. I just slipped.'

Behind her, inside the steamy bathroom, Tully could see wet streaks on the floor and a bath stool lying on its side. He helped Dorothy to her feet and she braced herself for a moment against the doorframe of her bedroom, striking almost exactly the same pose that Melanie had downstairs.

Tully looked over her head into the dark bedroom, and then stepped backwards and considered the unlit stairs up to the third floor. Neither Dorothy nor Melanie noticed. Dorothy stumbled forwards into the bedroom, muttering that she would just lie down for a minute, while Melanie leaned back against the wall and closed her eyes.

What Tully had realised was that, in the space of a few seconds as he had run up the stairs, or possibly during an even shorter span of time after he had reached the top, the air of menace coiling around the old house had gone. The darkness was just darkness. The woman tentatively feeling her way into her bedroom was just a woman who had slipped over; she was under no unnatural threat. The girl sprawling at the top of the stairs was a normal, slightly drunk teenager back late from an evening out with friends, exuding nothing, no inner tension, nothing that might initiate any threat.

Suddenly Tully felt like an intruder.

'Uh... I'll make some tea.'

'Cocoa,' said Dorothy Viviani, a little faintly, as she eased herself into bed without turning on any lights.

Tully watched her for a moment, able to see in the radiance from the hallway that she sighed deeply and closed her eyes. He suspected that she would not stay awake long enough for a cup of cocoa. He glanced at the bedroom curtains and the half-open door to the en suite bathroom. He remembered looking into the bedroom, just the evening before, and thinking that he would not have been surprised to see something strange happen—the door inexplicably move, or the curtains open. Now he felt no such sense of strangeness or menace. Whatever it was that had been hanging over the old house and its occupants for the last few weeks had vanished utterly, as if it had never existed.

Melanie roused herself and followed Tully downstairs to the kitchen.

'Sorry,' she said. He divined that she was referring to the way in which she had failed to answer his questions.

'Okay,' he said.

'I don't feel so good.'

Tully grinned. He opened cupboards at random. Eventually Melanie showed him where the tin of cocoa was stored.

'Want some?'

Melanie grimaced and shook her head.

'Must not have been footsteps,' she said. 'Must have been Mum knocking over that stool. And falling over,' she added.

'Could be,' said Tully. He glanced at her out of the corner of his eye, wondering if she realised that the timing wasn't right. He had heard Dorothy falling as he raced up the stairs, which would be when she knocked the stool over. The footsteps, or whatever they were, had sounded long, long seconds before that. It was as a *result* of hearing the footsteps that he had raced up the stairs. He tried to envision Dorothy knocking over the stool in such a way that it bumped repeatedly, sounding like footsteps; tried to envision her not falling over at the same time but some fifteen or twenty seconds later. He supposed it was possible. That was the trouble: something was always possible. He sighed.

'Mr Tully?'

'Nothing. Here, could you take this up to your mum?'

Melanie took the mug and stood for a moment, her head bowed. 'I'll be back down,' she said, and again Tully divined the subtext: we'll talk.

In the living room he picked up the papers which had slipped off the sofa, and poked the fire into some semblance of life, not noticing the handful of paper ashes lying between charred remains of logs. As he sat down, Melanie reappeared.

'She's fast asleep.'

'I thought she might be.'

Melanie perched on the edge of a chair and rubbed at her eyes.

'What's happening, Mr Tully? What's been going on?'

Tully noted that she seemed very tired, but less woozy. He decided on a direct approach.

'Ever since we first met—you remember, when I came with Harry, during the storm...?' She nodded. 'Ever since then I've wondered if something had happened to you, or something was happening to you. Something which you bottled up.'

Melanie looked down at her hands twisting on her lap. She didn't answer.

'I mean, not about your father,' said Tully. 'Something else.' He paused, letting silence work its magic.

'No,' whispered Melanie. Her hands clasped and unclasped. She didn't look up but Tully knew that she knew the lie was obvious. Her shoulders slumped slightly. 'Yes,' she whispered. Then she did look up and said with a touch of defiance, 'But I don't want to talk about it.'

'Okay,' said Tully.

'I wanted to talk to my dad about it,' said Melanie, growing more agitated. 'But he wasn't there. I needed him and he wasn't there. He wasn't there.' Melanie put a hand over her eyes and stopped talking.

'I understand,' said Tully.

More silence. Tully glanced up sharply at a movement in the hallway and almost smiled as the grey ragged-ear cat skipped past.

'I couldn't talk to Mum,' said Melanie in a low voice. 'It was just... something I couldn't talk to Mum about.'

'Okay.' Tully regarded the defensive, huddled posture of the girl sitting opposite, her hand still covering her eyes. He guessed that he would never know what had been troubling her. 'But,' he said, 'something's different now, isn't it? Something's happened.' Inspiration struck him. 'Something happened in Glasgow, is that it, Miss Viviani? You're back late not just because the train was late.'

Melanie nodded and shook her head. 'The train *was* late,' she said, sounding somewhat muffled.

'You know what I mean.'

Melanie uncovered her eyes and looked up. Tully was not surprised to see tears.

What was she supposed to say? That her dad had been seeing a young girl, not just a girl—she made herself think it—an escort, but that she, Melanie, had liked the girl and that talking to her had resolved a whole lot of queries in her own mind, had solved a whole lot of problems which, she now realised, were... not trivial, no, certainly not trivial, but weren't going to produce the calamitous consequences that she had imagined.

No, she couldn't say all that. She couldn't tell Tully about Dr Graham Rowbotham any more than she could have told her mother, and she couldn't tell him about Claire, not even to say that she met somebody her father used to know, as these things had a way of getting out and she dreaded the thought that, sometime in the future, her mother might turn to her and say, 'Dear, I gather you met one of your father's friends in Glasgow that night. Who was it?'

So what was she supposed to say? 'Yes, Mr Tully, but I can't tell you about it, and I'd prefer it if you said nothing to my mother'? Yeah, right, thought Melanie. And then what would Tully report to her mother, and what questions would her mother come up with?

If only she'd been able to talk to her father. He would have sorted it all out. He would have found a way...

Oh. She drew a sharp breath. Oh.

She saw Tully raise an eyebrow at her and before his lips could form a question, she thought of that place on the pavement where her father died, the cream-coloured taxi slowly entering the storm-wracked cul-de-sac, the television, the towels, the mobile phone which she would never have picked up if it hadn't been for the strangeness overtaking their lives, Claire's shrieking voice, Claire's tiny flat, Claire's scoring system and her own sudden realisation that her problems compared with those of others, Claire included, were—yes, certainly not trivial but perhaps not as significant as she had thought—and her own conviction that her father would have found a way...

'Miss Viviani?'

'Oh.' Melanie felt the blood rush from her face and she felt truly dizzy.

He would have found a way...

Her eyes widened. Her mouth opened in a faint gasp.

'Miss Viviani?'

She looked at Tully without seeing him.

'Perhaps... he did...'

'What?'

Melanie sat motionless for long moments, turning things over in her mind. Then she seemed to remember where she was, and notice Tully sitting quietly on the sofa. Her eyes flicked to the fire as it hissed and spat.

'What is it, Miss Viviani? Are you all right?'

'I'm fine.' Melanie stood up. Tully sensed that she had changed again, become more assured, less... His brow creased. He couldn't figure this one out.

'Thank you,' said Melanie. 'I'm going up now. I'm very tired. But thank you.'

Tully wanted to ask, for what? but before he could ask, Melanie turned and walked from the room. Seconds later, he heard her climbing the stairs, and then the faint sound of her bedroom door closing. He sat back, sighed, and pinched at the bridge of his nose. There were no flames dancing in the fire now, but its dying glow washed the bookshelves on the adjacent wall in a warm red colour. Tully was reminded of 'The Thirteenth Bookshelf', and Mrs Viviani's assertion that her husband wrote it in bed, recovering from a fall.

'Well, George,' said Tully, 'I hope *you* know what's going on.'

<hr>

The young man watched as Claire sat up in bed and leaned forward, cradling one knee with her cupped hands. Moonlight filtered patterns across her naked body, turned her red hair a deep black.

He remembered the early days, when their locked gaze had cut through autumn sunlight; now moonlight painted everything black and white, but nothing was black and white any more.

He remembered the curly-haired man that she had been talking about, the father of that girl up from Ayr, saw in his mind the man advancing up Laburnum Crescent, almost dancing up Laburnum Crescent, his black shoes glossed and gleaming. He had been one of the few men who smiled as much going into the dilapidated building as he did when he came out an hour, or two hours, later. Funny; now he was dead, and his death had somehow upset Claire enough to drive her out of her flat, and across the road, into this flat, his flat, and into his bed. The curly-haired man's death had turned out to his advantage and probably Claire's too.

He reached out to put his hand on her shoulder, or on her back, but stopped. He rotated his fingers in the moonlight, committing to memory the way in which shadows played over them and through them, and thinking how odd it was that sunlight always showed up motes and dust bobbing in the air, but moonlight seldom did. Then he retracted his arm and rested it on the warm sheet where she had been lying. Either she would unclasp her hands, and lie back, and draw the covers about the two of them. Or she wouldn't.

He stepped back. 'Dear God, help me. I can't rouse him.' He stood looking at Richardson. The tape recorder turned soundlessly.

From the stairwell, Clabber heard the slow ascent of footsteps.

The Search for Joseph Tully
William Hallahan

'And he won his bets, rather! Just think, if ever she had gone into that room. Pretty horrible, eh?'

He nodded his head, grimly, and we four nodded back. Then he rose and took us collectively to the door and presently thrust us forth in friendly fashion onto the Embankment and into the fresh night air.

Carnacki the Ghost-finder
William Hope Hodgson

Acknowledgements

Thanks are due to members of the Glasgow SF Writing Circle, who gave Kindred Spirit their usual tough, no-nonsense critique, and persuaded me to change a few things.

Of course I must thank all at Sparsile Books, especially Lesley Affrossman (Creative Director), Jim Campbell (editor) and Madeleine Jewett (proofreader).

Further Reading

The Promise
When promises can cost lives

Simon's Wife
Time is running out, and history is
being rewritten by a traitor's hand.

The Unforgiven King
A forgotten woman and the most
vilified king in history

American Goddess
Ancient powers
and new forces

L. M. Affrossman

Science for Heretics
Why so much of science is wrong

The Tethered God
Punished for a crime he can't
remember

Barrie Condon

Pignut and Nuncle
When we are born, we cry that
we have come to this stage of fools
King Lear

Des Dillon

Two Pups
What makes us different. What makes
us the same.

Seona Calder

Comics and Columbine
An outcast look at comics, bigotry and
school shootings

Tom Campbell

Drown for your Sins
DCI Grant McVicar: Book 1

Dress for Death
DCI Grant McVicar: Book 2

Diarmid MacArthur

www.sparsilebooks.com